Dedication

For the Regency Silk & Scandal 'continuistas'

Author Note

Flying to India on holiday last year, I grew weary of the long flight, but I cheered up when I thought of how many months the passengers on the East India Company's ships plying to and from the Far East must have been at sea together. Intrigued, I read more—especially the memoirs of the rake William Hickey, who spent much of his legal career in India and who described in vivid detail life on-board ship.

The voyage had its dangers, as well as its discomforts, and shipwrecks were not uncommon. I began to wonder what would happen to the passengers who survived such a disaster: would the bonds forged during months together withstand such a trauma? How would the wreck affect friends and lovers ashore?

This book is the first in a trio of novels that explores that question. Shocking Lady Perdita Brooke and rakish adventurer Alistair Lyndon strike sparks off each other from the moment they meet—but what will happen when the *Bengal Queen* is wrecked on the treacherous rocks of the Isles of Scilly?

I hope you enjoy finding out as much as I did, and will follow their fellow passengers in the next two books as three love stories emerge from the shipwreck.

Louise Allen has been immersing herself in history, real and fictional, for as long as she can remember, and finds landscapes and places evoke powerful images of the past. Louise lives in Bedfordshire, and works as a property manager, but spends as much time as possible with her husband at the cottage they are renovating on the north Norfolk coast, or travelling abroad. Venice, Burgundy and the Greek islands are favourite atmospheric destinations. Please visit Louise's website—www.louiseallenregency.co.uk—for the latest news!

Novels by the same author:

VIRGIN SLAVE, BARBARIAN KING
THE DANGEROUS MR RYDER*
THE OUTRAGEOUS LADY FELSHAM*
THE SHOCKING LORD STANDON*
THE DISGRACEFUL MR RAVENHURST*
THE NOTORIOUS MR HURST*
THE PIRATICAL MISS RAVENHURST*
PRACTICAL WIDOW TO PASSIONATE MISTRESS†
VICAR'S DAUGHTER TO VISCOUNT'S LADY†
INNOCENT COURTESAN TO ADVENTURER'S BRIDE†

*Those Scandalous Ravenhursts
†The Transformation of the Shelley Sisters

and in Mills & Boon® Historical *Undone!* eBooks:

DISROBED AND DISHONOURED

Chapter One

7th December 1808—Calcutta, India

It was blissfully cool, Dita assured herself, plying her fan in an effort to make it so. This was the *cool* season, so at eight o'clock in the evening it was only as hot as an English August day. Nor was it raining, thank heavens. How long did one have to live in India to become used to the heat? A trickle of sweat ran down her spine as she reminded herself of what it had been like from March to September.

But there was something to be said for the temperature: it made one feel so delightfully loose and relaxed. In fact, it was impossible to be anything *but* relaxed, to shed as many clothes as decency permitted and wear exquisitely fine muslins and lawns and floating silks.

She was going to miss that cat-like, sensual, indolence when she returned to England, now her year of exile was over. And the heat had another benefit, she thought, watching the group of young ladies in the reception room off the great Marble Hall of Government House: it made the beautiful peaches-and-cream blondes turn red and blotchy whereas she, the gypsy, as they snidely remarked, showed little outward sign of it.

It had not taken long to adapt, to rise before dawn to ride in the cool, to sleep and lounge through the long, hot afternoons, saving the evenings for parties and dances. If it had not been for the grubby trail of rumour and gossip following her, she could have reinvented herself, perhaps, here in India. As it was, it had just added a sharper edge to her tongue.

But she wanted so much now to be in England. She wanted the green and the soft rain and the mists and a gentler sun. Her sentence was almost done: she could go home and hope to find herself forgiven by Papa, hope that her reappearance in society would not stir up the wagging tongues all over again.

And if it does? she thought, strolling into the room from the terrace, her face schooled to smiling confidence. *Then to hell with them, the catty ones with their whispers and the rakes who think I am theirs for the asking. I made a mistake and trusted a man, that is all. I will not do that again.* Regrets were a waste of time. Dita slammed the door on her thoughts and scanned the room with its towering ceiling and double rows of marble columns.

The *Bengal Queen* was due to sail for England at the end of the week and almost all her passengers were here at the Governor's House reception. She was going to get to know them very well indeed over the next few months. There were some important men in the East India Company travelling as supercargo; a handful of army officers; several merchants, some with wives and daughters, and a number of the well-bred young men who worked for the Company, setting their feet on the ladder of wealth and power.

Dita smiled and flirted her fan at two of them, the Chatterton twins on the far side of the room. Lazy, charming Daniel and driven, intense Callum—Mama would not be *too* displeased if she returned home engaged to Callum, the unattached one. Not a brilliant match, but they were younger brothers of the Earl of Flamborough, after all. Both were amusing company, but neither stirred more than a flutter in her heart. Perhaps no one would ever again, now she had learned to distrust what it told her.

Shy Averil Heydon waved from beside a group of chaperons. Dita smiled back a trifle wryly. Dear Averil: so well behaved, such a perfect young lady—and so pretty. How was it that Miss Heydon was one of the few eligible misses in Calcutta society whom she could tolerate? Possibly because she was such an heiress that she was above feeling delight at an earl's daughter being packed off the India in disgrace, unlike those who saw Lady Perdita Brooke as nothing but competition to be shot down. The smile hardened; they could certainly try. None of them had succeeded yet, possibly because they made the mistake of thinking that she cared for their approval or their friendship.

And Averil would be on the *Bengal Queen*, too, which was something to be grateful for—three months was a long time to be cooped up with the same restricted company. On the way out she'd had her anger—mostly directed at herself—and a trunk full of books to sustain her; now she intended to enjoy herself, and the experience of the voyage.

'Lady Perdita!'

'Lady Grimshaw?' Dita produced an attentive expression. The old gorgon was going to be a passenger, too, and Dita had learned to pick her battles.

'That is hardly a suitable colour for an unmarried girl. And such flimsy fabric, too.'

'It is a sari I had remade, Lady Grimshaw. I find pastels and white make me appear sallow.' Dita was well aware of her few good features and how to enhance them to perfection: the deep green brought out the colour of her eyes and the dark gold highlights in her brown hair. The delicate silk floated over the fine lawn undergarments as though she was wearing clouds.

'Humph. And what's this I hear about riding on the *maidan* at dawn? Galloping!'

'It is too hot to gallop at any other time of day, ma'am. And I did have my *syce* with me.'

'A groom is neither here nor there, my girl. It is fast behaviour. Very fast.'

'Surely speed is the purpose of the gallop?' Dita said sweetly, and drifted away before the matron could think of a suitably crushing retort. She gestured to a servant for a glass of punch, another fast thing for a young lady to be doing. She sipped it as she walked, wrinkling her nose at the amount of arrack it contained, then stopped as a slight stir around the doorway heralded a new arrival.

'Who is that?' Averil appeared at her side and gestured towards the door. 'My goodness, what a very good-looking man.' She fanned herself as she stared.

He was certainly that. Tall, lean, very tanned, the

thick black silk of his hair cut ruthlessly short. Dita stopped breathing, then sucked down air. No, of course not, it could not be Alistair—she was imagining things. Her treacherous body registered alarm and an instant flutter of arousal.

The man entered limping, impatient, as though the handicap infuriated him, but he was going to ignore it. Once in, he surveyed the room with unhurried assurance. The scrutiny paused at Dita, flickered over her face, dropped to study the low-cut neckline of her gown, then moved on to Averil for a further cool assessment.

For all the world like a pasha inspecting a new intake for the seraglio, Dita thought. But despite the unfamiliar arrogance, she knew. Her body recognised him with every quivering nerve. *It is him. It is Alistair.* After eight years. Dita fought a battle with the urge to run.

'Insufferable,' Averil murmured. She had blushed a painful red.

'Insufferable, no doubt. Arrogant, certainly,' Dita replied, not troubling to lower her voice as he came closer. *Attack*, her instincts told her. *Strike before you weaken and he can hurt you again.* 'And he obviously fancies himself quite the romantic hero, my dear. You note the limp? Positively Gothic—straight out of a sensation novel.'

Alistair stopped and turned. He made no pretence of not having heard her. 'A young lady who addles her brain with trashy fiction, I gather.' The intervening years had not darkened the curious amber eyes that as a child she had always believed belonged to a tiger. Memories surfaced, some bittersweet, some simply bitter, some so shamefully arousing that she felt quite dizzy. She felt her

chin go up as she returned the stare in frigid silence, but
he had not recognised her. He turned a little more and
bowed to Averil. 'My pardon, ma'am, if I put you to the
blush. One does not often see such beauty.'

The movement exposed the right side of his head.
Down the cheek from just in front of the ear, across the
jawbone and on to his neck, there was a half-healed scar
that vanished into the white lawn of his neckcloth. His
right hand, she saw, was bandaged. The limp was not
affectation after all; he had been hurt, and badly. Dita
stifled the instinct to touch him, demand to know what
had happened as she once would have done, without
inhibition.

Beside her she heard her friend's sharp indrawn
breath. 'I do not regard it, sir.' Averil nodded with cool
dismissal and walked away towards the chaperons,
then turned when she reached their sanctuary, her face
comically dismayed as she realised Dita had not followed her.

I should apologise to him, Dita thought, *but he ogled
us so blatantly. And he cut at me just as he had that last
time.* Furthermore, he apologised only to Averil; her own
looks would win no compliments from this man.

'My friend is as gracious as she is beautiful,' she said
and the amber eyes, still warm from following Averil's
retreat, moved back to hers. He frowned at the tart sweetness of her tone. 'She can find it in herself to forgive
almost anyone, even presumptuous rakes.' *Which is what
Alistair appeared to have grown into.*

And on that note she should turn on her heel, perhaps
with a light trill of laughter, or a flick of her fan, and
leave him to annoy some other lady. But it was difficult

to move, when wrenching her eyes away from his meant they fell to his mouth. It did not curve—he could not be said to be smiling—but one corner deepened into something that was almost a dimple. Not, of course, that such an arrogant hunk of masculinity could be said to have anything as charming as a dimple. That mouth on her skin, on her breast…

'I am rightly chastised,' he said. There was something provocative in the way that he said it that sent a little shock through her, although she had no idea why. Then she realised that he was speaking to her as a woman, not as the girl he had thought her when he had so cruelly dismissed her before. It was almost as though he was suggesting that she carry out the chastisement more personally.

Dita told herself that one could overcome blushes by sheer force of will, especially as she had no very exact idea what she was blushing about now. He did not recognise her; even if he did, what had happened so long ago had been unimportant to him, he had made that very clear at the time. 'You do not appear remotely penitent, sir,' she retorted. Sooner or later he would realise who he was talking to, but she was not going to give him the satisfaction of acknowledging him and thinking she attached any importance to it.

'I never said I was, ma'am, merely that I acknowledged a reproof. There is no amusement in penitence—why, one would have to either give up the sin or be a hypocrite—and where's the fun in that?'

'I have no idea whether you are a hypocrite or not, sir, but certainly no one could accuse you of gallant behaviour.'

'You struck first,' he pointed out, accurately and unfairly.

'For which I apologise,' Dita said. She was not going to act as badly as he. Even as she made the resolution her tongue got the better of her. 'But I have no intention of offering sympathy, sir. You obviously enjoy fighting.' He had always been intense, often angry, as a youth. And that intensity had miraculously transmuted into fire and passion when he made love.

'Indeed.' He flexed the bandaged hand and winced slightly. 'You should see the other fellow.'

'I have no wish to. You appear to have been hacking at each other with sabres.'

'Near enough,' he agreed.

Something in the mocking, cultured tones still held the faintest burr of the West Country. A wave of nostalgia for home and the green hills and the fierce cliffs and the cold sea gripped her, overriding even the shock of seeing Alistair again.

'You still have the West Country in your voice,' Dita said abruptly.

'North Cornwall, near the boundary with Devon. And you?' He did not appear to find the way she had phrased the statement strange.

He misses it, too, she thought, hearing the hint of longing under the cool tone. 'I, too, come from that area.' Without calculation she put out her hand and he caught it in his uninjured, ungloved, left. His hand was warm and hard with a rider's calluses and his fingertips rested against her pulse, which was racing. Once before he had held her hand like this, once before they had stood so close and she had read the need in his eyes and she had misunderstood and acted with reckless innocence. He had taken her to heaven and then mocked her for her foolishness.

She could not play games any longer. Sooner or later he would find out who she was, and if she made a mystery of it he would think she still remembered, still attached some importance to what had happened between them. 'My family lives at Combe.'

'You are a Brooke? One of the Earl of Wycombe's family?' He moved nearer, her hand still held in his as he drew her to him to study her face. Close to he seemed to take the air out of the space between them. *Too close, too male. Alistair. Oh my lord, he has grown up.* 'Why, you are never little Dita Brooke? But you were all angles and nose and legs.' He grinned. 'I used to put frogs in your pinafore pocket and you tagged along everywhere. But you have changed since I last saw you. You must have been twelve.' His amusement stripped the eight years from him.

'I was sixteen,' she said with all the icy reserve she could manage. *All angles and nose.* 'I recall you—and your frogs—as an impudent youth while I was growing up. But I was sixteen when you left home.' *Sixteen when I kissed you with all the fervour and love that was filling me and you used me and brushed me aside. Was I simply too unskilled for you or too foolishly clinging?*

A shadow darkened the mocking eyes and for a moment Alistair frowned as though chasing an elusive memory.

But he doesn't seem to remember—or he is not admitting it. But how could he forget? Perhaps there have been so many women that one inept chit of a girl is infinitely forgettable.

'Sixteen? Were you?' He frowned, his eyes intent on her face. 'I don't…recollect.' But his eyes held questions and a hint of puzzlement as though he had been reminded of a faded dream.

'There is no reason why you should.' Dita pulled her hand free, dropped the merest hint of a curtsy and walked away. *So, he doesn't even remember! He broke my foolish young heart and he doesn't even remember doing it. I was that unimportant to him.*

Daniel Chatterton intercepted her in the middle of the room and she set her face into a pleasant smile. *I am not plain any more*, she told herself with a fierce determination not to run away. *I am polished and stylish and an original. That is what I am: an original. Other men admire me. It is good that I have met Alistair again— now I can replace the fantasy with the reality.* Perhaps now the memories of one shattering, wonderful hour in his bed would leave her, finally.

'Never tell me that you do not idolise our returning adventurer, Lady Perdita.' Apparently her expression was not as bland as she hoped. She shrugged; no doubt half the room had heard the exchange. She could imagine the giggles amongst the cattery of young ladies. Chatterton gestured to a passing servant. 'More punch?'

'No. No, thank you, it is far too strong.' Dita took a glass of mango juice in exchange. Was the arrack responsible for how she had felt just now? Without it perhaps she would have seen just another man and the glamour would have dropped away, leaving her untouched. As she raised her drink to sip, she realised her hand retained the faintest hint of Alistair's scent: leather, musk and something elusive and spicily expensive. He had never smelled like that before, so complex, so intoxicating. He had grown up with a vengeance. But so had she.

'If you mean Alistair Lyndon, the insolent creature who spoke to Miss Heydon and me just now, I knew him when he was growing up. He was a care-for-nothing then and it seems little has changed.' Now she was blushing again. She *never* blushed. 'He left home when he was twenty, or thereabouts.'

Twenty years, eleven months. She had bought him a fine horn pocket comb for his birthday and painstakingly embroidered a case for it. It was still in the bottom of her jewel box where it had stayed, even when she had eloped with the man she had believed herself in love with.

'He is Viscount Lyndon, heir to the Marquis of Iwerne, is he not?'

'Yes. Our families' lands march together, but we are not great friends.' Not, at least, since Mama was careless enough to show what she thought of the marquis's second wife, who was only five years older than Dita. With some friction already over land, and no daughters in the Iwerne household to promote sociability, the families met rarely and there was no incentive to heal the rift.

'Lyndon left home after some disagreement with his father about eight years ago,' she added in an indifferent tone. 'But I don't think they ever got on, even before that. What is he doing here, do you know?' It was a reasonable enough question.

'Joining the party for the *Bengal Queen* passengers. He is returning home, I hear. The word is that his father is very ill; Lyndon may well be the marquis already.' Chatterton looked over her shoulder. 'He is watching you.'

She could feel him, like the gazelle senses the tiger lurking in the shadows, and fought for composure. Three months in a tiny canvas-walled cabin, cheek by jowl with a man who still thrived, she was certain, on dangerous mischief. It wouldn't be frogs in pinafore pockets these days. If he even suspected how she felt, *had* felt, about him, she had no idea how he would react.

'Is he, indeed? How obvious of him.'

'He is also watching me,' Chatterton said with a rueful smile. 'And I do not think it is because he admires my waistcoat. I am beginning to feel dangerously *de trop*. Most men would pretend they were not observing you— Lyndon has the air of a man guarding his property.'

'Insolent is indeed the word for him.' He did not regard her as his property, far from it, but he had bestowed his attention upon her just now and she had snubbed him, so he would not be satisfied until he had her gazing at him cow-eyed like all the rest of the silly girls would do.

Now Dita turned slightly so she was in profile to the viscount and ran a finger down Daniel Chatterton's waistcoat. 'Lord Lyndon might not admire it, but is certainly a very fine piece of silk. And you look so handsome in it.'

'Are you flirting with me by any chance, Lady Perdita?' Chatterton asked with a grin. 'Or are you trying to annoy Lyndon?'

'Me?' She opened her eyes wide at him, enjoying herself all of a sudden. She had met Alistair again and the heavens had not fallen; perhaps she could survive this after all. She gave Daniel's neckcloth a proprietorial tweak to settle the folds, intent on adding oil to the fire.

'Yes, you! Don't you care that he will probably call me out?'

'He has no cause. Tell me about him so I may better avoid him. I haven't seen him for years.' She smiled up into Daniel's face and stood just an inch too close for propriety.

'I shall have to try that brooding stare myself,' Chatterton said, with a wary glance across the room. 'It seems to work on the ladies. All I know about him is that he has been travelling in the East for about seven years, which fits with what you recall of him leaving home. He's a rich man—the rumour is that he made a killing by gem dealing and that his weakness is exotic plants. He's got collectors all over the place sending stuff back to somewhere in England—money no object, so they say.'

'And how did he get hurt?' Dita ran her fan down Daniel's arm. Alistair was still watching them, she could feel him. 'Duelling?'

'Nothing so safe. It was a tiger, apparently; a man-eater who was terrorising a village. Lyndon went after it on elephant-back and the beast leapt at the howdah and dragged the *mahout* off. Lyndon vaulted down and tackled it with a knife.'

'Quite the hero.' Dita spoke lightly, but the thought of those claws, the great white teeth, made her shudder. What did it take to go so close, risk such an awful death? She had likened it to a sabre wound; the claws must have been as lethal. 'What happened to the mahout?'

'No idea. Pity Lyndon's handsome face has been spoiled.'

'Spoiled? Goodness, no!' She forced a laugh and deployed her fan. *His face? He could have been killed!* 'It will soon heal completely—don't you know that scars like that are most attractive to the ladies?'

'Lady Perdita, you will excuse me if I tear my brother away?' It was Callum Chatterton, Daniel's twin. 'I must talk tiresome business, I fear.'

'He's removing me from danger before I am called out,' Daniel interpreted, rolling his eyes. 'But he'll make me work as well, I have no doubt.'

'Go then, Mr Chatterton,' she said, chuckling at his rueful expression. 'Work hard and be safe.' She stood looking after them for a moment, but she was seeing not the hot, crowded room with its marble pillars, but a ripple in the long, sun-bleached grass as gold-and-black-striped death padded through it; the explosion of muscles and terror; the screaming *mahout* and the man who had risked his life to save him. Her fantasy of Alistair's eyes as being like those of a tiger did not seem so poetic now.

She turned, impulsive as always. She should make amends for her remark, she should make peace. That long-ago magic, the hurt that had shattered it, had meant nothing to him at the time and it should mean nothing to her now. Alistair Lyndon had haunted her dreams for too long.

But Alistair was no longer watching her. Instead, he stood far too close to Mrs Harrison, listening to something she was virtually whispering in his ear, his downturned gaze on the lady's abundantly displayed charms.

So, the intense young man she had fallen for so hard was a rake now, and the attention he had paid her and Averil was merely habitual. A courageous rake, but a rake none the less. And he was just as intrigued to find his plain little neighbour after all these years, which would account for his close scrutiny just now.

It smarted that he did not even seem to remember just what had happened between them, but she must learn to school her hurt pride, for that was all it could be. And he had found a lady better suited to his character than she to talk to; Mrs Harrison's reputation suggested that she would be delighted to entertain a gentleman in any way that mutual desire suggested.

Dita put down her glass with a snap on a side table, suddenly weary of the crowd, the noise, the heat and her own ghosts. As she walked towards the door her bearer emerged from the shadows behind the pillars.

'My chair, Ajay.' He hurried off and she went to tell Mrs Smyth-Robinson, who was obliging her aunt by acting as chaperon this evening, that she was leaving.

She was tired and her head ached, and she wished she was home in England and never had to speak to another man again and certainly not Alistair Lyndon. But she made herself nod and wave to acquaintances, she made herself walk with the elegant swaying step that disguised the fact that she had no lush curves to flaunt, and she kept the smile on her lips and her chin up. One had one's pride, after all.

Alistair was aware of the green-eyed hornet leaving the room even as he accepted Claudia Hamilton's invitation to join her for a nightcap. He doubted the lady was interested in a good night's sleep. He had met her husband in Guwahati buying silk and agreed with Claudia's obvious opinion that he was a boor—it was clear she needed entertaining.

The prospect of a little mutual *entertainment* was interesting, although he had no intention of this developing into an *affaire*, even for the few days remaining before he sailed. Alistair was not given to sharing and the lady was, by all accounts, generous with her favours.

'There goes the Brooke girl,' Claudia said with a sniff, following his gaze. 'Impudent chit. Just because she has a fortune and an earl for a father doesn't make up for scandal and no looks to speak of. She is going back to England on the *Bengal Queen*. I suppose they think that whatever it was she did has been forgotten by now.'

'Her family are neighbours of mine,' Alistair remarked, instinct warning him to produce an explanation for his interest. 'She has grown up.' He wasn't surprised to hear of a scandal—Dita looked headstrong enough for anything. As a gangling child she had been a fearless and impetuous tomboy, always tagging along at his heels, wanting to climb trees and fish and ride unsuitable horses. And she had been fiercely affectionate.

He frowned at the vague memory of her wrapping her arms around his neck and kissing him. That had been the day before he packed his bags and shook the dust of Castle Lyndon from his shoes.

He had been distracted with grief and humiliated anger and she had tried to comfort him, he supposed. Probably he had been abrupt with the girl. He had been drinking, too, the best part of a bottle of brandy and wine as well, if his very faint recollection served him right. But then his memory of that day and night were blurred and the dreams that still visited him about that time were too disturbing to confront. Dita… No, the dreams had not been of an affectionate kiss from a tomboy but of a slender, naked body, of fierce passion. Hell, he still felt guilty that his drink-sodden nightmares could have produced those images of an innocent girl.

Alistair glanced towards the door again, but the emerald silk had whisked out of sight. Dita Brooke was no longer a child, but she had most certainly developed into a dangerous handful for whichever man her father was aiming to marry her off to.

'You think her lacking in looks?' It was amusing to see the venom in Claudia's eyes as she thought about the younger woman. He had no intention of asking her to speculate about the scandal. Given the repressive English drawing rooms he remembered, it had probably been something as dreadful as being caught kissing a man on the terrace during a ball. Dull stuff.

'No figure, too tall, her face lacks symmetry, her nose is too long, her complexion is sallow. Other than that I am sure she is tolerable.'

'A catalogue of disasters to be sure, poor girl,' Alistair agreed, his fingertip tracing lazy circles in Claudia's palm. She made a sound like a purr and moved closer.

She was right, of course, all those things could be said of Lady Perdita. Little Dita Brooke had been as plain and ungainly as a fledgling in a nest. And yet, by some alchemy, she had overcome them to become a tantalising, feminine creature. Poise, exquisite grooming and sheer personality, he supposed. And something new—a tongue like an adder. It might be amusing to try his luck as a snake charmer on the voyage home.

Chapter Two

'Steady, Khan.' Dita smoothed her hand along the neck of the big bay gelding and smiled as he twitched one ear back to listen to her. 'You can run in a minute.' He sidled and fidgeted, pretending to take violent exception to a passing ox cart, a rickshaw, a wandering, soft-eyed sacred cow and even a group of chattering women with brass bowls on their heads. The Calcutta traffic never seemed to diminish, even at just past dawn on a Wednesday morning.

'I wish I could take you home, but Major Conway will look after you,' she promised, turning his head as they reached one of the rides across the *maidan*, the wide expanse of open space that surrounded the low angular mass of Fort William. Only one more day to ride after today; best not to think about it, the emotions were too complicated. 'Come on, then!'

The horse needed no further urging. Dita tightened her hold as he took off into a gallop from almost a standing start and thundered across the grass. Behind her she heard the hoofbeats of the grey pony her *syce* Pradeep rode, but they soon faded away. Pradeep's pony could never catch Khan and she had no intention of waiting for him. When she finally left the *maidan* he would come cantering up, clicking his tongue at her and grumbling as always, 'Lady Perdita, *memsahib*, how can I protect you from wicked men if you leave me behind?'

There aren't any wicked men out here, she thought as the Hooghly River came in sight. The soldiers patrolling the fort saw to that. Perhaps she should take Pradeep with her into the ballroom and he could see off the likes of Alistair Lyndon.

She had managed about three hours' sleep. Most of the night had been spent tossing and turning and fuming about arrogant males with dreadful taste in women—and the one particular arrogant male she was going to have to share a ship with for weeks on end. Now she was determined to chase away not only last evening's unsettling encounter, but the equally unsettling dreams that had followed it.

The worst had been a variation on the usual nightmare: her father had flung open the door of the chaise and dragged her out into the inn yard in front of a stagecoach full of gawking onlookers and old Lady St George in her travelling carriage. But this time the tall man with black hair with her was not Stephen Doyle, scrambling out of the opposite door in a cowardly attempt to escape, but Alistair Lyndon.

And Alistair was not running away as the man she had talked herself into falling for had. In her dream he turned, elegant and deadly, the light flickering off the blade of the rapier he held to her father's throat. And then the dream had become utterly confused and Stephen in a tangle of sheets in the inn bed had become a much younger Alistair.

And that dream had been accurate and intense and so arousing that she had woken aching and yearning and had had to rise and splash cold water over herself until the trembling ceased.

As she had woken that morning she had realised who Stephen Doyle resembled—a grown-up version of Alistair. Dita shook her head to try to clear the last muddled remnants of the dreams out of her head. Surely she hadn't fallen for Stephen because she was still yearning for Alistair? It was ludicrous; after that humiliating fiasco—which he had so obviously forgotten in a brandy-soaked haze the next morning—she had fought to put that foolish infatuation behind her. She had thought she had succeeded.

Khan was still going flat out, too fast for prudence as they neared the point where the outer defensive ditch met the river bank. Here she must turn, and the scrubby trees cast heavy shadow capable of concealing rough ground and stray dogs. She began to steady the horse, and as she did so a chestnut came out of the trees, galloping as fast as her gelding was.

Khan came to a sliding halt and reared to try to avoid the certain collision. Dita clung flat on his neck, the breath half-knocked out of her by the pommel. As the mane whipped into her eyes she saw the other rider wrench his animal to the left. On the short dusty grass the fall was inevitable, however skilled the rider; as Khan landed with a bone-juddering thud on all four hooves the other horse slithered, scrabbled for purchase and crashed down, missing them by only a few yards.

Dita threw her leg over the pommel and slid to the ground as the chestnut horse got to its feet. Its rider lay sprawled on the ground; she ran and fell to her knees beside him. It was Alistair Lyndon, flat on his back, arms outflung, eyes closed.

'Oh, my God!' *Is he dead?* She wrenched open the buttons on his black linen coat, pushed back the fronts to expose his shirt and bent over him, her ear pressed to his chest. Against her cheek the thud of his heart was fast, but it was strong and steady.

Dita let all the air out of her lungs in a whoosh of relief as her shoulders slumped. She must get up and send for help, a doctor. He might have broken his leg or his back. But just for a second she needed to recover from the shock.

'This is nice,' remarked his voice in her ear and his arm came round her, pulled her up a little and, before she could struggle, Alistair's mouth was pressed against hers, exploring with a frank appreciation and lack of urgency that took her breath away.

Dita had never been kissed by a man who appeared to be taking an indolently dispassionate pleasure in the proceeding. When she was sixteen she had been in Alistair's arms when she was ignorant and he was a youth and he had still made her sob with delight. Now he was a man, and sober, and she knew it meant nothing to him. This was pure self-indulgent mischief.

Even so, it was far harder to pull away than it should be, she found, furious with herself. Alistair had spent eight years honing his sexual technique, obviously by practising whenever he got the opportunity. She put both hands on his shoulders, heaved, and was released with unflattering ease. 'You libertine!'

He opened his eyes, heavy-lidded, amused and golden, and sat up. The amusement vanished in a sharp intake of breath followed by a vehement sentence in a language she did not recognise '…and bloody hell,' he finished.

'Lord Lyndon,' Dita stated. It took an effort not to slap him. 'Of course, it had to be you, riding far too fast. Are you hurt? I assume from your language that you are. I suppose you are going to say your outrageous behaviour is due to concussion or shock or some such excuse.'

The smouldering look he gave her as he scrubbed his left hand through his dusty, tousled hair was a provocation she would not let herself rise to. 'Being a normal male, when young women fling themselves on my chest I do not need the excuse of a bang on the head to react,' he said. He wriggled his shoulders experimentally. 'I'll live.'

Dita resisted the urge to shift backwards out of range. There was blood on his bandaged hand, the makings of a nasty bruise on his cheek; the very fact he had not got to his feet yet told her all she needed to know about how his injured leg felt.

'Are *you* hurt?' he asked. She shook her head. 'Is my horse all right?

'Pradeep,' she called as the *syce* cantered up. 'Catch the *sahib*'s horse, please, and check it is all right.' She turned back, thankful she could not understand the muttered remarks Lyndon was making, and tried to ignore the fact that her heart was still stuck somewhere in her throat after the shock. Or was it that kiss? How he *dared*! How she wanted him to do it again.

'Now, what are we going to do about you?' she said, resorting to brisk practicality. 'I had best send Pradeep to the fort, I think, and get them to bring out a stretcher.' At least she sounded coherent, even if she did not feel it.

'Do I look like the kind of man who would put up with being carted about on a stretcher by a couple of sepoys?' he enquired, flexing his hand and hissing as he did so.

'No, of course not.' Dita began to untie her stock. Her hands, she was thankful to see, were not shaking. 'That would be the rational course of action, after all. How ludicrous to expect you to follow it. Doubtless you intend to sit here for the rest of the day?'

'I intend to stand up,' he said. 'And walk to my horse when your man has caught it. Why are you undressing?'

'I am removing my stock in order to bandage which-ever part of your ungrateful anatomy requires it, my lord,' Dita said, her teeth clenched. 'At the moment I am considering a tourniquet around your neck.'

Alistair Lyndon regarded her from narrowed eyes, but all he said was, 'I thought that ripping up petticoats was the standard practice under these circumstances.'

'I have no intention of demolishing my wardrobe for you, my lord.' Dita got to her feet and held out her hand. 'Are you going to accept help to stand up or does your stubborn male pride preclude that as well?'

When he moved, he moved fast and with grace. His language was vivid, although mostly incomprehensible, but the viscount got his good leg under him and stood up in one fluid movement, ignoring her hand. 'There is a lot of blood on your breeches now,' she observed. She had never been so close to quite this much gore before but, by some miracle, she did not feel faint. Probably she was too cross. And aroused—she could not ignore that humiliating fact. She had wanted him then, eight years ago when he had been a youth. Now she felt sharp desire for the man he had become. She was grown, too; she could resist her own weaknesses.

'Damn.' He held out a hand for the stock and she gave it to him. She was certainly not going to offer to bandage his leg if he could do it himself. Beside any other consideration, the infuriating creature would probably take it as an invitation to further familiarities and she had the lowering feeling that touching him again would shatter her resolve. 'Thank you.' The knot he tied was workmanlike and seemed to stop the bleeding, so there was no need to continue to study the well-muscled thigh, she realised, and began to tidy her own disarranged neckline as well as she could.

'Your wounds were caused by a tiger, I hear,' Dita remarked, feeling the need for conversation. Perhaps she was a trifle faint after all; she was certainly oddly light-headed. Or was that simply that kiss? 'I assume it came off worst.'

'It did,' he agreed, yanking his cuffs into place. Pradeep came over, leading the chestnut horse. 'Thank you. Is it all right?'

'Yes, *sahib*. The rein is broken, which is why the *sahib* was not able to hold it when he fell.' The *syce* must think he required a sop to his pride, but Alistair appeared unconcerned. 'Does the *sahib* require help to mount?'

He'll say no, *of course*, Dita thought. *The usual male conceit.* But Lyndon put his good foot into the *syce*'s cupped hands and let Pradeep boost him enough to throw his injured leg over the saddle.

It was interesting that he saw no need to play-act the hero—unlike Stephen, who would have doubtless managed alone, even if it made the wound worse. She frowned. What was she doing, thinking of that sorry excuse for a lover? Hadn't she resolved to put him, and her own poor judgement, out of her head? He had never been in her heart, she knew that now. But it was uncanny, the way he was a pale imitation of the man in front of her now.

'What happened to the *mahout?*' she asked, putting one hand on the rein to detain Lyndon.

'He survived.' He looked down at her, magnificently self-assured despite his dusty clothes and stained bandages. 'Why do you ask?'

'You thought he was worth risking your life for. Many *sahibs* would not have done so.' It was the one good thing she had so far discovered about this new, adult, Alistair. 'It would be doubly painful to be injured and to have lost him.'

'I had employed him, so he was my responsibility,' Lyndon said.

'And the villagers who were being attacked by the man-eater? They were your responsibility also?'

'Trying to find the good side to my character, Dita?' he asked with uncomfortable perception. 'I wouldn't stretch your charity too far—it was good sport, that was all.'

'I'm sure it was,' she agreed. 'You men do like to kill things, don't you? And, of course, your own self-esteem would not allow you to lose a servant to a mere animal.'

'At least it fought back, unlike a pheasant or a fox,' he said with a grin, infuriatingly unmoved by her jibes. 'And why did you put yourself out so much just now for a man who obviously irritates you?'

'Because I was riding as fast as you were, and I, too, take responsibility for my actions,' she said. 'And you do not irritate me, you exasperate me. I do not appreciate your attempts to tease me with your shocking behaviour.'

'I was merely attempting to act as one of your romantic heroes,' he said. 'I thought a young lady addicted to novels would expect such attentions. You appeared to enjoy it.'

'I was shocked into momentary immobility.' Only, her lips had moved against his, had parted, her tongue had touched his in a fleeting mutual caress... 'And I am not *addicted*, as you put it. In fact, I think you are reading too many novels yourself, my lord,' Dita retorted as she dropped the rein and turned away to where Pradeep stood holding Khan.

Alistair watched her walk, straight-backed, to her groom and spend a moment speaking to him, apparently in reassurance, while she rubbed the big gelding's nose. For all the notice she took of Alistair he might as well not have been there, but he could sense her awareness of him, see it in the flush that touched her cheekbones. *Momentary immobility*, his foot! She had responded to his kiss whether she wanted to admit it or not.

The *syce* cupped his hands and she rose up and settled in the saddle with the lack of fuss of a born horsewoman. And a fit one, he thought, appreciating the moment when her habit clung and outlined her long legs.

In profile he could see that Claudia had been right. Her nose *was* too long and when she had looked up at him to ask about the *mahout* her face had been serious, emphasising the slight asymmetry that was not apparent when she was animated. And a critic who was not contemplating kissing it would agree that her mouth was too wide and her figure was unfashionably tall and slim. But the ugly duckling had grown into her face and, although it was not a beautiful one, it was vividly attractive.

And now he need not merely contemplate kissing her, he knew how she tasted and how it was to trace the curve of her upper lip with his tongue. The taste and feel of her had been oddly familiar.

He knew how she felt, her slight curves pressed to his chest, her weight on his body, and oddly it was as though he had always known that. It was remarkably effective in taking his mind off the bone-deep ache in his thigh and the sharp pain in his right hand. Alistair urged the bay alongside her horse as Dita used both hands to tuck up the strands of hair that had escaped from the net. The collar of her habit was open where the neckcloth was missing and his eyes followed the vee of pale skin into the shadows.

Last night her evening gown had revealed much more, but somehow it had not seemed so provocative. When he lifted his eyes she was gathering up the reins and he could tell from the way her lips tightened that she knew where he had been looking. If he had stayed in England, and watched the transformation from gawky child into provocatively attractive woman, would the impact when he looked at her be as great—or would she just be little Dita, grown up? Because there was no mistaking what he wanted when he looked at her now.

'We are both to be passengers on the *Bengal Queen*,' he said. It was a statement of the obvious, but he needed to keep her here for a few more moments, to see if he could provoke her into any more sharp-tongued remarks. He remembered last night how he had teased her with talk of chastisement and how unexpectedly stimulating that had been. The thought of wrestling between the sheets with a sharp-tongued, infuriated Lady Perdita who was trying to slap him was highly erotic. He might even let her get a few blows in before he…

'Yes,' she agreed, sounding wary. Doubtless some shadow of his thoughts was visible on his face. Alistair shifted in the saddle and got his unruly, and physically uncomfortable, imaginings under control. Better for now to remember the gawky tomboy-child who had always been somewhere in the background, solemn green eyes following his every move. 'You will be anxious to get home, no doubt,' she said with careful formality. 'I was sorry to hear that Lord Iwerne is unwell.'

'Thank you.' He could think of nothing else to say that was neither a lie nor hypocritical. From the months'-old news he had received from Lyndonholt Castle there was a strong chance that he was already the marquis, and try as he might to summon up appropriate feelings of anxiety and sadness for his father, he could not. They had never been close and the circumstances of their parting had been bitter. And even if his father still lived, what would he make of the hardened, travelled, twenty-nine-year-old who returned in the place of the angry, naïve young man who had walked away from him?

And there was his stepmother, of course. What would Imogen be expecting of the stepson who had not even stayed to see her wed?

She was in for a shock if she thought he would indulge her or had any tender feelings left for her. She could take herself off to the Dower House with her widow's portion and leave the Castle for the bride he fully intended to install there as soon as possible. And that bride would be a gentle, obedient, chaste young lady of good breeding. He would select her with care and she would provide him with heirs and be an excellent hostess. And she would leave his heart safely untouched—love was for idealists and romantics and he was neither. Not any more.

'A rupee for your thoughts?' Dita said, her wary expression replaced with amusement at his abstraction. It almost had him smiling back, seeing a shadow of the patient child in an unusual young lady who did not take offence at a man forgetting she was there. But then, she was probably relieved his attention was elsewhere. 'Are you daydreaming of home?'

'Yes,' he agreed. 'But the thought was hardly worth a rupee. Ma'am, it was a pleasure.' He bowed his hatless head for a moment, turned his horse towards Government House and cantered off.

For a moment there he had been tempted to stay, to offer to escort her back to wherever she was living. He must have hit his head in that fall, Alistair thought, to contemplate such a thing. He was going to be close to Dita Brooke for three months in the narrow confines of the ship, and he had no intention of resuming the role of elder brother, or however she had seen him as a child. He was not going to spend his time getting her out of scrapes and frightening off importunate young men; it made him feel old just thinking about it. As for that impulsive kiss, she had dealt with it briskly enough, even if she *had* responded to it. She was sophisticated enough to take it at face value as part of the repertoire of a rake, so nothing to worry about there.

Alistair trotted into the stable yard of Government House and dismounted with some care. The Governor General was away, but he was interested in plant hunting, too, and had extended a vague invitation that Alistair had found useful to take up for the few weeks before the ship sailed.

Damn this leg. He supposed he had better go and show it to the Governor's resident doctor and be lectured on his foolishness in riding so hard with it not properly healed. But the prospect of weeks without energetic exercise had driven him out to ride each day for as long as the cool of the morning lasted. No doubt Dita had been motivated by the same considerations.

Which led him to think of her again, and of violent exercise, and the combination of the two was uncomfortably vivid. No, his feelings were most definitely not brotherly, any more than those damnably persistent dreams about her were. 'Bloody fool,' he snapped at himself, startling the *jemahdar* at the front door.

Intelligent, headstrong, argumentative young women

with a scandal in their past and a temper were not what he was looking for. A meek and biddable English rose who would give him no trouble and cause no scandal was what he wanted and Dita Brooke had never been a rosebud, let alone a rose. She was pure briar with thorns all the way.

Chapter Three

$\sim\!\!\!\sim\!\!\!\sim$

As Alistair limped up the staircase to the first floor he thought of Dita's threat to apply a tourniquet around his neck and laughed out loud at the memory of her face as she said it. The two men coming out of an office stopped at the sound.

'Hell's teeth, Lyndon, what's happened to you?' It was one of the Chatterton twins, probably Daniel, who had been flirting with Perdita last night. 'Found that tiger again?'

'My horse fell on the *maidan* and I've opened up the wound in my thigh. I'd better get a stitch in it—have you seen Dr Evans?' Stoicism was one thing, being careless with open wounds in this climate quite another.

'No, no sign of him—but we only dropped in to leave some papers, we haven't seen anyone. Let's get you up to your room while they find Evans. *Daktar ko bulaiye,*' one twin called down to the *jemahdar*.

That was Callum, Alistair thought, waving away the offer of an arm in support. The responsible brother, by all accounts. 'I can manage, but come and have a *chota peg* while they find him. It's early, but I could do with it.'

They followed him up to his suite and settled themselves while his *sirdar* went for brandy. 'Horse put its foot in a hole?' Daniel asked.

'Nothing so ordinary. I damn nearly collided with Lady Perdita, who was riding as if she'd a fox in her sights. I reined in hard to stop a crash and the horse over balanced. She wasn't hurt,' he added as Callum opened his mouth. 'Interesting coincidence, meeting her here. My family are neighbours to hers, but it is years since I have seen her.'

'Did you quarrel in those days?' Daniel asked, earning himself a sharp kick on the ankle from his brother.

'Ah, you noticed a certain friction? When we were children I teased her, as boys will torment small and unprepossessing females who tag around after them. I was not aware she was in India.'

'Oh, well, after the elopement,' Daniel began. 'Er… you did know about that?'

'Of course,' Alistair said. Well, he had heard about a scandal yesterday. That was near enough the truth, and he was damnably curious all of a sudden.

'No harm in speaking of it then, especially as you know the family. My cousin wrote all about it. Lady P. ran off with some fellow, furious father found them on the road to Gretna, old Lady St George was on hand to observe and report on every salacious detail—all the usual stuff and a full-blown scandal as a result.'

'No so very bad if Lord Wycombe caught them,' Alistair said casually as the manservant came back, poured brandy and reported that the doctor had gone out, but was expected back soon.

'Well, yes, normally even Lady St George could have been kept quiet, I expect. Only trouble was, they'd set out from London and Papa caught them halfway up Lancashire.'

'Ah.' One night, possibly two, alone with her lover. A scandal indeed. 'Why didn't she marry the fellow?' Wycombe was rich enough and influential enough to force almost anyone, short of a royal duke, to the altar and to keep their mouths shut afterwards. A really unsuitable son-in-law could always be shipped off to a fatally unhealthy spot in the West Indies later.

'She wouldn't have him, apparently. Refused point blank. According to my cousin she said he snored, had the courage of a vole and the instincts of a weasel and while she was quite willing to admit she had made a serious mistake she had no intention of living with it. So her father packed her off here to stay with her aunt, Lady Webb.'

'Daniel,' Callum snapped, 'you are gossiping about a lady of our acquaintance.'

'Who is perfectly willing to mention it herself,' his twin retorted. 'I heard her only the other day at the picnic. Miss Eppingham said something snide about scandalous goings-on and Lady Perdita remarked that she was more than happy to pass on the benefits of her experience if it prevented Miss Eppingham making a cake of herself over Major Giddings, who, she could assure her, had the morals of a civet cat and was only after Miss E.'s dowry. I don't know how I managed not to roar with laughter.'

That sounded like attack as a form of defence, Alistair thought as Daniel knocked back his brandy and Callum shook his head at him. Dita surely couldn't be so brazen as not to care and he rather admired the courage it showed to acknowledge the facts and bite back. He also admired Wycombe's masterly manner of dealing with the scandal. He had got his daughter out of London society and at the same time had placed her in a situation where it would be well known that she was not carrying a child. Three months' passage on an East Indiaman gave no possibility of hiding such a thing.

But what the devil was Dita doing running off with a man she didn't want to marry? Perhaps he was wrong and she really was the foolish romantic he had teased her with being. She certainly knew how to flirt—he had seen her working her wiles on Daniel Chatterton last night—but, strangely, she had not done so with him. Obviously he annoyed her too much.

But, whatever she thought of him, the more distance there was between them mentally, the better, because there was going to be virtually none physically on that ship and he was very aware of the reaction his body had to her. He wanted Perdita Brooke for all the wrong reasons; he just had to be careful that wanting was all it came to. Alistair leaned back and savoured the brandy. Taking care had never been his strong suit.

'Perdita, look at you!' Emma Webb stood in the midst of trunks and silver paper and frowned at her niece. 'Your hair is half down and your neckcloth is missing. What on earth has occurred?'

'There was an accident on the *maidan*.' Dita came

right into the room, stripped off her gloves and kissed her aunt on the cheek. 'It is nothing to worry about, dearest. Lord Lyndon took a fall and he was bleeding, so my neckcloth seemed the best bandage.' She kept going, into the dressing room, and smiled at the *ayah* who was pouring water for her bath from a brass jug.

'Oh?' Her aunt came to the door, a half-folded shawl in her hands. 'Someone said you were arguing with him last night. Oh dear, I really am not the good chaperon my brother expected.'

'We have not seen each other since I was sixteen, Aunt Emma,' Dita said, stepping out of her habit. 'And we simply picked up the same squabble about a frog that we parted on. He is just as infuriating now as he was then.'

And even more impossibly attractive, unfortunately. In the past, when she had told herself that the adult Alistair Lyndon would be nothing like the young man she had known and adored eight years ago, she had never envisaged the possibility that he would be even more desirable. It was only physical, of course. She was a grown woman, she understood these things now. She had given him her virginity: it was no wonder, with no lover since then, that she reacted to him.

It was a pity he did not have a squint or a skin condition or a double chin or a braying laugh. It was much easier to be irritated by someone if one was not also fighting a most improper desire to…

Dita put a firm lid on her imagination and sat down in eight inches of tepid water, an effective counter to torrid thoughts. It was most peculiar. She had convinced herself that she wanted to marry Stephen Doyle until he had tried to make love to her; then she had been equally convinced that she must escape the moment she could lay her hands on his wallet and her own money that was in it.

She was equally convinced now that Alistair Lyndon was the most provoking man of her acquaintance as well as being an insensitive rake—and yet she wanted to kiss him again until they were both dizzy, which probably meant something, if only that she was prone to the most shocking desires and was incapable of learning from the past.

'I think everything is packed now,' Emma said with satisfaction from the bedchamber. 'And the trunks have gone off to the ship, which just leaves what you need on the voyage to be checked. Twelve weeks is a long time if we forget anything.' She reappeared as Dita stepped out of the bath and was wrapped in a vast linen sheet. 'I do hope Mrs Bastable proves as reliable as she appears. But she seems very happy to look after you and Miss Heydon.'

Averil was going to England for the first time since she was a toddler in order to marry Viscount Bradon, a man she had never met. *Perhaps I should let Papa choose me a husband*, Dita thought. *He couldn't do much worse than I have so far.* And her father was unlikely to pick on a pale imitation of Alistair Lyndon as she had done so unwittingly, it seemed. 'It isn't often that we see brides going in that direction,' Lady Webb added.

'Do you think me a failure?' Dita asked, half-serious, as her maid combed out her hair. 'After all, I came over with the Fishing Fleet and I haven't caught so much as a sprat.' *And do I want to marry anyway? Men are so fortunate, they can take a lover, no one thinks any the worse of them. I will have money of my own next year when I am twenty five…*

'Oh, don't call it that,' her aunt scolded. 'There are lots of reasons for young ladies to come India, not just to catch husbands.'

'I can't think of any,' Dita said. 'Other than escaping a scandal, of course. I am certain Papa was hoping I would catch an up-and-coming star in the East India Company firmament, just like you did.'

'Yes, I did, didn't I?' Lady Webb said happily. 'Darling George is a treasure. But not everyone wants to have to deal with the climate, or face years of separation for the sake of the children's health.' She picked up a list and conned it. 'And you will be going home with that silly business all behind you and just in time for the Season, too.'

That silly business. Three words to dismiss disillusion and self-recrimination and the most terrible family rows. Papa had been utterly and completely correct about Stephen Doyle, which meant that her own judgement of men must be utterly and completely at fault. On that basis Alistair Lyndon was a model of perfection and virtue. Dita smiled to herself—no, she was right about him, at least: the man was a rake.

10th December 1808

'Two weeks to Christmas,' Dita said as she hugged her aunt on the steps of the *ghat*. 'It seems hard to imagine in this climate. But I have left presents for you and Uncle on the dressing table in my room, and something for all the servants.' She was babbling, she knew it, but it was hard to say goodbye when you had no idea if you would ever see the person again.

'And I have put something in your bag,' Emma said with a watery smile. 'Goodness knows what happens about Christmas celebrations on board. Now, are you sure you have everything?'

'I went out yesterday,' her uncle assured her, patting his wife on the shoulder and obviously worried that she would burst into tears. 'You've got a nice compartment in the roundhouse below the poop deck, just as I was promised. That will be much quieter and the odours and noise will be less than in the Great Cabin below. It is all ladies in there as well, and you will be dining at the captain's table in the cuddy with the select passengers.'

'But those wretched canvas partitions,' his wife protested. 'I would feel happier if she was in a cabin with bulkheads.'

It had been a subject for discussion and worry for weeks. 'The partitions give better ventilation,' Dita said. 'I felt perfectly secure on the outward passage, but that was in a compartment forward of the Great Cabin and it was so very stuffy.' And revoltingly smelly by the time they had been at sea for a month.

'And all your furniture is in place and secured,' her uncle continued. *All* made it sound as though she was occupying a suite. The box bed that was bolted to the deck was a fixture, but passengers were expected to supply anything else they needed for their comfort in the little square of space they could call their own. Dita had a new coir mattress and feather pillow, her bed linen and towels, an ingenious dressing chest that could support a washbasin or her writing slope and an upright chair. Her trunk would have to act as both wardrobe and table and her smaller bags must be squashed under the bunk.

'And there are *necessaries* for the passengers' and officers' use on this ship,' Lord Webb added. Which was a mercy and an improvement on a slop bucket or the horrors of the heads—essentially holes giving on to the sea below—that had been the only options on the outward passage.

'I shall be wonderfully comfortable,' Dita assured them. 'Look, they want us to go down to the boats now.'

Plunging into the scrimmage of passengers, porters, beggars, sailors and screaming children was better than dragging out this parting any longer, even if her stomach was in knots at the thought of getting into the boat that was ferrying passengers to the ship. It hurt to part with two people who had been understanding and kindly beyond her expectations or deserts, and she feared she would cling and weep and upset her aunt in a moment.

'I love you both. I've written, it is with the Christmas presents. I must go.' Her uncle took her arm and made sure the porter was with them, then, leaving her aunt sniffing into her handkerchief, he shouldered his way to the uneven steps leading down into the fast-running brown water.

'Hold tight to me! Mind how you go, my dear.' The jostling was worse on the steps, her foot slipped on slime and she clutched wildly for support as the narrow boat swung away and the water yawned before her.

'Lady Perdita! Your hand, ma'am.' It was Alistair,

standing on the thwarts. 'I have her, sir.' He caught her hand, steadied her, then handed her back to one of the Chatterton twins who was standing behind him.

'Sit here, Lady Perdita.' This twin was Callum, she decided, smiling thanks at him and trying to catch her breath while her uncle and Alistair organised her few items of hand baggage and saw them stowed under the plank she was perched on. 'An unpleasant scrum up there, is it not?'

'Yes.' She swallowed hard, nodded, managed a smile and a wave for her uncle as the boat was pushed off. Alistair came and sat opposite her. 'Thank you. I am the most terrible coward about water. The big ship is all right. It is just when I am close to it like this.' She was gabbling, she could hear herself.

'What gave you a fear of it?' Alistair asked. He held her gaze and she realised he was trying to distract her from the fact that they were in an open boat very low in the water. 'I imagine it must have been quite a fright to alarm someone of your spirit.'

'Why, thank you.' Goodness, he was being positively kind to her. Dita smiled and felt the panic subside a little.

'Presumably you got into some ridiculous scrape,' he added and the smile froze as the old guilt washed through her.

Without meaning, to she gabbled the whole story. 'I was walking on the beach with my governess when I was eight and a big wave caught me, rolled me out over the pebbles and down, deep.' She could still close her eyes and see the underneath of the wave, the green tunnel-shape above her, trapping her with no air, beating her down on to the stones and the rocks. 'Miss Richards went in after me and she managed to drag me to the beach. Then the next wave took her. She nearly drowned and I couldn't help her—my leg was broken. The poor woman caught pneumonia and almost died.'

'Of course you couldn't have helped,' Callum said firmly. 'You were a child and injured.'

'But Lord Lyndon is correct—I had disobeyed her and was walking too close to the water. It was my fault.' No one had beaten her for her bad behaviour, for Miss Richards had told no one. But the guilt over her childish defiance had never gone away and the fear of the sea at close quarters had never left her.

'It has not prevented you from taking risks,' Alistair said dispassionately.

'Lyndon.' Chatterton's tone held a warning.

Alistair raised one eyebrow, unintimidated. 'Lady Perdita prizes frankness, I think.'

'It is certainly better than hypocrisy,' she snapped. 'And, no, it did not stop me taking risks, only, after that, I tried to be certain they were my risks alone.'

'My leg is much better.' Alistair delivered the apparent *non sequitur* in a conversational tone.

'I cannot allow for persons equally as reckless as I am,' Dita said sweetly. 'I am so glad you are suffering no serious consequences for your dangerous riding.'

'We're here,' Chatterton said with the air of a man who wished he was anywhere rather than in the middle of a polite aristocratic squabble.

'And they are lowering a bo'sun's chair for the ladies,' said Alistair, getting to his feet. 'Here! You! This lady first.'

'What? No! I mean I can wait!' Dita found herself ruthlessly bundled into the box-like seat on the end of a rope and then she was swung up in the air, dangled sickeningly over the water and landed with a thump on the deck.

'Oh! The wretched—'

'Ma'am? Fast is the best way to come up, in my opinion, no time to think about it.' A polite young man was at her elbow. 'Lady Perdita? I'm Tompkins, one of the lieutenants. Lord Webb asked me to look out for you. We met at the reception, ma'am.'

'Mr Tompkins.' Dita swallowed and her stomach returned to its normal position. 'Of course, I remember you.'

'Shall I show you to your cabin, ma'am?'

'Just a moment. I wish to thank the gentleman who assisted me just now.'

The ladies and children continued to be hoisted on board with the chair. Most of them screamed all the way up. *At least I did not scream*, she thought, catching at the shreds of her dignity. What had she been thinking of, to blurt out that childhood nightmare to the men? Surely she had more control than that? But the tossing open boat had frightened her, fretting at nerves already raw with the sadness of departure and the apprehension of what was to come in England. And so her courage had failed her.

Dita gritted her teeth and waited until the men began to come up the rope ladder that had been lowered over the side, then she walked across to Alistair where he stood with Callum Chatterton.

'Thank you very much for your help, gentlemen,'

she said with a warm smile for Callum. 'Lord Lyndon, you are *so* masterful I fear you will have to exercise great discretion on the voyage. You were observed by a number of most susceptible young ladies who will all now think you the very model of a man of action and will be seeking every opportunity to be rescued by you. I will do my best to warn them off, but, of course, they will think me merely jealous.'

She batted her eyelashes at him and walked back to Lieutenant Tompkins. Behind her she heard a snort of laugher from Mr Chatterton and a resounding silence from Alistair. This time she had had the last word.

Chapter Four

Dita sat in her cabin space and tried to make herself get up and go outside. Through the salt-stained window that was one of the great luxuries of the roundhouse accommodation she could see that they were under way down the Hooghly.

Every excuse she could think of to stay where she was had been exhausted. She had arranged her possessions as neatly as possible; thrown a colourful shawl over the bed; hung family miniatures on nails on the bulkhead; wedged books—all of them novels—into a makeshift shelf; refused the offer of assistance from Mrs Bastable's maid on the grounds that there was barely room for one person, let alone two, in the space available; washed her face and hands, tidied her hair. Now there was no reason to stay there, other than a completely irrational desire to avoid Alistair Lyndon.

'Perdita? We'll be sailing in a moment—aren't you coming on deck?' Averil called from the next compartment, just the other side of one canvas wall.

Courage, Dita, she thought, clenching her hands into tight fists. *You can't stay here for three months*. She had grown up knowing that she was plain and so she had learned to create an aura of style and charm that deceived most people into not noticing. She was rebellious and contrary and she had taught herself to control that, so when things went wrong it was only she who was hurt. Or so she thought until her hideous mistake with Stephen Doyle meant the whole family had had to deal with the resulting gossip. And in India she had coped with the talk by the simple method of pretending that she did not care.

But I do, she thought. *I do care. And I care what Alistair thinks of me and I am a fool to do so.* The young man she had adored had grown up to be a rake and the heir to a marquisate and she could guess what he thought about the girl next door who had a smirched reputation and a sharp tongue. *Hypocrisy.* Had the tender intensity with which he had made love to her eight years ago been simply the wiles of a youth who was going to grow up into a rake? It must have been, for he showed no signs of remembering; surely if he had cared in the slightest, he would recall calling her his darling Dita, his sweet, his dear girl…

'I'm coming!' she called to Averil, fixing a smile on her face because she knew it would show in her voice. 'Just let me get my bonnet on.' She peered into the mirror that folded up from the dressing stand and pinched the colour into her cheeks, checked that the candle-soot on her lashes had not smudged, tied on her most becoming sunbonnet with the bow at a coquettish angle under her chin and unfastened the canvas flap. 'Here I am.'

Averil linked arms with the easy friendliness that always charmed Dita. Miss Heydon was shy with strangers, but once she decided she was your friend the reserve melted. 'The start of our adventure! Is this not exciting?'

'You won't say that after four weeks when everything smells like a farmyard and the weather is rough and we haven't had fresh supplies for weeks and you want to scream if you ever see the same faces again,' Dita warned as they emerged on to the deck.

'I was forgetting you had done this before. I cannot remember coming to India, I was so young.' Averil unfurled her parasol and put one hand on the rail. 'My last look at Calcutta.'

'Don't you mind leaving?' Dita asked.

'Yes. But it is my duty, I know that. I am making an excellent marriage and the connection will do Papa and my brothers so much good. It would be different if Mama was still alive—far harder.'

In effect, Dita thought, *you are being sold off to an impoverished aristocratic family in return for influence when your family returns to England.* 'Lord Bradon is a most amiable gentleman,' she said. It was how she had described him before, when Averil had been excited to learn that Dita knew her betrothed, but she could think of nothing more positive to say about him. *Cold, conventional, very conscious of his station in life*—nothing there to please her friend. And his father, the Earl of Kingsbury, was a cynical and hardened gamester whose expensive habits were the reason for this match.

She only hoped that Sir Jeremiah Heydon had tied

up his daughter's dowry tightly, but she guessed such a wily and wealthy nabob would be alert on every suit.

'You'll have three months to enjoy yourself as a single lady, at any rate,' she said. 'There are several gentlemen who will want to flirt.'

'I couldn't!' Averil glanced along the deck to where the bachelors were lining the rail. 'I have no idea how to, in any case. I'm far too shy, even with pleasant young men like the Chatterton brothers, and as for the more… er…' She was looking directly at Alistair Lyndon.

As if he had felt the scrutiny Alister looked round and doffed his hat. 'Indeed,' Dita agreed, as she returned the gesture with an inclination of the head a dowager duchess would have been proud of. Alistair raised an eyebrow—an infuriating skill—and returned to his contemplation of the view. 'Lord Lyndon is definitely *er*. Best avoided, in fact.'

'But he likes you, and you are not afraid of him. In fact,' Averil observed shrewdly, 'that is probably *why* he likes you. You don't blush and mumble like I do or giggle like those silly girls over there.' She gestured towards a small group of merchants' daughters who were jostling for the best position close to the men.

'*Likes* me?' Dita stared at her. 'Alistair Lyndon hasn't changed his opinion of me since that encounter at the reception, and the accident we had on the *maidan* only made things worse. And don't forget he knew me years ago. To him I am just the plain little girl from the neighbouring estate who was scared of frogs and tagged along being a nuisance. He was kind to me like a brother is to an irritating little sister.' *And who then grew up to discover that she was embarrassingly besotted by him.*

'Well, you aren't plain now,' Averil said, her eyes fixed on the shore as the *Bengal Queen* slipped downriver. 'I am pretty, I think, but you have style and panache and a certain something.'

'Why, thank you!' Dita was touched. 'But as neither of us are husband-hunting, we may relax and observe our female companions making cakes of themselves without the slightest pang—which, men being the contrary creatures they are, is probably enough to make us the most desirable women on board!'

Dinner at two o'clock gave no immediate opportunity to test Dita's theory about desirability. The twenty highest-ranking passengers assembled in the cuddy, a few steps down from the roundhouse, and engaged in polite conversation and a certain jostling for position. Everyone else ate in the Great Cabin.

Captain Archibald had a firm grasp of precedent and Dita found herself on his left with Alistair on her left hand. Averil was relegated to the foot of the table with a mere younger son of a bishop on one side and a Chatterton twin on the other.

'Is your accommodation comfortable, my lord?' she ventured, keeping a watchful eye on the tureen of mutton soup that was being ladled out to the peril of the ladies' gowns.

'It is off the Great Cabin,' Alistair said. 'There is a reasonable amount of room, but there are also two families with small children and I expect the noise to be considerable. You, on the other hand, will have the sailors traipsing about overhead at all hours and I rather think the chickens are caged on the poop deck. You are spared the goats, however.'

'But we have opening windows.'

'All the better for the feathers to get in.'

Dita searched for neutral conversation and found herself uncharacteristically tongue-tied. This was torture. The way they had parted—even if he had no recollection of it—made reminiscence of their childhood too painful. She was determined not to say anything even remotely provocative or flirtatious and it was not proper to discuss further details of their accommodation.

'How do you propose to pass the voyage, my lord?' she enquired at last when the soup was removed and replaced with curried fish.

'Writing,' Alistair said, as he passed her a dish of chutney.

The ship was still in the river, its motion gentle, but Dita almost dropped the dish. 'Writing?'

'I have been travelling ever since I came to the East,' he said. 'I have kept notebooks the entire time and I want to create something from that for my own satisfaction, if nothing else.'

'I will look forward to reading it when it is published.' Alistair gave her a satirical look. 'I mean it. I wish I had been able to travel. My aunt and uncle were most resistant to the idea when I suggested it.'

'I am not surprised. India is not a country for young women to go careering around looking for adventures.'

'I did not want to *career around*,' Dita retorted, 'I wanted to observe and to learn.'

'Indeed.' His voice expressed polite scepticism. 'You

had ambitions of dressing up as a man and travelling incognito?'

'No, I did not.' Dita speared some spiced cauliflower and imagined Alistair on the end of her fork. 'I am simply interested in how other people live. Apparently this is permissible for a man, according to you, but not for a woman. How hypocritical.'

'Merely practical. It is dangerous'. He gestured with his right hand, freed now of its bandage.

Dita eyed the headed slash across the back, red against the tan. 'I was not intending to throw myself at the wildlife, my lord.'

'Some of the interesting local people are equally as dangerous and the wildlife, I assure you, is more likely to throw itself at you than vice versa. It is no country for romantic, headstrong and pampered young females, Lady Perdita.'

'You think me pampered?' she enquired while the steward cleared the plates.

'Are you not? You accept the romantic and headstrong, I note.'

'I see nothing wrong with romance.'

'Except that it is bound to end in disillusion at the very best and farcical tragedy at the worst.' He spoke lightly, but something in his voice, some shading, hinted at a personal meaning.

'You speak from experience, my lord?' Dita enquired in a tone of regrettable pertness to cover her own feelings. He had fallen in love with someone and been hurt, she was certain. And she was equally certain he would die rather than admit it, just as she could never confess how she felt for him. How she had once felt, she corrected herself.

'No,' he drawled, his attention apparently fixed on the bowl of fruit the steward was proffering. 'Merely observation. Might I peel you a mango, Lady Perdita?'

'They are so juicy, no doubt you would require a bath afterwards,' she responded, her mind distracted by the puzzle of how she felt about him now. Had she ever truly been in love with him, and if so, how could that die as it surely had, leaving only physical desire behind? It must have been merely a painful infatuation, the effect of emotion and proximity when she was on the verge of womanhood, unused to the changes in her body and her feelings. It would have passed, surely, if she had not stumbled into his arms at almost the moment she had realised how she felt.

But if it was merely infatuation, why had she been so taken in by Stephen? Perhaps one was always attracted to the same looks in a man…Then she saw the expression on Lady Grimshaw's face. Oh goodness, what had she just said?

'*Bath,*' Alistair murmured. He must have seen the look of panic cross her face. 'How fast of you to discuss gentlemen's ablutions, Lady Perdita,' he added, loudly enough for the elderly matron's gimlet gaze to fix on them intently.

'Oh, do hush,' she hissed back, stifling the giggle that was trying to escape. 'I am in enough disgrace with her already.'

Alistair began to peel the mango with a small, wickedly sharp knife that he had removed from an inner pocket. 'What for?' he asked, slicing a succulent segment off the stone and on to her plate.

'Existing,' Dita said as she cut a delicate slither and tried it. 'Thank you for this, it is delicious.'

'You have been setting Calcutta society by the ears, have you?' Alistair gestured to the steward who brought him a finger bowl and napkin. 'You must tell me all about it.'

'Not here,' Dita said and took another prim nibble of the fruit. Lady Grimshaw turned her attention to Averil, who was blushing at Daniel Chatterton's flirtatious remarks.

'Later, then,' Alistair said and, before she could retort that he was the last person on the ship to whom she would confide the gossip that seemed to follow her, he turned to Mrs Edwards on his other side and was promptly silenced by her garrulous complaints on the subject of the size of the cabins and the noise of the Tompkinson children.

Dita fixed a smile on her lips and asked the captain how many voyages he had undertaken; that, at least, was a perfectly harmless topic of conversation.

When dinner was over she went to Averil and swept her out of the cuddy and up on to the poop deck.

'Come and look at the chickens, or the view, or something.'

'Are you attempting to avoid Lord Lyndon, by any chance?' Averil lifted her skirts out of the way of a hen that had escaped from its coop and was evading the efforts of a member of the crew to recapture it.

'Most definitely,' Dita said. 'The provoking man

seems determined to tease me. He almost made me giggle right under Lady Grimshaw's nose and I have the lowering suspicion that he has heard all about the scandal in England and has concluded that I will be receptive to any liberties he might take.'

The fact that she knew she would be severely tempted if Alistair attempted to kiss her again did nothing to calm her inner alarm.

'Forgive me for mentioning it,' Averil ventured, 'but perhaps if one of the older ladies were to hint him away? If he has heard of the incident and has wrongly concluded that you... I mean,' she persisted, blushing furiously, 'if he mistakenly thinks you are not...'

'I spent two nights in inn bedchambers with a man to whom I was not married,' Dita said. 'An overrated experience, I might add.'

It had been a dreadful disillusion to discover that the man she had thought was perfect in looks and in character was a money-hungry boor with the finesse of a bull in a china shop when it came to making love.

The realisation that she had made a terrible mistake had begun to dawn on her by the time the chaise hired with her money had reached Hitchin. Stephen had no longer troubled to be charming, to be witty, to converse or to show the quick appreciation of her thoughts he had always counterfeited before. He had fretted about pursuit and asked interminable questions about her access to her funds. When the postillions, who quite obviously realised that an elopement was afoot, became impertinent he blustered ineffectually and Dita had to snub them with a few well-chosen words.

By the time they had stopped for the first night Dita

decided she had had enough and declared that she would
hire another chaise and return alone. It was then that she
discovered that Stephen was quite capable of forcing
her into the inn and up to a bedchamber and that he had
removed all the money from her luggage and reticule.

The effort to keep him from her bed involved a sleepless night and a willingness to stab him with a table knife
after he had run the gamut from trying to charm her, to
attempting to maul her, to a desperate attempt to force
her.

The second day had been worse. He had been furious
and sulky and every pretence that this was anything but
an abduction had gone. Papa had caught up with them
as they had arrived in Preston and by that time she was
so exhausted by lack of sleep that she had simply flung
herself on his chest and sobbed, unconscious of the audience in the inn yard and uncaring about his anger.

Averil was blushing, but it did not stop her putting
the question she was obviously dying to ask. 'Is it really
horrid? You know, one hears such things.'

'With the wrong man it is,' Dita said with feeling.
And that had been without the actual act taking place.
She shuddered to think what it would have been like
if Stephen had forced her. 'With the right one—' She
stopped on the verge of admitting that it was very plea-
surable indeed.

'I am sure it would be wonderful,' she said, as if
she did not know. There was no point in making Averil
fearful of her own nuptials, even if she suspected that
her betrothed had no finesse to speak of. Dita shivered
a little, wondering what would happen if another man
tried to make love to her.

Oh, but she had enjoyed Alistair's impertinent kiss on the *maidan*. The cockerel in the chicken coop flapped up on to the perch and crowed loudly, ruffling his feathers and throwing his head back. 'Yes, you are a fine fellow,' she said to him and he crowed again. Male creatures were all the same, she told herself. They needed feminine admiration and attention all the time. And Alistair had sensed she had enjoyed that meeting of lips, she was certain. No wonder he was so confident about teasing her. It would be well to exercise considerable caution if he was to not to guess the way she felt about him now— which could be summed up in three words: desirable, treacherous, trouble.

'Let us walk,' she said firmly. 'We must exercise every day, it will help keep us healthy.'

They strolled round and round the poop deck, both of them sunk, Dita guessed, in rather different thoughts about wedding nights. The view was not particularly diverting, for the river banks were hardly higher than the water, here in the delta of the Ganges, and mud banks, fields covered in winter stubble and herds of buffalo were all that could be seen between the small villages that dotted the higher ground.

'I had better go and unpack,' Averil said after a while. 'I can see now why I was advised to bring a hammer and nails to hang things up. I cannot imagine how I am ever going to fit everything in and still live in that space. It is a quarter the size of my dressing room at home!'

Dita could well believe it. For all that she was unpretentious and unspoiled, Averil was used to considerable luxury. She wondered what she would make of the chilly Spartan grandeur of her betrothed's home. But doubtless her own money would go a long way to making it comfortable.

When her friend went below Dita leaned her forearms on the rail and let herself fall into a daydream. Soon the rhythms of shipboard life would assert themselves and the passengers would develop a routine that could become quite numbing until landfalls, quarrels or hurricanes enlivened things. On the way out she had read her way through a trunk full of books, determined to keep her mind off her problems with light fiction. Now she was equally determined to face the reality of her future. There was only one problem, Dita realised: she had no idea what she wanted that to be.

'That was a big enough sigh to add speed to the sails.'

She turned her head, but she had no need to look to know who that was, lounging against the rail beside her. Her biggest problem, in the flesh.

'I was trying to decide what life will be like when I return to England,' she replied with total honesty. 'What I want it to be like.' *Whatever was the matter with me when I was sixteen? Perhaps all girls that age believe themselves in love without receiving the slightest encouragement.* Only she had received rather more than a little encouragement. She sighed again, thinking of the girl newly emerged from childhood, suddenly realising the boy she had idolised had turned into a young man, just as she was becoming a woman.

'Will the scandal be forgotten?' Alistair asked.

Dita blinked at him. Most people politely pretended they knew nothing about it, to her face at least. Only the more catty of the young women would make snide remarks, or the chaperons hint that she needed to be particularly careful in what she did.

'You know about it?'

'You eloped and your father caught up with you after two nights on the road and you refused to marry the man concerned.' Alistair shifted so that his elbow almost met hers on the rail. Her breath hitched as though he had touched her. 'Is that a fair summary?'

'Fair enough,' Dita conceded.

'Why did you refuse?'

'Because I discovered he was less than the man I thought he was.'

'In bed?'

'No! What a question!' The laugh was surprised out of her by his outrageous words. She twisted to stare at him. No, this was not the boy she remembered, but that boy was still there in this man. The trouble was, every feminine instinct she possessed desired him. Him, Alistair, as he was now.

He was waiting for her answer and she made herself speak the truth. 'He was after my money. Which wouldn't have been so bad if he hadn't been a bore and a lout into the bargain. He must be a very good actor.' *Or I must have been blinded by the need to escape the Marriage Mart, the restrictions of life as a single young woman.*

'Or you are a very poor judge of men?' Alistair suggested.

'Perhaps,' Dita conceded. 'But I have *your* measure, my lord.'

He was staring out to sea and she could study his profile for a moment. She had been correct when she had told Daniel Chatterton that the savage slash of the scar on his face would only enhance his attractiveness. Combined with the patrician profile and his arresting eyes, it gave him a dangerous edge that had been missing before.

Then he turned his head and she looked into his eyes and realised that the edge had been there already: experience, intelligence, darkness. 'Oh yes?'

She straightened up, pleased to find she could face him without a blush on her cheeks; it had felt for a moment as though every thought was imprinted on her forehead. Alistair turned so he lounged back against the rail, shamelessly watching her. She tried not to stare back, but it was hard. He looked so strong and free. Bareheaded, the breeze stirred his hair and the sun gilded his tanned skin. *I want him. He fills me with desire, quite simple and quite impure.*

'You have a great deal in common with that creature there.' She nodded towards the cockerel's cage. 'You are flamboyant, sure of yourself and dangerous to passing females.'

There was no retort, not until she was halfway across the deck and congratulating herself on putting him firmly—safely—in his place. His crack of laughter had her pursing her lips, but his words sent her down the companionway with something perilously close to an angry flounce.

'Why, thank you, Dita. I shall treasure the compliment.'

Chapter Five

After their exchange on the poop deck Dita did her best to avoid Alistair without appearing to do so, and flattered herself that she was succeeding. It did not prevent the disturbing stirring in her blood when she saw him, but it gave her a feeling of safety that, in the restless small hours, she suspected was illusory.

She was helped by the captain relaxing his seating plans at dinner. Having clearly established precedent, he acknowledged that to keep everyone tied to the same dining companions for three months was a recipe for tedium at best and squabbles at worst.

Breakfast and supper were informal meals and by either entering the cuddy with a small group, or after he was already there, Dita ensured she was always sitting a safe distance from Alistair.

During the day, when she was not in her cabin reading or sewing alone or with Averil, she sought out the company of the other young women on deck. They were all engaged in much whispering and secrets, making and wrapping Christmas gifts, teasing each other about who was giving what to which of the men.

They irritated her with their vapid conversation, giggling attempts to flirt with any passing male and obsession with clothes and gossip, but they provided concealment, much, she thought wryly, as one swamp deer is safer from the tiger in the midst of the herd.

Alistair had no way of realising that this was not her natural habitat, she thought, as she watched him from under the tilted brim of her parasol while Miss Hemming confided her plan to get Daniel Chatterton alone under the stars that evening.

It was on the tip of her tongue to point out that Mr Chatterton was already betrothed, and had been for years to a young woman who awaited him in England, and that with the amount of cloud cover just now there would be no stars to flirt beneath. But she bit her lip and kept the tart remarks to herself. Alistair bowed slightly as he passed the group, accepting both the wide-eyed looks, nervous titters and her own frigid inclination of the head with equal composure.

Now, why is Dita so set on avoiding me, I wonder? Those chattering ninnies are boring her to distraction and in five days I cannot believe we have not sat next to each other for a meal simply by chance. That kiss on the maidan*? Surely not. Dita has more spirit than to flee because of that, even if she knows I want to do it again. And more. And I'll wager so does she.*

'Oh, Lord Lyndon!' It was one of the Misses Whyton, indistinguishable from each other and with a tendency to speak in exclamations.

He stopped and bowed. 'Miss Whyton?'

'What is your favourite colour, Lord Lyndon?'

Ah, Christmas gifts. He had hoped to escape that by the simple expedient of not flirting with any of the little peahens, but it was obviously not working. 'Black,' he drawled, producing what he hoped was a sinister smile.

'Ooh!' She retreated to her sister's side, a frown giving her face more expression than it usually bore. Apparently whatever she was making would not work well in mourning tones.

He glanced across and saw Dita's head bent over a book. Now, it would be amusing to surprise her with a Christmas gift. What a pity he had no mistletoe to accompany it.

Or, perhaps he could improvise; he certainly had the berries. Smiling to himself as he plotted, Alistair strolled along the main deck to where the Chatterton twins and a few of the other young men had gathered. With the captain's permission they were going to climb the rigging. After a few days out most of them were already feeling the lack of exercise and it seemed an interesting way of stretching muscles without overly shocking the ladies. Wrestling, sparring or singlestick bouts would have to be indulged in only when a female audience could be avoided.

Daniel and Callum had already taken off their coats and were eyeing the network of ropes as they soared up the main mast. 'It looks easy enough,' Daniel said. 'Climb up on the outside and you are leaning into the rigging the whole way.'

'Until you get to the crow's nest,' his brother pointed

out. 'Then you have to swing round to the inside and climb up the hole next to the mast.'

'Bare feet,' Alistair said. Like the other younger men he was wearing loose cotton trousers. He heeled off his shoes as he looked up. 'I tried this on the way out.' He squinted up at the height and added, 'Smaller ship, though!'

'We cannot all get up there at once, not with a sailor already in the crow's nest,' Callum pointed out, and the others moved off to stand at the foot of the smaller foremast, leaving the Chattertons and Alistair in possession of the main mast.

'We three can if we move out along those ropes the sailors stand on to bundle up the sails,' Daniel pointed out. 'And don't snort at me, Cal, I don't know the name of them and neither do you, I wager.'

'Sounds as though that will work.' Alistair took a yard in his hand and swung up to stand on the rail. 'Let's try it.'

The tarred rope was rough under the softer skin of his arches, but it gave a good grip and his hands were toughened by long hours of riding without gloves. It felt good to reach and stretch and use his muscles to pull himself up and to counteract the roll of the ship, one minute dropping him against the rigging, the next forcing him to hang on with stretched arms and braced legs over the sea.

The newly healed wound in his thigh reminded him of its presence with every contraction of the muscle, but it was the ache of under-use and weakness, not the pain of the wound tearing open. His right hand was not fully right either, he noticed with clinical detachment, and compensated by taking more care with the grip.

The wind blew his hair off his face and ripped through his thin shirt and Alistair found he was grinning as he climbed. Daniel appeared beside him, panting with effort as he overtook. From below Callum called, 'It isn't a race, you idiot!'

But Daniel was already twisting around the edge of the rigging to hang downwards for the few perilous feet up into the crow's nest. Alistair heard the look-out greeting Chatterton as he reached the top spar of the mainsail himself and eyed the thin rope swinging beneath it. It was a tricky transfer, but if sailors could do it in a storm, he told himself, so could he. There was an interesting moment as the sail flapped and the foot rope swayed and then he was standing with his body thrown over the spar, looking down at the belly of the sail.

Callum appeared beside him. 'I wouldn't want to do this in a gale at night!' he shouted.

'No. Damn good reason not to get press-ganged,' Alistair agreed as he twisted to look back over his shoulder. The young women had stopped all pretence of ignoring the men and were standing staring up at them. Dita, hatless, was easy to pick out, her face smoothed into a perfect oval by the distance.

'We have an audience,' he remarked.

'Then let's get down before Daniel and make the most of the admiration,' Callum said with a grin.

Going down was no easier, as Alistair remembered. As he glanced down at the ladies, and to set his feet right on the rigging, the scene below seemed to corkscrew wildly, as though the top of the mast was fixed and the ship moved beneath it.

'Urgh,' Callum remarked, and climbed down beside him. 'Remind me why this is a good idea.'

'Exercise and impressing the ladies, if that appeals.' Alistair kept pace with him as the rigging widened out. His leg was burning now with the strain, but it would hold him. He'd be glad to relax his hand, though. 'It is Daniel who is betrothed, is it not?'

'Yes,' Callum agreed, somewhat shortly. 'A childhood friend,' he added after another rung down. 'I'm not looking for a wife myself, not yet while I don't know whether the Company wants me to come back out or work in London.' After another two steps down he seemed to unbend a trifle. 'What about you?'

'I certainly require a wife,' Alistair agreed. 'There's the inheritance to think of. I shall no doubt be braving the Marriage Mart this Season in pursuit of a well-bred virgin with the requisite dowry and connections, not a thought in her brain and good child-bearing hips.'

Callum snorted. 'Is there no one below us right this minute with those qualifications? What about Lady P—?'

He broke off, obviously recalling that Dita fell scandalously short of one of Alistair's stated requirements. 'Er, that is—'

'That is, Lady Perdita has enough thoughts in her brain to keep any man in a state of perpetual bemusement,' Alistair said, taking pity on him. 'I have had my fill of troublesome women, I want a placid little English rose.'

And besides, he thought as he jumped down on to the

deck and held out a hand to steady Callum, *she certainly hasn't got child-bearing hips. She's still the beanpole she always was.*

A beanpole, he was startled to realise, who stood regarding him with wide-eyed interest. So, she was not above getting in a flutter over displays of male prowess. How unexpected. How stimulating. She came up to him as he shrugged back into his coat and he braced himself for gushing admiration.

'That looks wonderful!' Dita exclaimed, her eyes fixed on the crow's nest and not on him, or any of the men. 'I would love to do that.'

'No! Of course you can't, you're a girl!' It was the response that had become automatic through years of her tagging along behind him. 'A lady,' he corrected himself as the wide green eyes focused on his face, and he was conscious of an odd feeling of disappointment.

'That's what you always said,' she retorted. 'You always snubbed me, and I always got my way. I climbed the same trees, I learned to swim in the lake—I even rode a cow backwards when you did. Do you remember?'

'Vividly,' Alistair said. 'I got a beating for that. But what you did when you were eight has nothing to do with this. Besides anything else, you couldn't climb rigging in skirts.'

'That is a very good point,' she said, bestowing a smile on him that left him breathless. Before he could think of a response she turned away.

Dita Brooke had obviously been taking lessons in witchcraft, he concluded, wondering whether he was foolishly suspicious to read a promise of trouble into that radiant smile.

'Ooh! Lord Lyndon, you must be ever so strong to do that!' One of the merchants' daughters, he had no idea which, gazed at him in wide-eyed adoration.

'Not at all,' he said, lowering his voice into a conspiratorial whisper. 'I get dizzy at heights and had to be helped by Mr Chatterton there. Fine physical specimen, and all that money, too…' He let his voice trail off in admiration and watched with wicked pleasure as she hurried off to hang on Callum's arm.

Alistair sauntered back to his cabin to wash. He took care not to limp and reflected that unless he wanted to become a circus turn it would be better to confine vigorous exercise to the early morning before the ladies were about.

It was not until he had stripped off his shirt and was pouring water over his head that he identified the strange feeling of disappointment that had hit him during that brief exchange at the foot of the mast. Dita had wanted the adventure, the experience, but for the first time, she did not want it in order to follow him.

But why should she? he thought. He was no longer thirteen, she was no longer eight, and she was most certainly not the troublesome little sister he had always thought of her as. But she was going to be trouble for someone.

Dita retreated to her cabin and piled all the items from on top of her trunk on to the bed so she could open it. She was restless and impatient and they had only been at sea a few days; she needed exercise and adventure and she was going to get it, even if it meant getting up an hour early.

The fact that the close proximity of Alistair Lyndon was contributing to the restlessness could not be helped. She closed her eyes and let her memory bring back the sight of him, his thin shirt flattened against his back by the wind, the muscles in his forearms standing out like cord as he gripped the ropes, the curiously arousing sight of his bare feet. He had always been tall, but the lanky youth had filled out into a well-muscled man.

She had watched him like a hawk for any signs of weakness from his wounds, but he had shown nothing, not until he had strolled away and she had seen what she doubted anyone else had: the effort not to limp. He should take it more easily.

Then she gave herself a little shake. Alistair could look after himself and there was no point in torturing herself with worry about him. She should think about her own plans. Alistair was right, she could not climb in skirts and she couldn't climb at all if the captain realised what she was about, so it was a good thing that she had packed her Indian clothes.

Dita dug out a pile of cottons and laid them on the bed. She had beautiful *shalwa kameezes* in silk, but she had stowed those in the trunks below decks. In her cabin luggage she had kept the simple cotton ones for lounging in comfort in the privacy of her cabin.

She shook out a pair of the trousers, tight in the lower leg, comfortably roomy around the waist and hips: perfect for climbing. And she had a *kurta*, the loose shirt that reached well down her thighs. That would give her plenty of room to move. All she had to do was to wake at dawn.

* * *

The deck was cool and damp under her bare feet, still not dry after the early morning holystoning it had received. Most of the crew on deck were gathered near the main mast, with few close to the shorter of the three masts nearest the stern.

Dita dropped her heavy plait of hair down inside the *kurta*, used a coil of rope as a step and climbed on to the rail, her hands tight on the rigging, her eyes fixed on a point above her head and not on the sea. Her heart pounded and for a moment she thought her fear of the water would root her to the spot, but it was far enough below.

No one had noticed her in the early light, they were too busy with their tasks and she had deliberately chosen garments dyed the soft green that, improbably, cow dung produced.

She stepped on to the first horizontal rope in the rigging that tapered upward to the crow's nest and grimaced at the tarry smell and the roughness under her hands and feet. But it felt secure and after a moment she began to climb, slowly and steadily, not looking down.

It was harder than it had looked when the men had done it, but she had expected that. After several minutes she rested, hooking her arms through the ropes and letting her body relax into the rhythm of pitch and roll. Perhaps that was far enough for today; there was a burn in her muscles that warned her they were overstretched and when she risked a downwards glance the deck seemed a dizzying distance below.

Yes, time to get down. As she hung there, deciding how much longer to rest, a figure came out on to the deck. Even foreshortened she recognised Alistair in his shirtsleeves. He seemed to be holding a pole of some kind. He turned as though to climb the companionway to the almost deserted poop deck and as he did so he glanced up.

Dita froze. Would he would recognise her?

'Get down here this instant!' He did not shout, but his voice carried clearly.

Defiant, Dita shook her head and began to climb. She had rested; she could do it and she was not going to come down just because Alistair told her to. A rapid glance showed he was climbing after her and she kept going. But she was slow now, slower than he was, and he reached her as she neared the top where the rigging narrowed sharply.

'Dita, don't you dare try to get into the crow's nest!'

She glanced down to the wind-tousled black head on a level with her ankles, suddenly very glad he was there. 'I have no intention of trying,' she admitted. 'I'll just have a rest and then I'll come down.'

'You are tired?' His face was tipped up to her now, and the world below him—one moment the sea, the next the hard and unforgiving white deck planks—twisted and turned in the most disconcerting manner.

'Just a little.'

'Hell. Keep still and hang on.'

'I have no intention of doing anything else. Alistair! What on earth are you doing?' He climbed up beside her and then swung over so his body bridged hers and his hands gripped the rope either side of her wrists.

'Stopping you falling off. Your face has gone the nasty

shade of green I remember from when you climbed the flagpole on the church tower.'

'Oh.' She certainly felt green now. 'Alistair, you can't do this, I'll push you off.'

'There's hardly any bulk to you,' he said. 'Put one foot down. Good, now the other.'

Awkwardly they began to descend. When the ship swung one way his body crushed hers into the rigging, even though she could feel him fighting to keep his weight off her. When it went the other way she knew his arms would be stretched by the extra extension her body created. She glanced over to his right hand and watched the way his knuckles whitened and the tendons stood out under the strain.

His breath was hot on her neck, her cheek, her ear, and she could feel his heartbeat when his chest pressed into her back. And, as her mind cleared and she gained enough confidence to think of other things, she realised that he was also finding this proximity stimulating— with his groin crushed into her buttocks with every roll of the ship there was no disguising it.

The realisation almost made her lose concentration for a moment. She was enjoying the feel of his body so close too, frustrating though it was to be pinned down like this, unable to do anything but place hands and feet at his command. *I remember how his body felt over mine on a bed. I remember the scent of his skin and his hands on my...*

'We're at the rail. Slide round in front of me and jump down,' Alistair ordered, shaking her out of her sensual reverie.

Dita very much doubted her legs were up to jumping,

but she had too much pride to argue. With an awkward twist she swung down from the rigging and landed on the deck on all fours with an inelegant thump. 'Thank you.'

Alistair's face as he straightened up beside her showed nothing but anger. If he had enjoyed being so close to her, it did not show now. 'You idiot! What the blazes do you think you were doing? You could have been killed.'

'I doubt it.' They were attracting attention from some of the deck hands; Dita turned on her heel and walked away towards the cuddy, her shoulders braced against the coming storm. Behind her she could hear the slap of Alistair's bare feet on the deck.

The space was empty, she was relieved to see, and the stewards had not begun to lay the table and set out breakfast. There was little hope of outdistancing Alistair and reaching the roundhouse, although she was going to try—he could hardly pursue her into that all-female sanctuary. Dita lengthened her stride, then his grip on her shoulder stopped her dead in her tracks. His hand was warm and hard and the thin cotton caught in the roughness of his palm. Struggling would be undignified, she told herself.

'I should go and change,' Dita said, her back still turned.

'Not until you give me your word you will not try that damn-fool trick again.' The thrust of his hand as he spun her round was not gentle, nor was the slap of his other palm as he caught her shoulder to steady her. 'Are you all about in your head, Perdita?'

She tipped up her chin and stared back into the furious tiger eyes with all the insolence she could muster.

'Perdita? Now that *is* serious—you never called me that unless you were very angry with me.' Alistair's eyes narrowed. 'Let me see. The last time must have been when I borrowed your new hunter and rode it.'

'Stole,' he said between gritted teeth. 'And *tried* to ride it. I can recall hauling you out of the ditch by your collar.'

'And you called me *Perdita* for a week afterwards.' She remembered his strength as he had lifted her, the fear in his voice for her—and how that had changed to anger the moment he realised she was unhurt. He had never failed to rescue her then, however much she annoyed him.

'And it is not funny!'

She must have been smiling at the memory. He took a step forwards; she slid back, still in his grasp.

'And I am very angry now and I am not fifteen and you are not a child and a fall from a horse is not the same as plunging into the sea from a great height.'

'No,' she agreed. The door was quite close. If she just edged a little more to the right and ducked out of his grip… She needed to distract him. 'You enjoyed that.'

His brows snapped together as he took the step that brought them toe to toe. 'What do you mean?'

'We were pressed very close together. Did you think I would not notice, or not understand? I am not an innocent.' What had possessed her to say that? The fact that he was obviously thinking of her as a child to be extracted from scrapes, even though his body was well aware of her age? *He really does not remember that last night*, she thought. He had been drinking, a little, when she had gone into his arms; she had tasted the brandy on his lips, but he had not been drunk.

'No, you're not, are you?' Alistair agreed, his voice silky as he moved again, turning them both so that he was between her and the door. Once she had been small and lithe enough to slip from his hands, evade his clumsy adolescent attempts to control her. Now he was a mature man, with a man's strength, and he was not going to let her go. Not until he was ready. She was angry and a little frightened and, it was disturbing to realise, aroused by the fact. 'You would be wise to behave as though you were.'

'I mean—' Dita bit her tongue. But she was not going to explain herself to Alistair and tell him that her only experience was their eager, magical, lovemaking. If he chose to believe that she had lost her virginity to Stephen Doyle, that was up to him. She could hardly accuse him of failing to understand her, when she couldn't forgive herself for going off with the man. 'I mean, why should I trouble to pretend, with you?'

'Is that an invitation, Dita?' He was so close now that she had to tip her head back at an uncomfortable angle to look up at him. He gave her a little push and she was trapped against the massive table.

'No,' she said with all the composure she could muster. 'It is an acknowledgement that we were…friends, once, a long time ago and I do not think you have changed so much that you would deliberately hurt me now.'

'And an *affaire* would hurt?' He lowered his head so his mouth was just above hers. His lids were low over those dangerous eyes and she stared at the thick fringe of spiky black against his tanned cheek. Not a young man's fresh skin any more. There were small scars, fine lines at the corners of his eyes. Her gaze slid lower. He hadn't shaved yet that morning and the stubble showed darker than she remembered. Alistair's mouth was so close now that she could kiss him if she chose.

I do not choose, she told herself fiercely. 'Naturally.' *And an* affaire *is all you would consider, isn't it? You've as much pride as I have and you wouldn't offer to marry another man's leavings. And I am not the girl I was, the one who was dazzled by you and had no idea what the fire was she was playing with that night. I am the woman who desires you and who knows that to surrender would be my undoing and the last blow to my reputation. I* must *be sensible.*

She made herself shrug, then realised that her hands had come up to clasp his upper arms, her fingers pressed against the bulge of muscle. Dita made herself open her hands and pressed them instead to his chest. Pushing was hopeless, but it gave her at least the illusion of resistance.

'A dalliance with you, Alistair, would doubtless be delightful—you have so much experience, after all. But I have my future to consider. In this hypocritical world *you* may dally all you wish and still find yourself an eligible bride. I must do what I may to repair my image. One slip, with my name and my money, might be overlooked. Two, never.'

'You are very cool about it, Dita. Where's the impulsive little creature I remember?' His right hand moved up her shoulder and she stiffened, refusing to give in to the shiver of need running through her. Between her legs the intimate pulse throbbed with betraying insistence and she made herself stand still, expecting him to cup her head and hold her for his caress. Instead his hand curled round her neck and pulled the long plait out of the back of her shirt.

'Where's the intense, straightforward young man of my memory?' she countered as he twisted her hair around his hand and tugged gently.

'Oh, he is still intense,' Alistair said. 'Just rather less straightforward.' He was close enough for her to see the pulse in his throat, exposed by the open-necked shirt. Close enough to smell the fresh linen and the soap he had used that morning and the salt from the sea breeze and the sweat from that rapid climb to reach her.

Dita closed her eyes. He was going to kiss her and she was not strong-willed enough to stop him, nor, in her heart, did she want to. One kiss could not matter; it would not be of any importance to him. He pulled gently on the plait and she swayed towards him, blind, breathless, and felt his warmth against her upper body in the thin cotton. His knuckles brushed her cheek, his breath feathered over her mouth and she tipped her face up, remembering the feel of his lips on hers, the sensual slide of his tongue as he had explored her mouth while he sprawled on the ground.

Nothing happened. Confused, Dita opened her eyes and looked straight into his dark, amused amber gaze where her reflection was trapped like a fly. Alistair flicked the tip of her nose with the end of her plait and stepped back. She swayed and threw out her hands to grip the edge of the table to keep from falling

'As always, I will do my best to keep you out of trouble, Dita my dear.' He sauntered to the head of the companionway leading down to the lower deck and the Great Cabin and paused at the top. 'The stewards are on their way, Dita. What are you waiting for?'

Chapter Six

What am I waiting for? A kiss? An apology? The strength to walk over there and slap that beautiful, assured, sardonic face? Whatever it was, she was not going to let him see how shaken she felt, how close she was to reaching for him. Dita blinked back angry tears, furious with herself and with Alistair.

'Waiting for? Why, nothing.' It was quite a creditable laugh and really should have been accompanied by the flutter of a fan. 'I had thought you might have wanted a reward for your gallant rescue just now, but obviously you are not as predictable as I thought you were.' The door to the roundhouse was mercifully close. 'I will see you at breakfast perhaps, my lord.'

Something showed in his face, just for a second. Admiration? Regret? Dita got safely through the door and ran, her hand pressed against her mouth to stifle the furious sob that was struggling to emerge.

'Dita!' Averil's startled cry stopped her dead in

her tracks. 'What on earth are you doing dressed like that?'

Dita pushed back the canvas flap of her own cabin and pulled her friend inside. 'Shh!' The walls were the merest curtains, enough for an illusion of privacy only. She pulled Averil down to sit beside her on the bed. 'I have been climbing the rigging,' she muttered.

'No! Like that?' Averil whispered back.

'Of course, like this. I could hardly do it in a gown, now could I?'

'No. I suppose not. I was going to come and see if you were ready for a walk before breakfast. I thought if the other ladies weren't out there we could walk faster and stretch our legs.'

'Without having to stop every minute to exclaim over an undone bonnet ribbon or bat our eyelashes at a man?' Dita stood up to pull off the *kurta* and Averil modestly looked away as she tugged off the trousers. 'Pass my chemise, would you? Thank you.' Her stomach was churning with what she could only suppose was a mixture of unsatisfied desire and sheer temper.

'Did you really climb up? All the way? What if someone had seen you?' Averil clasped her hands together in horror.

'Someone did.' Dita unrolled a pair of stockings and began to pull them on. She had to tell someone, pour it all out, and Averil was the only person she could trust. 'Alistair Lyndon. And he climbed up after me and made me come down.'

'How *awful*!' Averil got up to help lace Dita's light stays.

'I was glad to see him, if truth be told,' she admitted,

prepared to be reasonable now that Averil was aghast. 'Or, rather, I was glad when he came after me. My first instinct when he told me to come down was to climb higher and then I wished I hadn't! It is much harder work than I realised and my legs were beginning to shake and when I looked down everything seemed to go round and round in circles.'

'What did he say when you reached the deck again? Was he angry? I would have sunk with mortification, but then you are much braver than I am.' Averil bit her lip in the silence as Dita, words to describe what had happened next completely deserting her, shook out her petticoats. 'It was rather romantic and dashing of Lord Lyndon, don't you think?'

It was and she would have died rather than admit it, even if what had happened next was anything but romantic. 'He lectured me,' Dita said, her head buried in her skirts as she pulled her sprig muslin gown on. Instinct was telling her to dress as modestly as she could. 'He thinks of me as a younger sister,' she added as she pinned a demure fichu over what bare skin the simple gown exposed. 'Someone to keep out of trouble.'

And that's a lie. That teasing near-kiss and the feeling of Alistair's hard, aroused body pressed against her had told her quite clearly that whatever his feelings were, they were not brotherly. He had felt magnificent and just thinking about it made her ache with desire. What would he have done just now if she had bent her head and kissed his bare throat, trailed her tongue down over the salty skin to where she could just glimpse a curl of dark hair?

She remembered the taste of him, the scent of his

skin. But there had not been so much hair on his chest eight years ago. *He's a man now,* she reminded herself. What if she had reached out and cupped her hand wantonly over the front of his trousers where his desire was so very obvious?

'What a pity,' Averil surprised her by murmuring as she stood up to tie the broad ribbon sash. 'Perhaps he'll change his mind. It is a long voyage.'

'He will do no such thing,' Dita said. 'He knows about my elopement. Bother, I must have an eyelash in my eye—it is watering. Oh, thank you.' She dabbed her eyes with Averil's handkerchief. 'That's better.' *I am not going to weep over him, not again. Not ever.*

'But you are Lady Perdita Brooke,' Averil protested. 'An earl's daughter.'

'And Alistair is about to become a marquis, if he isn't one already. He can look as high as he likes for a wife and he won't have to consider someone with a shady reputation. If we were passionately in love, then I expect he would throw such considerations to the wind. But we are not, of course.' *Merely in lust.* 'Not that I want him, of course,' she lied. *Marriage isn't what either of us wants; sin is.*

'I can't imagine why not,' Averil said with devastating honesty. 'I would think any unattached woman would be attracted to him. He *might* fall in love with you,' she persisted with an unusual lack of tact. Or perhaps Dita was being better at covering up her feelings than she feared.

'Love?' Dita laughed; if Averil noticed how brittle it was, she did not show it. 'Well, he had plenty of oppor-

tunity when we were younger.' She brushed out her hair
and twisted it up into a simple knot at her nape.

Not that it had occurred to her that what she felt for
him was more than childish affection, not until that
night when he had been so bitterly unhappy and she had
reached out to him, offering comfort that had become
so much more. But now she realised that he had hardly
cared who he was with, let alone been concerned about
her feelings, whatever endearments he had murmured as
he had caressed the clothes from her body. If he had, he
would never have rejected her so hurtfully afterwards.

It was a blessing that he had not understood, simply
seen the innocent love that burned in her eyes, the trust
that had taken her into his arms.

She could still feel the violence with which Alistair
had put her from him that last day, the rejection with
which he had turned his face from her. He had been
upset about something, desperately, wordlessly upset,
and he had been drinking alone, something that she had
never seen him do before, and her embrace had been
meant only to comfort, just as the eight-year-old Dita
would hug her idol when he fell and cut his head. But it
had turned into something else, something the sixteen-
year-old Dita could not control.

He had yanked her into his arms, met her upturned
lips in a kiss that had been urgent on his part, clumsy
and untutored on hers. And then it had all got completely,
wonderfully, out of control and she had discovered that,
however innocent she was, he was not and that he could
sweep away her fears, melt them in the delight of what
he was teaching her body—until he had pushed her

from him, out of his bedchamber, his words scathing and unjust.

For several months she had thought she had driven him away by her actions, had shocked him with her forwardness. After a while she had made up stories to console herself and blank out what had really happened; then she overheard her parents talking and learned that he had left after a furious quarrel with his father.

'When Alistair left home,' she told Averil as she stuck in combs to hold her hair, 'I had this fantasy that his father had refused to allow him to pay his addresses to me. Wasn't that foolish? There was absolutely no reason why we wouldn't have been a perfectly eligible couple then. In reality, they had a row over Alistair taking over one of the other estates, or something equally ridiculous to fall out about.'

'So you were in love with him then?' Averil asked.

'I fancied I was!' Dita was pleased with the laugh, and her smile, as she made the ready admission. 'I was sixteen and hopelessly infatuated. But I grew out of it and I would expire of mortification if he ever found out how I had worshipped him, so you must swear not to tell.' Hero worship, affection, calf love and desire: what a chaos of feelings to try to disentangle.

'I wouldn't dream of it,' Averil assured her. 'I would hate it if a man guessed something like that about me.'

'So would I,' Dita assured her as she adjusted her shawl. 'So would I.'

They managed a brisk walk around the deck, which Dita thought would account for any colour in her cheeks, and then went straight in to breakfast. Alistair was already at table, seated between the Chattertons; Dita deliberately sat opposite. The men half-rose, greeted them and resumed their conversation.

'I was going to try some singlestick exercises early this morning, but I got distracted,' Alistair said, continuing his conversation with Callum.

So that was what he was doing, up so early. Dita accepted a cup of coffee and took a slice of toast.

'I think I'll do that every morning,' he went on, without so much as a glance in her direction to accompany the warning. 'Why don't you two join me? We could box, wrestle, use singlesticks.'

'Good idea,' Callum agreed, with a nudge in the ribs for Daniel who was grumbling about early rising. 'We will be sure to avoid the ladies by doing that.'

And that put an end to any dawn exercise on her part, Dita recognised, slapping preserve on her toast with a irritable flick. It was easier to be angry with Alistair than to confront any of the other feelings he aroused in her.

'What a charming picture you two ladies make.' Alistair again, smiling now. Beside her Averil made a small sound that might have been pleasure at the compliment, or might have been nerves. 'So English in your muslins and lawns and lacy fichus.'

'You do not like Indian female dress, my lord?' Dita enquired. She was not going to allow him to needle her and she rather thought he knew exactly why she had changed into something so blandly respectable. It had been an error to show him that she cared for his opinion. She had morning dresses that would make him pant with desire, she told herself, mentally lowering necklines and removing lace trim from the contents of her trunk.

'It is suitable for Indian females, but not for English ones to ape.'

'But English gentlemen resort to Indian garb to relax in, do you not? Why should ladies not have the same comforts? But of course,' she added, 'you do not appreciate the wonderful freedom of casting off one's stays.'

Averil gave a little gasp of horrified laughter, Callum went pink and Alistair grinned. 'No, but I can imagine,' he said, leaving her in no doubt he was thinking of garments he had unlaced in the past.

She was not going to rattle him, she realised, and all she was succeeding in doing was embarrassing Averil and scandalising Callum Chatterton, who was too nice and intelligent a man to be teased.

'And how do you ladies intend passing the day?' Callum enquired, changing the subject with rather desperate tact.

'I am making Christmas gifts,' Averil confided. 'I thought that all of us who dine in the cuddy make up a house party, as it were. On Christmas Eve after supper it would be delightful to exchange little tokens, just as though we really were at a Christmas house party, don't you think?'

'Gifts for *everyone*?' Daniel asked, chasing some tough bacon around his plate.

'It would be invidious to leave anyone out, I think.' Averil frowned. 'Of course, it is not easy to prepare for this sort of thing, not knowing everyone who is of the party. But twenty small gifts are not so very hard to come up with.'

'Twenty-one with the captain,' Dita pointed out. 'I think it is a charming idea, but we should let everyone know we will do it, don't you think? In case there is anyone who had not thought of gifts and is embarrassed.'

'Oh. I had not considered that. If there are people with nothing suitable to exchange, it would indeed put them out.' Averil's face fell.

'If you mention it now, then anyone who needs to do last-minute shopping can go to the bazaars when we call at Madras,' Alistair suggested. Averil beamed at him and Dita found herself meeting his eyes with something like gratitude for his thoughtfulness to her friend.

'That was a kind thought,' she said across the table when Averil was distracted by Daniel teasing her about what she could possibly give the captain. 'Thank you.'

'I do occasionally have them,' he said laconically. 'Miss Heydon is a charming and kind young woman and I would not like to see her embarrassed.'

'I do not accuse you of being unkind,' Dita began. That had felt like an oblique slap at her, the young woman he had no compunction about embarrassing.

'You, my dear Dita, are a feline. You walk your own path, you guard your own heart and you will not yield to anything but your own desires. Miss Heydon is a turtle dove—sweet, loyal, affectionate. Although,' he added, glancing along the table to where Averil was fending off Daniel's wit with surprising skill, 'she has more intelligence and courage than at first appears. She would fight for what she loves.'

'Whereas you think me merely selfish?' Dita's chin came up.

'And intelligent and courageous and quite surprisingly

alluring. But you are going to find it hard to bend that self-will to a husband, Dita.'

'Why should I?' *Alluring?* The unexpected compliment was negated by the fact he found it surprising that she should be attractive. She sliced diagonally across the slice of toast with one sweep of her knife. 'Men do not have to compromise in marriage. I cannot imagine *you* doing so, for example, even for a woman you love.'

Alistair gave a harsh laugh. 'What has love got to do with it? That is the last thing I would marry for. Excuse me.' He pushed back his chair and left the table.

How had he let that betraying remark escape? Alistair wondered as he strode down to his tiny cubicle off the Great Cabin. Or was it only his acute consciousness of his own ghosts that made him fear his words would expose him?

Love brought blindness with it and rewarded trust with lies. It had blinded him, humiliated him—he was not going to give it a chance again. Physical love was easy enough to take care of, even if one was fastidious and demanding, as he knew himself to be. Alistair grimaced as he sat on his bunk and tried to remember what he had come down here for. Not to run away from Dita Brooke, he sincerely hoped, although the wretched chit was having the most peculiar effect on his brain.

Easier to think about sex than about emotion—and Dita seemed to produce emotional responses in him he rarely experienced: anxiety, protectiveness. Possessiveness, damn it. Yes, better to think about sex and she certainly made him fantasise about that, too.

He had dreamed about her for years, erotic, arousing,

frustrating dreams that had puzzled him as much as they had tormented him. They had been too real. Had he really thought about the girl he had grown up with in that way and suppressed it so the desire only emerged when he was asleep? Now it was damnably hard not to indulge in waking dreams about the adult woman.

Three months' celibacy was not something he would seek out, he had to admit. He was a sensual man by nature, but he prized control and he was not going to seek relief either here on board or in any of their ports of call. Fortunately there was no one on the *Bengal Queen* who attracted him in that way. No one except Lady Perdita Brooke, of course.

Hell. How could he feel responsible for her—a hangover from all those childhood years, he supposed—and yet want to do the very things he would kill another man for trying with her?

She was so responsive, with all the intensity and passion of the child grown into the woman. Her reckless riding, the way she had flung herself from her horse and run to him, her uninhibited attempts to care for him. That kiss. Alistair fell back on to the bed and relived those stimulating seconds.

He had enjoyed that, irresponsible as it had been. And so had Dita. And being Dita, when she thought he was offering to do it again she had wanted it, as filled with passionate curiosity for risk and experience as she always had been. Passion. A shiver ran through his long frame as he thought about passion and Dita.

Damn it, no. By all accounts she had been hurt enough by her own recklessness—the last thing she needed was an *affaire* with him. And the last thing *he* needed when he arrived in London for the Season was the rumour that he had been involved with the scandalous Lady Perdita. He was hunting for a bride as pure as the driven snow and for that he had to preserve the mask of utmost respectability that was expected in this artificial business. He owed it to his name. And he owed it to his own peace of mind not to become embroiled with a mistress who would expect far more than he was prepared to give.

Alistair sat up abruptly. He was leaping to conclusions about what Dita might expect. She knew he was no saint. His mouth curled into a sensual smile. If Dita wanted to pay games—well, there were games they could play, games that would be just as much fun in their own way as those innocent sports of their childhood.

Alistair left the cabin half an hour later, notebooks under one arm and his travelling inkwell in his hand. He had told Dita that he was going to write a book; now he must see whether he could produce prose that was good enough and turn his travels into something that would hold a reader's attention.

There was a lady seated at the communal table in the middle of the cabin, a sewing box open and items strewn around. Ah, yes, Mrs Ashwell, the wife of newly wealthy merchant Samuel Ashwell. He had seen her at work before, it was what had prompted his idea about mistletoe for Christmas.

'That is very fine, ma'am,' he observed.

She was instantly flustered. 'Oh! You mean my artificial flowers? I used to be… I mean, I always used to make them, for myself and friends, you understand. I enjoy the work…'

In other words, she had been an artificial flower maker before her husband made his money. He, no doubt, wished his wife to hide the fact, but she enjoyed the creativity. The products were as good as any society lady would buy.

'Can you make mistletoe?' Alistair asked. 'A spray of it that a lady might put in her hair?'

'Why, yes, I suppose so. I never have, but it should be straightforward.' She frowned and rummaged in her work box. 'This ribbon is the right green. But I would need white beads for the berries and I have none.'

'I have.' Alistair went back into his cabin and unlocked the small strong box he had bolted to the deck. 'Here.' He handed her a velvet bag. 'Use all of them if you can.' Now, how to recompense her for what would be a considerable amount of fiddling work without giving offence by offering payment?

'And thank you. You have rescued me from the embarrassing predicament of having no suitable gift for a lady. I do hope, when you are in London next, you will do me the honour of leaving your card? I would very much like to invite you and Mr Ashwell to one of the parties I will be giving.'

'My lord! But…I mean…we would be delighted.' He left her ten minutes later, flushed and delighted. If only pleasing a woman was always that easy.

Chapter Seven

20th December 1808—Madras

The *Bengal Queen* dropped anchor opposite Fort St George close to the mouth of the Kuvam River and the harassed ship's officers set about sorting out the groups of passengers. Some wanted to go ashore to shop in Madras; there were men who were eager to hire a boat and go upstream to shoot duck and the East India Company supercargo—very senior men indeed—demanded to be taken ashore to transact Company business with all speed.

'I really do not think we should go ashore without a gentleman to escort us,' Mrs Bastable said for the fourth time since breakfast. 'And Mr Bastable is clerking for Sir Willoughby and will be in the Company offices all day. Perhaps we could join the Whytons.'

Averil and Dita exchanged looks. The thought of a morning in the company of the Misses Whyton was excruciating. 'Um…I think they are already a very large group. I asked the Chattertons,' Dita said, 'but Daniel is committed to the shooting party and Callum is going to the offices with Sir Willoughby.' She surveyed the rest of the available men without much enthusiasm. 'I suppose I could ask Lieutenant Tompkins, if he is off duty.'

'A problem, ladies?'

Dita turned, her heart thumping in the most unwelcome manner. 'Merely a question of an escort to the markets, Lord Lyndon. Please, do not let us detain you—I am sure there are ducks awaiting slaughter.'

'I was not intending to join the shooting party and I have my own shopping to do.' He appeared to take their acceptance for granted. 'Are you ready?'

'Yes, we are. Thank you so much, my lord.' Mrs Bastable had no hesitation snatching at this promise of escort. 'Oh dear, though, there's that dreadful chair to negotiate.'

'Safest way down,' Alistair said. 'Let me assist you, ma'am. There you are.'

Averil and Dita watched their chaperon being whisked skywards. 'She's landed safely,' Averil announced. 'Look.'

'No, thank you.' Dita remained firmly away from the rail.

'Why do you climb the rigging if you won't look over the side?' Alistair demanded as Averil sat down in the bos'un's chair with complete unconcern.

'The further I get from the sea, the happier I am,' Dita said and turned her back firmly on the rail and all the activity around it. She fixed her gaze on Alistair's mouth, which was a reckless thing to do for the sake of her emotions, but was a great help in taking her mind off small boats and open water. 'Don't ask me to explain it, I know it is irrational.'

'That is no surprise, you are female after all,' Alistair remarked. She glanced up sharply and met a look that was positively lascivious.

Dita opened her mouth, shut it again with a snap at the expression in his eyes and took two rapid steps back. Alistair followed her, gave her a little push and she sat down with a thump in the chair.

'Why, you—' He flicked the rope across the arms and signalled to the sailors hauling it up. Seething, Dita found herself in the flat-bottomed boat being helped out by Averil.

'You devious, underhand, conniving creature,' she hissed as Alistair dropped into the boat from the ladder.

'It worked,' he said with a grin as he sat down beside her. 'And I take it back—you *are* irrational, but not because you are female. But I cannot apologise for any looks of admiration—you do look most charming.'

Dita sorted through the apology and decided she was prepared to accept it. 'Thank you. But you really are the most provoking man,' she added. 'I don't recall you being so—except when you wouldn't let me do something I wanted to, of course.'

'Which was most of the time. You always wanted to do the maddest things.'

'I did not!' The boat bumped alongside the *ghat*. 'You wretch! You are doing it again, arguing in order to distract me.'

'I have no idea why you are complaining,' Alistair said, as he got out on to the stone steps and held out his hand to Mrs Bastable, who glanced from one to the other with a puzzled frown. 'You have made the transition from ship to shore without turning green in the slightest.'

They were enveloped in the usual crowd of porters jostling for business, trinket sellers, garland merchants and beggars. Alistair dropped into rapid, colloquial Hindi as he cleared a way through for the ladies to climb the steps; by the time they had reached the top they had two of the more respectable men at their heels.

...double that when we get back here with all our packages intact, Dita translated when she could hear more clearly. Coins changed hands, the men grinned and set off.

'I told them I wanted the best general market,' Alistair said as they followed, skirting a white-clad procession bearing a swathed body towards the burning *ghats*.

'Oh, I can never get used to that,' Mrs Bastable moaned, turning her head away. 'I so long for the peace of a green English churchyard.'

'But not yet, I hope,' Alistair murmured. Dita caught his eye and stifled a choke of laughter. Now that she had recovered from his trickery she discovered that today she was quite in charity with the man, which was dangerous. She reflected on just how dangerous as she picked her way round potholes and past a sacred cow that had come to a dead halt beside a vegetable stall and was placidly eating its way through the wretched owner's produce.

'And cows that stay in a field would be nice,' she remarked.

The market they were guided to was down the usual narrow entrance that opened out into a maze of constricted alleys, lined on each side with tiny stalls and booths, many of them with the owner sitting cross-legged on the back of the counter.

'Do you know what you want?'

'Not fish!' Mrs Bastable turned with a shudder from the alley to their left, its cobbles running with bloody water, the flies swarming around the silvery heaps.

'Down here.' Averil set off confidently down another lane and they soon found themselves amidst stalls selling spices, baskets of every kind, toys, small carvings and embroidery. 'Perfect!'

Soon their porters were hung around with packages. Mrs Bastable fell behind to haggle over a soapstone carving and Alistair stayed with her to help.

'We'll be in the next alley on the right,' Averil called back. 'I can see peacock-feather fans. They are charming and useful,' she said as they stood examining them. 'We could buy a dozen between us; they will do very well for gifts.'

'Yes, I—what's that?' Both swung round at the sound of screams and running feet and a deep-throated snarling. The alleyway cleared as though a giant broom had swept through it. Men leapt on to counters, dragging women with them as a small boy ran down, screeching in fear, followed by a dog, snarling and snapping, its mouth dripping foam.

'Up!' Dita grabbed Averil and thrust her towards the fan seller, who took her wrists and dragged her on to the narrow counter amidst a heap of feathers. Time seemed to slow to a crawl as the boy and the dog hurtled towards her and she realised there was no room on any of the stalls now and the alley was a dead end. Dita snatched the child as he reached her and clambered up a pile of baskets as though it were a stepladder until they were perched on the top of the teetering heap, the dog leaping and snarling at the foot.

'*Hilo dulo naha,*' she murmured to the boy as he clutched her, his dirty, skinny little body wrapped around hers. But he needed no warning to keep still and, as their fragile sanctuary began to tilt with an ominous cracking sound, he seemed to stop breathing.

The dog leapt at them, clawing at the baskets. It was mad, there was no mistaking it. Dita tried to put out of her mind the memory of their *jemahdar* who had been bitten. His death had been agonising and inevitable. She had to stay calm. If the baskets collapsed—*when* they collapsed—she would throw the boy to Averil and pray she was strong enough to hold him. And she would try and get behind the baskets...

Something flew through the air and hit the dog and it turned, yelping. Alistair, a long, bloody knife in his hand, came down the alley at the run and kicked out as the dog leapt for him, catching it under the chin. As it spun away he lunged with the knife, but his foot slipped on rotting vegetables in the gutter and he went down on to the snapping, snarling animal.

Dita screamed as she slid down the baskets and thrust the little boy into Averil's reaching arms. As she hit the ground, groping for the stone he had thrown, Alistair got to his feet. The dog, throat cut, lay twitching in the gutter.

'Did it bite you?' Frantic, she seized his hands, used her skirts to wipe the blood away. 'Are you scratched? Have you any cuts on your hands?'

Alistair dropped the knife and caught at her wrists. 'I'm all right. Dita, stop it.'

'You fell hard, you might not have felt a bite.' She tried to see if there were any tears in his coat or the light trousers he wore. 'Alistair, don't you know what happens if you've been bitten, even a graze—'

'Yes, I know. I am all right,' he repeated. 'Dita you are getting covered in blood. What the devil were you thinking of, scrambling up there with that child?'

'There was nowhere else to go,' she protested as the alley began to fill up. One man, a fish seller by the state of his clothes, picked up the bloody knife and walked away with it. A woman, weeping loudly, ran and snatched the child from Averil. The noise was deafening.

'It wouldn't bear the weight of both of you.' Alistair released her and she began to shake. 'It was going to collapse at any moment.'

'I know that. I couldn't leave him!'

'Most people would have.' Someone brought a bowl of water and Alistair plunged his hands into it. Dita held her breath until they emerged, the skin unbroken. His coat was stained, but she could see no evidence of teeth marks on it, or tears in his trousers.

Alistair gestured for more water. When it was poured he took her hands in his and washed them and she thought back over the crowded, terrified, minutes. 'You came to rescue the child,' she said. 'You must have gone for the knife the moment you heard him scream, or you wouldn't have got here with it when you did.'

'Well, that's two of us who are sentimental,' he said, his voice harsh, but his eyes as he looked at her held admiration and the shadow of fear, not for himself, but for her. 'Don't do that to me again, Dita. My nerves won't stand it. The mast was bad enough, this—'

They stood, their hands clasped in the reddening water and the noise of the crowd faded. Dita wondered if she was going to faint. Alistair was staring at her as though he had never seen her before.

'Dita! Dita, are you all right?' She looked round, dazed and a little dizzy, to see her friend supporting their weeping chaperon. 'I don't think Mrs Bastable can walk back.'

'Rickshaw,' Alistair snapped at their two porters. 'Two. Can you help Lady Perdita, Miss Heydon?' As Averil's hand came under her elbow he scooped Mrs Bastable up and followed the porters out of the market.

'Oh, my,' Averil said with a laugh that broke on a sob. 'She's gone all pink. At least it has stopped her weeping.'

'Are you all right?' Better to think about Averil than what might have happened to the child, to Alistair, to her.

'Me? Oh, yes. I've feathers sticking in me and doubt-less any number of bruises, but if it wasn't for you I don't know what would have happened. You are a heroine, Dita.'

'No, I'm not,' she protested. 'I'm shaking like a leaf and I would like to follow Mrs Bastable's example and have hysterics right here and now.' *I wish he was holding me. I wish...*

Mrs Bastable sank into the rickshaw with a moan. 'I'll get in with her,' Averil said. 'I have a vinaigrette in my reticule and a handkerchief.'

Dita held on to the side of the other rickshaw while Alistair got Averil settled. She would like to sit down, but she didn't think she could climb in unaided. Her legs had lost all their strength and the bustling street seemed to be growing oddly distant.

'Don't faint on me now.' Alistair scooped her up, climbed into the rickshaw and sat down with her still in his arms.

'Can't I?' she murmured against his chest. 'I would like to, I think. But I never have before.'

'Very well, if you want to.' There was the faintest thread of amusement in his voice and he shifted on the seat so he could get both arms around her as it tilted back and the man began to trot forwards between the shafts.

'Perhaps I won't. This is nice.' *That was he said when he kissed me on the* maidan. *Nice.* 'Where's my bonnet?'

'Goodness knows. Lie still, Dita.'

'Hmm? Why?' *He is very strong, all those muscles feel so good.* His chest was broad, his arms were reassuring and his thighs…she really must stop thinking about his thighs.

'Never mind.' He was definitely amused now, although there was something else in his voice. Shock, of course. Alistair wasn't made of stone and that had been a terrifying few minutes.

'You are all right, aren't you?' she asked after a moment, the panic spiking back. 'You would tell me if you had been bitten or scratched?'

'I am all right. And I would tell you if I had been bitten.' Alistair added the lie as he bent his head so his mouth just touched the tangled brown mass of her hair. He was still shaken to find that his skin was unbroken and his stomach cramped at the thought of those few seconds after the dog had collapsed twitching into the gutter and he had looked, felt, for any wound on his body and on hers.

It was good that he was holding Dita, because he suspected his hands would shake if he was not. Never, in his life, had he been more afraid—for himself, for another person. She thought he had grabbed the knife when he heard the screams because he wanted to save the child and he could not tell her the truth, that he had reacted purely on instinct: she was where those screams had come from.

'Something smells of fish,' she said. She still sounded drugged with shock; the sooner she was in bed, warm, the better. Despite the heat she was shivering.

'I do. That was a fish-gutter's knife and I ran through those puddles by their stalls to get it.'

She chuckled and he tightened his arms and made himself confront the nightmare that was gibbering at the back of his brain. If he had been bitten, then he would have shot himself. He had seen a man die of the bite of a mad dog and there didn't seem to be any worse way to go. But what if it had bitten Dita? What if he had arrived just too late? The vision of her slender white throat and the knife and his bloody hands and the dog's foaming muzzle shifted and blurred in his imagination.

'Ouch,' she murmured and he made himself relax his grip. All his young life it seemed he had looked out for Dita, protected her while she got on with being Dita. Eight years later and, under the desire he felt for her, he still felt the need to do that—but would he have had the courage to do for her what he would have done for himself? Would it have been right?

'Alistair? What is wrong?' She twisted round and looked up at him, her green eyes dark with concern, and he shook himself mentally and sent the black thoughts back into the darkness where they belonged. The worst hadn't happened, they were both all right, the child was safe and he had to keep his nightmares at bay in case she read them in his face and was frightened.

'Our wardrobes are wrecked, I smell of fish and now you probably do too, we haven't finished our Christmas shopping, Mrs Bastable is still wailing—it is enough to send a man into a decline.'

Her face broke into a smile of unselfconscious amusement and relief. 'Idiot.'

It was the least provocative thing to say, the least flirtatious smile, but the desire crashed over him like a wave hitting a rock. He wanted her, *now*. He wanted her hot and trembling and soft and urgent under him. Somehow he knew how she would feel, the scent of her skin, of her arousal. He wanted to take her, to bury himself in her heat and possess her. He wanted her with all the simple urgency of a man who had felt death's breath on his face and who had tasted more fear in a few seconds than he would surely ever feel for the rest of his life.

She was still looking at him; her wide mouth was still smiling and sweet and her eyes held something very close to hero worship. Alistair bent and kissed her without finesse, his tongue thrusting between lips that parted in a gasp of shock, his hands holding her so that her breasts were crushed against him; the feel of soft, yielding curves against his chest, against his heart, sent his body into violent arousal.

Dita must have felt his erection and she could not escape the message of a kiss that was close to a brutal demand, but she did not fight him. She melted against him, her mouth open and generous, her tongue tangling with his, her hands clinging while he tasted and feasted and felt the need and the primitive triumph surge through him. He had killed the beast for her and now she was his prize.

The seat tilted sharply, almost throwing them out of the rickshaw as the man lowered the shafts to the ground. Alistair grabbed the side with one hand and held tight to Dita with the other, shaken back into reality and the realisation that he had damn near ravished a woman in a rickshaw on the streets of Madras.

'Hell.'

She stared at him, apparently shocked speechless by what they had just done, then scrambled down on to the ground unaided and went to the other rickshaw.

Alistair got out, paid the drivers, found the boat, paid off the porters and oversaw loading the parcels before he turned to the three women. By then, he hoped, he would have himself under control again. Mrs Bastable was leaning on Averil's arm, fanning herself, but looking much more composed. Averil smiled. Dita, white-faced, just looked at him with no expression at all, although if either of the others had been themselves they could not have failed to see her mouth was swollen with the force of his kisses. She had said nothing, he realised.

He got them into the boat, the three women in a row, and sat down opposite them so he could look at Dita.

She sat contemplating her clasped hands, calm while they were rowed out, calm when he helped her into the chair, last of the three so he could get up the ladder and be there when she landed on the deck.

'I'll take Lady Perdita to her cabin,' he said to Averil and picked her up before either of them could react.

'Second on the left,' she called after him. 'I'll come in a moment.'

If there was anyone in the cuddy he didn't see them. He fumbled a little with the ties on the canvas flap, uncharacteristically clumsy with delayed shock, then he had her inside and could put her on the bed.

'I'm sorry,' he said as she raised her eyes to meet his. 'It happens, it's a male reaction to danger, fear—we want sex afterwards. It doesn't mean anything… It wasn't you. Don't think it was your fault.'

'Oh.' She arched her brows, aloof, poised, the acid-tongued lady from Government House despite her stained, torn gown and tumbling hair and bruised mouth and shaking hands. 'Well, as long as it wasn't *me*. I would hate to think I was responsible for that exhibition.' He could not read her eyes as she watched him and her smile when it came did not reach them. 'Thank you for saving my life. I will never forget that.'

'Dita?' Averil said from outside. 'May I come in?'

'Ma'am.' He opened the flap and stepped out, holding it for her to enter. 'I'll have the parcels sent down to the cuddy.'

'Oh, Dita.' Averil sat down on the trunk. 'What a morning. Mrs Bastable is resting and I've asked the steward to make tea.'

'Thank you. A cup of tea would be very welcome.' Incredibly she could still make conversation. Alistair had kissed her as though he was starving, desperate—for her. And she had kissed him back with as much need and desire and with the certainty that he wanted her. And then he said it wasn't *her*. That any woman would have provoked that storm of passion. That kissing her as she had always dreamt he would kiss her meant absolutely nothing to him. He needed sex as Mrs Bastable had needed to have hysterics.

That time when they had made love fully, gloriously, he had looked at her as she had smiled up at him dreamily afterwards and told her harshly to get out, to go, all his tenderness and passion hardening into rejection and anger.

Alistair had saved her life, risked a hideous death, behaved like the hero she had always known him to be—and stamped on her heart all over again.

'Oh, don't cry!' Averil jumped up with a handkerchief. *She must have an inexhaustible supply*, Dita thought, swallowing hard against the tears that choked her throat.

'No, I won't. It is just the shock. I think I will lie down for a while. That would be sensible, don't you think?'

'Yes.' *Poor Averil, she doesn't need another watering pot on her hands.* 'You get into bed and I'll bring your tea and tuck you in. I'll put all our shopping in my cabin; you just rest, dear.'

Chapter Eight

24th December 1808

They rounded the southern tip of India and headed across the ocean towards Mozambique as dinner was served on Christmas Eve. The stewards had brought a load of greenery on board from Madras and the Great Cabin and cuddy were lavishly decorated with palm fronds and creepers.

The ladies cut both red and gold paper into strips to weave amongst it and there were garlands of marigolds that had been kept in the cool of the bilges and were only a little worn and wilted if one looked too close.

'At least that reduces the look of Palm Sunday in church that all those fronds produced,' Averil observed as they made table decorations to run down the length of the long board.

The captain had decreed a return to formality and precedence, Dita noticed as the stewards began to set out place cards with careful reference to a seating plan.

It meant she would be sitting next to Alistair. She had been avoiding any intimacy ever since their return on board ship, despising herself for cowardice even as she did so.

She had tried not to be obvious about it: she owed the man her life, after all. But it was torture to be close to him. She wanted to touch him, to have him take her lips again, and yet she knew that the passion he had shown her would have been the same for any woman. It was not much consolation that he appeared to have been avoiding her, too.

'We can put out the presents now,' Averil said. 'The place cards will help.' Dita made herself concentrate on the task at hand. The stewards were having a difficult time of it, trying to lay an elaborate formal setting while ladies ducked and wove between them, heaping up little parcels that slid about with the motion of the ship, but the mood was good natured and, as Miss Whyton said, sorting out the gifts could only add to the jollity.

Dita juggled her pile of packages, squinting at labels and tweaking ribbons while she tried to avoid thinking about the fact that there was one person she had no gift for. Alistair wouldn't notice, she tried to tell herself, not with such a pile of parcels in front of him. But she suspected he would. It was not that she wanted to snub him, but she had had no idea what to give him. A trivial token was just that: trivial. She could not insult the man who had saved her life with a trinket. A significant gift— and she was a good enough needlewoman to make a handsome waistcoat from the silks in her trunk if she applied herself—would cause comment.

There was only one thing and it nagged at the back

of her mind until the last teetering pile was stabilised with tightly rolled napkins.

'Just time to get changed,' Averil said as they all stood back to admire the effect, then Dita followed her to their cabins.

The jewellery box was locked in her trunk and she lifted it out and set it on the bunk. Emeralds for dinner, she decided, and lifted out the necklace and earrings and set them aside.

Her hands went back to the box, hesitated, then she lifted out the top tray, then the items below until it appeared to be empty. There was a pin to be pulled, a narrow panel to be pushed and then the secret drawer slid out. In it was a slim oblong package wrapped in tarnished silver paper. The amber velvet ribbon was frayed and the label, *Alistair, Happy Birthday with love from Dita XXX*, was crumpled.

It was almost nine years since she had wrapped it up. The stitches might be embarrassingly clumsy—she should check. Certainly it needed rewrapping. Dita hesitated, then lifted out the package, slid it into her reticule just as it was, and reassembled the box before she locked it safely away.

The cuddy was filling up as she returned and the noise level was rising, helped by bowls of punch and glasses of champagne. The doors had been thrown open to the deck so the sea breezes could mitigate the heat of twenty-one bodies, hot food and scurrying stewards and some of the sailors had been posted on the deck to play fiddles and pipes.

'Lady Perdita.' Captain Archibald bowed over her hand and handed her wine.

'You look, if I may be so bold, utterly stunning, Lady Perdita.' Daniel Chatterton appeared at her side, his gaze frankly appreciative as he took in her amber silk gown and the glow of the emeralds. 'You look so...uncluttered—' he glanced towards some of the other ladies, weighted down with jewellery and feathers '—and that shows off your beauty.'

There was no denying the pleasure his words gave her. She had deliberately set out to dress her hair without ornament, only one long brown curl brushing her shoulder. The emeralds were simply cut and simply mounted to achieve their effect by their size and quality and her gown shimmered in the light.

But it was not Daniel Chatterton she had dressed for. It was a satisfying statement of the polished style she had made her own and it was a defiant gesture to Alistair. *See what you spurn.*

He was on the opposite side of the cabin, talking to Averil, making her laugh and blush, and Dita allowed herself a moment's indulgence to admire the dark tail-coat, the tight breeches, immaculate striped stockings, exquisite neckcloth. He would look perfectly at home in a London drawing room, she thought. Then he moved and the play of muscle disturbed the cut of the coat and the look he swept round the crowded room held the alertness of the hunter. *He isn't quite civilised any more*, she thought, and found she was running her tongue over dry lips.

The gong sounded, the patterns shifted and broke up as people went to their places, the chaplain said grace and then went below decks to do the same in the Great Cabin, and Alistair was holding her chair for her. She smiled her thanks and he smiled back. No one looking at them could have imagined that kiss in the rickshaw, she thought. It almost seemed like a dream now. But, of course, he didn't want her, so there would be nothing in his look to betray him.

The meal passed in a noise-filled blur. The food was good, but too rich, the wine flowed too freely, Alistair made unexceptional, entertaining small talk, first to her, then to his other partner. Dita nodded and chatted and smiled and plied her fan and drank a second glass of wine and wondered if the room was spinning or whether it was her head.

Finally the dishes were cleared, fruit was set out, more wine was poured and the captain raised his glass. 'A toast, my lords and gentlemen, to the ladies who have created this festive table.'

The men rose and drank, the ladies smiled and bowed and the captain picked up his first present, the signal for them all to begin.

There were shrieks and laughter and people calling their thanks down the length of the board. It would be impossible, Dita thought, to notice if someone had omitted to give you a present unless you were looking for one gift in particular. The Chattertons waved and mouthed *Thank you* for the watercolour sketches she had done of them. Averil seemed delighted with the notebook she had covered in padded silk and the captain was most impressed with her drawing of the *Bengal Queen*'s figurehead.

Her own collection of gifts was delightful, too. Thoughtful, handmade presents from some people, well intentioned but prosaic ones from others. The Chattertons had given her a pair of beautiful carved sandalwood boxes, Averil a string of hand-painted beads. There was nothing from Alistair.

Dita carefully folded up the wrapping paper, handed it to a steward and glanced around the table. No, no unclaimed gift, nothing had fallen to the floor. He had not given her a present—that would teach her to be complacent and expect something.

'What a clever idea these knots made into paperweights are,' she remarked to Alistair with a bright smile, holding out her own gift from the captain. 'You have a different knot, I see.'

'Yes,' he agreed as he pushed back his chair. 'Please excuse me.'

Dita watched him leave the cuddy. He had gone down to the Great Cabin, she realised, hearing the noise coming up the companionway from the company below. Why? Was he going to come back? On the impulse Dita got to her feet and followed him. She would give Alistair her gift even if he scorned it. It was that or throw it over the side.

There was a passage at the foot of the steps formed by the screens that divided up the cabins down on this deck. To her right she could hear the passengers in the Great Cabin toasting each other amidst much laughter. A small boy ran out astride a hobby horse, a toy trumpet in one hand. He stared at her, then rushed back.

This was foolish. She could hardly confront Alistair with her tattered little parcel in front of everyone down here; she would go back and lay it at his place. Even as she thought it he emerged from the same opening that the child had run through.

'Dita?'

'I have a gift for you.'

'And I one for you. Come down here.' Alistair led her past several doors and along the cramped passageway, lit only by a few lanterns. They turned a corner and were quite alone, even the noise from the Great Cabin fading into a murmur like the sea. In the shadows he seemed larger than ever and somehow mysterious.

'I realised there would be one thing missing from a traditional Christmas, beside a flaming Yule log and snow.' He held something in his hand, a spray of foliage that caught the light with a myriad of soft creamy orbs.

'Oh, how lovely! Mistletoe—where on earth did you get it?' Dita reached for it, but he held it just out of her reach.

'Magic.'

She could believe that. The ship pitched and she stumbled towards him and was caught in his free arm. 'Will you trust me with a kiss now?'

'I thought you didn't want me. You said you did not.'

'I said that the way I kissed you then was simply a reaction to danger, to fighting. It was wrong to have done it like that, then. But I would have to be dead not to want to kiss you, Dita.'

'Oh. I see. I thought—' *So he does want me, just*

as I want him. 'Yes.' Her heart soared and she did not hesitate now. Trust him? It was herself she could not trust, here in the semi-darkness, but she was not going to fight the way she felt. He was so close, and what she could not see clearly she could read with every other sense. He smelled of wine and smoke and she leaned a little closer to inhale clean, hot male and the scent that was his alone. His breathing was slow and calm, but she could detect just the slightest hitch in it as though he was controlling it consciously. And touch—solid, strong male in clothing she wanted to rip from his body.

Around her waist his hand held her steady and she fought the need to press against it, to feel those long fingers move on her skin. She wanted them on her, all over her. In her. Dita blushed in the shadows, hot with desire and shaken by her own imaginings and memories.

Alistair's free hand moved and touched her hair and she felt him fasten the mistletoe sprig in amongst the heaped curls before he drew her to him with both hands.

'Just a kiss,' he murmured as he bent his head.

'Yes,' she agreed and reached up her own hands to touch his hair. It was soft and strong, thick and rebellious under her fingers and she recalled the unruly length of it when he had been younger, long enough for him to tie back with a cord when he was outside. When they had been in bed together she had untied the cord and run her fingers into the silk of it. 'I like this short, it feels like fur.' She stroked as she would a cat and he pushed against the caress, his eyes hooded and heavy.

Just a kiss, a Christmas kiss. The taste of him when he touched his mouth to hers had her closing her eyes and opening her lips. The darkness was arousing, gave an edge of danger now she could not see him, only feel and smell and taste. Alistair kissed her as deeply as he had in the rickshaw, but with no desperation, as leisurely as he had on the *maidan*, but with no mockery; she sighed into his mouth as their tongues met and tangled and stroked, sharing the wet heat and the intimacy and the trust.

Just a kiss, he had said. Dita wanted more, more of him. She pressed close, feeling the ache as her breasts crushed against the silk of his waistcoat, the heat as his erection pressed against her and she rocked into him, moaning now because a sigh was not enough for the need inside her. The man knew how to tantalise and prolong as his young self had not.

'Dita.' He lifted his head and she caught his ear between her teeth as he bent to kiss her neck, his hands sliding up to cup her breasts. Stephen had done that and she had recoiled and his hungry grasp had hurt her; now the pressure made her want to rub herself shamelessly against Alistair. It was an effort not to bite and she forced herself to concentrate on licking, nibbling, probing the intriguing whorls of his ear.

'Perfect,' Alistair murmured as his fingers found the edge of her bodice and began to stroke the aureole of her nipple. Her breast ached and swelled, heavy and tight in the silken bodice, and she moved under his hands, restless, needing to be free of corsets and camisole, needing his hands on her bare flesh.

He bent to kiss the swell of her breast above the silk, his teasing fingers fretting at the nipple until it was tight to the point of an exquisite pleasure that was almost pain.

Dita gasped and Alistair lifted his head, his eyes glinting in the lantern light. 'Did I hurt you?'

'No. No…kiss me.'

It was almost too much, the heat of his mouth on hers, the demanding pressure, the tug at her breast that went deep, deep into her belly, down to where she felt the heat building and twisting into something that made her arch to rub against him—but that only made the ache worse. Her back was against the panelling now, Alistair's weight pressing her, the thick length of his erection just where she needed him to be.

There was something behind her, digging into her back, and she shifted, felt it move and the wall vanished.

Alistair caught her as she stumbled back. 'The door must have been unlocked,' he said as she stared about her, confused. 'It's an empty cabin.' There was just enough light to see. Alistair reached outside, lifted a lamp from the wall and came in, closing the door behind him. She heard the click of the key as he stood there, the light spilling out over the bare deck, the unmade bed with its coir mattress. 'Alistair—'

'Yes,' he said, putting down the lantern and coming to pull her into his arms. 'What do you want, Dita?'

'I don't know.' She tugged at his waistcoat buttons. 'You.'

'I want you, too,' he said as she undid the last of them and began to pull his shirt from his waistband. 'I only meant to kiss you: I should have known it wouldn't stop there. Trust me a little more, Dita? Trust me to pleasure you?'

'Yes,' she said, not quite understanding what he was

asking, what it meant. 'I need to touch you. *Aah…*' Her hands slid around his waist against the hot skin and she stood there, resting against him, catching her breath and feeling him tense under her caress.

That evening so long ago, there had been no time to simply hold each other. He had reached for her, she had stumbled into his arms, thinking to give comfort for whatever was causing him such pain, finding her innocent intentions going up in a blaze of scarce-understood desire in the arms of a young man who had been, it seemed, as desperate as she had been and who had somehow found the control to be gentle despite their urgency.

Alistair moved and lifted her and then they were lying on the bunk and her skirts were around her thighs and her hand was cupped around his erection through his trousers and he groaned as he stroked up her legs. She trembled as he pressed them apart, opened her, slid his fingers into the slick folds that parted for him with no resistance. She had fought Stephen off before he touched her with such intimacy; now she had no shame and no fear, only the desperate need for this man.

That time before she had been passive and uncertain under his seeking hands and urgent mouth; now she wanted to touch him, all of him.

'Touch me,' he said against her mouth, echoing her thoughts, and she struggled to understand for a moment. She was touching him… Then she found the fall of his trousers and somehow undid them, slid her hand inside, found the hot, hard length of him and closed her fingers. 'More. Dita…'

She squeezed and stroked and he shuddered and

slipped one finger inside her as she clung to him. Then another, and his thumb found a place that felt hard and tight with tension and stroked and she cried out until he stopped her mouth with his, pressing into her circling hand, stroking and squeezing until she screamed silently, arching upwards as everything broke inside her and he surged in her grasp and shuddered above her and the world spun out of its orbit.

'Dita, sweetheart. Are you all right?'

'Hmm?' She was on a bed, in a strange cabin, with Alistair, and he had made love to her—and she had made love to him and it had been everything she remembered yet different. 'Yes. Yes, I am quite all right.'

He was sitting up, putting his clothing to rights and she lay there, just looking at him in the lamplight. Beautiful, mysterious, male. Even more mysterious now he had let her come so close to him again. As close, almost, as it was possible to be. Alistair gave her his handkerchief and got up, his back turned, while she tidied herself and got unsteadily to her feet.

'Are you all right?' He turned to look at her in the lamplight and she smiled. 'That wasn't what I really want, you know that.' He reached out and began to put her hair into order. 'There. I'll leave the mistletoe in place for some other lucky fellows to snatch a kiss.'

'What *do* you want?' she asked, ignoring her hair, not caring about any other men and their kisses.

'To make love with you, fully. But I won't take that risk, Dita. You said it yourself—one slip would be fatal to your reputation. This was certainly a slip—but I think we'll get away with it.' He pulled her closer. 'Was it all right for you, our loving, even though it was not complete?'

She answered him truthfully. 'You gave me more pleasure just now than Stephen did in two days and nights.' *You gave me as much pleasure as that boy had done, so long ago, even though I ache because I need you inside me.*

Alistair laughed and caught her to him for another kiss. As they stood there, her arms twined round his neck she said, 'Do you want your gift?

'Of course!' He sounded eager, almost the young Alistair that the present had been intended for all those years ago.

'Where is my reticule?' They found it on the floor and she pulled out the package and handed it to him and watched as he flattened out the crumpled label.

'Happy birthday?'

'I was going to give it to you the day you left home. I tossed it into the secret drawer of my jewellery box when I realised you were gone. Then I found it again, quite recently. I thought it might amuse you.' She shrugged, 'I will not vouch for the embroidery—I think I will have improved since I was sixteen.'

'You were sixteen when I left?' He frowned at her. 'I suppose you must have been. Dita, did we quarrel, that last day? There was something, some memory in the back of my mind that I cannot catch hold of. Dreams like smoke. A kiss? But that cannot be right: I would not have kissed you.' She thought he muttered, *Let alone more*, but she was not certain. 'God, I was drunk that night. The whole thing was such a hellish mess I can't recall properly.'

'Yes, we quarrelled,' she lied. *He does not recall making love, his anger, the things he said afterwards. He must have been beside himself.* 'And I cried and you... I left.'

'Ah.' The tarnished silver paper flashed in the light as he turned it over in his hands. 'What are you going to give me for my birthday this year if I open this now?'

'It depends upon what you deserve,' she said, and tried to keep her voice light to match his tone.

'Mmm.' The low growl held a wealth of promise as the paper tore away to reveal the comb case, wavy stripes of amber and gold and black on one side, on the other a tiger, copied painstakingly from a print in her father's library. The stitching was a little uneven, the sewing not quite smooth.

'You made me a tiger?' Alistair slid the comb out and then back, turning the case in his hands. 'You had powers of prediction?'

'No. I always thought you had tiger's eyes,' she confessed. 'When I was a little girl I used to dream you would turn into a tiger at night and stalk the corridors of the castle.'

Alistair stared at her from those same uncanny amber eyes. 'I frightened you that much?'

'No, of course not. I thought it was exciting. You know you never frightened me, even when you were angry with me. You looked after me.'

'I did, didn't I.' There was a silence that was strangely awkward while he stood there, quite still except for the restless fingers that turned the comb case over in his hands. Then, just as she opened her mouth to break it, he pushed the gift into his pocket and took up the lantern.

'We shouldn't have done that, Dita,' he said flatly. She stared at him as he turned the magic of their love-making into an ill-judged romp with his matter-of-fact words. 'You look a little ruffled—we had best go up the companionway at the end here and account for that with some sea air. Ready?'

It was as though another man entirely had come into the cabin: brisk, efficient and practical. 'A good idea,' Dita said, chilled, and followed him as he stepped with wary care into the corridor.

Chapter Nine

$\infty\!\!\curvearrowleft\!\!\otimes\!\!\curvearrowright\!\!\infty$

Alistair looked from the charming, slightly clumsy piece of embroidery in his hands and up to the generous mouth he had kissed until it was red and swollen. And then up again and into the green eyes that were Dita's, just as they always looked, unchanged even though he had taken her with careless lust. He had seen the sophisticated, adult Dita at Government House and somehow she and the girl in his memory had seemed separate individuals; now, with her gift in his hand, the two slid together, became one.

It had been very strange, that feeling that they had done this before, that she had lain in his arms, that his lips had tasted the tender skin of her breasts, stroked those long, slim legs. It must be because he had known her so well. And those frequent dreams: confused, erotic, troubling dreams touched with anger and betrayal, all mixed with the memories of how he had left home.

The last thing he needed was her becoming in some way attached to him. Lovemaking was all very well, but perhaps he had underestimated her experience. His brain felt as though he had a fever, but one thing was clear: Dita might not be a virgin, but she was inexperienced. The man she had eloped with had obviously been a clumsy boor and now he had shown her a glimpse of what lovemaking could be like. He suspected he had given her her first orgasm.

Alistair led her up the companionway and on to the foredeck. Other passengers had come out, too, but they were laughing and talking and listening to the sailors playing, not paying any attention to two of their number who appeared to have strayed a little further along the deck to catch the warm breeze.

'There—safe,' he said, giving his neckcloth a final tug.

'Indeed.' Dita was a good actress, he thought with gratitude. Her voice was cool even though she looked flushed and a little…a little *loved*. He had thought her still a skinny beanpole, but now he had caressed those slight curves he knew he had been wrong: she was perfect and made for his touch. Her skin glowed under its slight golden tan, her lower lip pouted with a fullness that held the promise of passion with its potential still unfulfilled. Dita raised one hand and curled the loose ringlet around it and his body tightened at the memory of those slender fingers circling his flesh, the ache to sheathe himself in her tight, wet heat.

Perhaps he had been worrying unnecessarily and she was sophisticated enough for these kind of games. He would wait and see.

Some of the passengers had begun to dance a country jig. Alistair caught Dita's hand and almost ran down to join them, whirling her into the end of the line next to the elder Miss Whyton and Lieutenant Tompkins.

'Mistletoe!' Miss Whyton cried as Dita was spun past her, on down between the row of dancers by the lieutenant. 'Wherever did you get that?'

But she was safely down to the other end now and Alistair made himself focus on the steps as he caught her hands and waited for their turn to dance to the other end.

By the time the fiddler drew out the last chord everyone was flushed and laughing, the ladies fanning themselves, the men pretending to pant with exertion. Alistair saw Callum Chatterton admire Dita's hair ornament and then snatch a kiss, followed by his brother. A positive queue of gentlemen formed.

'I will lend it to you,' Dita said to Daniel, 'and then you may go and make mischief.'

Averil began to unfasten it for her, then stopped, the spray in her hands, and stared. Alistair strolled a little closer.

'But these berries are pearls, Dita! *Real* pearls—you could make an entire necklace there are so many.'

Callum took the spray out of her hands and turned it close in front of his eyes. 'And fine ones at that. You should have them locked in the strongbox, Lady Perdita, not be dancing a jig on the open deck in something this valuable.'

'How lovely they are.' Mrs Bastable came over to join the group, her arm linked through that of her taciturn husband. 'But you ought to replace the pearls with glass beads, for safety. Who gave them to you, dear?'

'Someone I was friends with a long time ago.' Dita

said. 'I don't think I know him any more.' She looked up from the mistletoe and caught Alistair looking at her. Her eyes were bleak. 'Excuse me. I will take your advice and lock them away.'

Alistair held the door to the cuddy open for her and she paused on the threshold. 'I would have lain with you for glass beads, or none,' she said in a vehement whisper. 'You had no need to buy me with pearls. I am not a professional. Nor am I an innocent girl who has no idea what is happening when a man kisses her. Don't behave as though we have just done something regrettable; something *silly*. If you want someone to patronise, go and flirt with Dotty Whyton.'

'Damn it!' The accusation was so unfair, and yet such an accurate stab at his conscience, that Alistair let go of the door and it slammed, shutting them off from the others.

'Give them back, then,' he said, smiling, not troubling to keep that devil out of his eyes.

'No.' She put up her chin. 'I shall keep them to remind myself of the folly of passion. They will make a very lovely necklace.'

They were fortunate with the weather, everyone agreed. The wind held, the storms were not severe and they reached Cape Town a week ahead of Captain Archibald's most optimistic prediction.

'I will be so glad to stretch my legs on a surface that does not go up and down,' Averil said as she tied her bonnet ribbons under her chin and tried to see the result in the small mirror that hung on her wall.

'The land will go up and down just as much as the

ship seemed to,' Dita told her from her perch on Averil's bunk. 'You have got your sea legs now. What do you intend to do today? The captain says we have two days here.'

'Lord Lyndon has asked me to form one of a party going to the Company's gardens. Apparently they have the most wonderful collection from all over the world, and a menagerie as well. But surely he has asked you, too?'

'He did, but I have shopping to do, so I refused.' Dita met Averil's questioning gaze with a look of bright interest. 'I saw the gardens on my way out. They are very fine—you will enjoy yourself.'

'I am sure I will.' Averil stuck a hatpin in her pincushion and fidgeted about tidying her things. Dita waited for the next question.

'Shopping for two days?'

'I have something to take to the jewellers and then I must collect it the next day.'

'Is there something wrong between you and Lord Lyndon?' Averil went slightly pink; she was not given to intrusive personal questions.

'Yes,' Dita said. There was no point in lying about it.

'Since Christmas Eve.' Averil nodded to herself. 'That is what I guessed. Whatever is the matter?'

'We had a…a misunderstanding.' *Or, at least, I misunderstood. I thought he cared for me and wanted to make love to me because of that. How naive! He wanted to make love and so he* seemed *to care and once he had, then he was all cool practicality.* It was a mercy he had held back from entering her. She was shamefully aware that she would not have stopped him.

'I thought you liked him very well.'

'I do…did. I find him too…attractive for prudence with a man like that.'

'Oh.' Averil fiddled some more, dropped her gloves and blurted out, 'Did he overstep the mark?'

'Overstep it? Yes, I think you could say he over-leapt it. I should have known better—' Dita broke off, but the sound she heard had been from above their heads, not from anyone returning to the roundhouse, and the windows were closed.

'Dita—you didn't *sleep* with him?'

'Absolutely no sleeping occurred. Oh, I am sorry, I should not be so flippant. No, if you mean did anything occur that might lead to, say, pregnancy. I was more intimate with him than I should have been, and, it is fair to say, we are both regretting that now.'

'So he kissed you very passionately?' Dita reminded herself that Averil was a virgin, and a well-behaved one at that, and nodded. 'But if you are both regretting it, could you not put it behind you now?'

'It is one thing both of you regretting something at the same time,' Dita said, jamming her own hat on her head as she got to her feet. 'That indeed might lead to eventual harmony. What is not…flattering is when the man shows every sign of wanting to run a mile within moments of the encounter.'

'Oh, no! How—'

'Humiliating, is the word you are looking for. The fact that this is, of course, the most sensible and prudent outcome does not help in the slightest.'

'No, I can see that.' Averil gathered up her parasol, reticule and shawl and opened the canvas flap. 'What a pity. I thought he was perfect for you.'

Perfect. He is beautiful and insanely courageous and intelligent and apparently rich and he makes love like an angel and he…he is no angel. An angel would bore me.

'Lady Perdita, Miss Heydon. Good morning.' It was Dr Melchett, a tough old survivor of everything India could throw at a man. Except possibly tigers, Dita thought.

'Good morning, Dr Melchett. Are you going with the party to the gardens?'

'I am not, Lady Perdita. I have seen them several times and I have every intention of buying gifts for my godsons. Might I escort you ladies, if you are also looking for bargains? Ostrich feathers, for example?'

'Thank you, I would be glad of your company, sir. Miss Heydon is bound for the gardens, so I will be your only companion.'

He was a dry and witty escort, Dita discovered, and the perfect antidote to troubling and handsome young men. He tempted her into buying a huge ostrich feather fan and plumes for her next court appearance and then enchanted her by taking her to a wood carver to buy amusing carved animals for his godchildren.

'Oh, look.' It was a small oval box, no bigger than a large snuffbox, with Noah's Ark carved in low relief on the lid. When the lid was opened it was full of minute animals, each in exquisite detail and so small that she could sit the elephant on her little fingernail.

Dita played with it for several minutes before she found the pair of tigers and remembered Alistair and her reason for coming shopping.

'Is there a good jeweller's shop, do you know, Doctor?' Reluctantly she slid the lid closed and handed the box back to the dealer. She already had a number of larger carved animals for nephews and nieces and they were all too young for anything so delicate.

'You are not intending to buy gemstones? You would have done better in India. There is one along here, I seem to recall. Ah, yes, here we are.'

'I need a necklace stringing,' she explained as the jeweller came to greet them. 'These. They are already drilled.' She poured the pearls out on to the velvet pad on the counter. 'Can you do it for tomorrow? I want them in one simple string.'

'I can do it for tomorrow morning, madam.' He produced his loupe and picked up a handful. 'These are very fine and well matched. Indian?'

'Yes.' They agreed a price and she let the doctor take her arm and find a carriage back to the ship.

'Your mistletoe pearls?'

'They are.' She gazed out of the window, willing the doctor to change the subject.

'Interesting young man, that. And generous.' So he had guessed who had given them to her.

'We knew each other as children.' *Talk about something else. Please.*

'And yet you are no longer friends.' The old man rested his clasped hands on the top of his walking cane and regarded her with faded blue eyes. 'A pity to fall out with old friends. When you reach my age you appreciate the value of all of them.'

'It is his birthday tomorrow,' Dita said. There was a lump in her throat for some reason. 'I… Perhaps I should buy him a present.'

'What would he like, do you think?' Doctor Melchett sat up straight, a twinkle of interest in his eyes.

'I do not know. He can afford whatever he wants and it is too late to make anything.'

'Then give him simplicity and something to make him smile. He does not smile enough, I suspect.'

'The Noah's Ark!'

'That would make me smile if a lovely young lady gave it to me,' the old man said with a chuckle, pulling the check string and ordering the carriage back to the shopping district.

After breakfast Dita waited until Alistair strolled out on to the deck alone. If he snubbed her, she did not want an audience.

'Happy birthday.' She could have sworn she had made no sound as she walked towards him where he leaned against the rail, but he did not start at the sound of her voice right behind him. Nor did he look round.

'Thank you.' She waited, despite her instinct to turn on her heel, and eventually he shifted until he faced her. 'You are speaking to me again?'

'And you to me. Kindly do not imply I have been sulking.' She drew down a deep breath: this was not how she had meant this encounter to go. 'You are the most infuriating man. I was determined to be all sweetness and light and in less than a dozen words you have me scratching at you.'

'Sweetness and light?' He smiled and she found herself smiling back with wary affection. *Thank you, Dr Melchett.* 'That I would like to see.'

'I would like to forget Christmas Eve, to put it behind us. I wish we could just be friends again and not think about who was to blame or who said what.'

His smile was wicked. 'I would suggest that staying in plain view of at least three fellow passengers at all times might be a good idea if that is your plan. You might want to be *just friends*, Dita, I would be a liar if I said I did. And I am not sure I believe you either.'

'Have you no self-control?' she snapped, then threw up her hands. 'I am sorry. Doubtless you are right. It was both of us, I know that. Can we not forget it?'

'We could pretend to forget it,' Alistair said, watching her. Could he sense how aroused he made her feel, just standing there? She had kissed his mouth, just there. Those long, clever fingers had touched her there and there and… 'Would that do?' he asked. Something in his expression made her doubt he intended pretending for very long.

'It will have to, I suppose.' Dita brought her hands out from behind her back to reveal the box. 'This is for your birthday. It is quite useless—its only purpose is to make you smile.'

'That seems a good purpose.' He reached out and took it, his fingers scrupulously avoiding touching hers. 'Local work?'

'Yes. Best to open it over a flat surface and out of the breeze, I think.'

It was reward enough, just to sit and watch his face, intent over the box, his fingers delicately lifting each tiny creature on to the table, arranging them in pairs, finding the miniature gangplank that could slope up to the box. 'Here is Noah.' He lifted the final piece out and looked up at her, smiling. She swayed towards him a little, drawn by the curve of his lips.

'Thank you, this is exquisite.' He lifted a finger and touched her cheek. 'It makes you smile, too. I hated that I killed your smiles, Dita.'

'You did not,' she said, stiffening. He had only to touch her, it seemed, and her self-control wilted. Attack seemed the only defence. 'You have an exaggerated idea of the influence you have over me. If I have seemed sombre, it is no doubt because I have been reflecting on the folly of allowing myself to be attracted to a person-able rake.'

'Attracted?' That smile was back. He must practise it to have such a devastating effect, she thought, fighting down equal measures of panic and arousal.

'Do stop fishing for compliments, Alistair.' Dita pushed back her chair and stood up and he rose, too, the movement of his linen coat scattering the tiny animals across the table. 'Of course *attracted*. I would hardly make love with a man for whom I felt no attraction.'

'Wouldn't you? I really have no idea what you might do, Dita, if the fancy took you.' The amusement had drained out of his expression, leaving it bleak and arrogant.

'You are suggesting that I would—' *What? Sleep with any man I fancied, on a whim?* She almost asked the question, then bit it back; she did not want to hear him say *yes*.

'That so-called chaperon of yours, sweet lady though she is, just isn't up to your weight, Dita.'

'I am not a damned horse!'

Alistair's eyes narrowed into an insolent scrutiny that had her balling her fists at her sides in an effort not to slap him. 'No. You don't need a jockey, you go fast enough as it is. What you need, Perdita my love, is a husband.'

'Perhaps I do,' she said with every ounce of sweetness she could get into her voice. 'Perhaps, somewhere, there is a man who is not patronising, arrogant, domineering or interested only in my money or my body. On the evidence so far, however, I am finding that hard to believe.'

Behind them the door opened, bringing with it the sea air and the sound of shouted orders to the men in the rigging. Dita whirled round and walked out, almost colliding with Dr Melchett on the threshold. She managed a thin-lipped smile as she passed, intent on reaching the prow of the ship before anyone, anyone at all, spoke to her.

Chapter Ten

'Happy birthday, my lord.'

Alistair looked up from collecting up the tiny animals. It took steady fingers and had to be done before they were scattered and damaged, whatever else he wanted to do. Like kicking the panelling or getting drunk. 'Doctor Melchett. Thank you, sir. How did you—? Ah, yes, you knew Lady Perdita bought the Ark for me, I assume.'

'I went shopping with her yesterday,' the older man said as he sat down opposite Alistair. 'Charming young lady. Intelligent, lovely and high spirited.'

'She is certainly all those things.' Alistair continued to slot each fragile piece into place.

'You did not like her gift?'

'Very much; it is a work of art.' Dr Melchett was silent. Alistair recognised the technique: keep quiet and eventually your opponent will start babbling. He considered playing the game and saying nothing, but that would be disrespectful to an old man. 'Lady Perdita is not certain she likes me.'

'Ah.' The doctor fumbled in his pocket, brought out a snuffbox and offered it to Alistair. He didn't use the stuff himself, but he recognised the friendly overture and took a pinch. 'Difficult thing, love,' Melchett mused.

'What?' A minute elephant went skidding out of his hand and across the table.

The doctor picked it up and peered at it. 'Love. Old friends, aren't you?'

'Yes. Not lovers.' He examined the last half-hour in painful detail and shrugged. 'We were friends, as children, as much as one can be with a six-year age gap. We have apparently grown out of it.'

'Love, lovers, in love, loving… So many shades of meaning to that word.' Melchett sighed. 'You were fond of her as a boy?'

'She was a burr under my saddle,' Alistair said evenly as he slid the box lid closed. 'A pestilential little sister.' He grinned reluctantly, remembering. 'I suppose I was fond of her, yes.'

'And you still want to protect her.'

No, he did not want to protect her—he wanted to make love to her for the rest of the voyage. 'Lady Perdita requires protecting from herself, mainly,' Alistair said as he put the box in his pocket. 'But of course I keep an eye on her; she is the daughter of neighbours, after all.'

Melchett got to his feet. 'That's the ticket: neighbourliness. Now you know what it is, you won't fret over it so much.' He chuckled. 'Nothing like a proper diagnosis for making one feel better. Don't let me disturb you,' he added as Alistair stood. 'Have a pleasant birthday, my lord.'

What the devil was that about? Neighbourliness? Diagnosis indeed! He didn't need medical assistance to know that he was suffering from a mixture of exasperation and frustration. And just a tinge of guilt.

He wanted Dita: wanted her in bed, under him, around him. He wanted her screaming his name, wanted her begging him to make love to her again, and again. Alistair took a deep breath and thought longingly of cold rivers.

He also wanted to box her ears half the time. That was nothing new—he had spent most of his boyhood in that frame of mind, when she wasn't making him laugh. Not that he had ever given in to the temptation: one did not strike a girl under any circumstances, however provoking she was.

Unfair that, he thought with a slight smile. *Spanking, now…* The word brought a vision of Dita's small, pert backside delightfully to mind.

Which brought him neatly back to the guilt. It was not an emotion he was much prone to. He certainly hadn't felt guilt over leaving home. Since then he had done few things that caused him regret; all experience had some value. The problem was, he saw with a flash of clarity, he was not feeling guilty over wanting to make love to Dita, he was feeling guilty because he couldn't be sorry about it.

Damn it. It would be a good thing when she was home safely, despite her best efforts otherwise, and when she *was* home he hoped she would do her utmost to find a decent husband, although her list of requirements from this paragon probably meant the man did not exist. He could watch this while he searched for a wife—who should be easy to identify when he met her. She would be precisely the opposite of Lady Perdita Brooke in every particular.

'If I never see St Helena again it will be too soon,' Mrs Bastable remarked as the island vanished over the horizon. 'A more disagreeable place I cannot imagine, and the food was dreadful.'

'There's Ascension next; we can pick up some turtles and have splendid soup,' Alistair remarked from his position on the rail, surrounded by a group of ladies, amongst whom the elder Miss Whyton was prominent. 'And from there, if we have good fortune, perhaps only another ten weeks sailing.'

'The Equator soon,' Callum Chatterton added. 'But no sport to be had there—we got everyone who had never crossed before on the way out from Madras.'

Alistair ducked under the sailcloth and sat down on one of the chairs under the awning that sheltered Dita, Averil and Mrs Bastable. He chose one opposite her and not the vacant one by her side, much to her relief. Then she realised that from where he was sitting he could meet her eyes. He seemed intent on doing just that. She held the amber gaze and her breath hitched, shortened, as his lids drooped sensually and the colour seemed to darken.

'How are you entertaining yourselves?' he asked, his tone at variance with the messages his eyes were sending. 'I find I am growing blasé about flying fish and whales.'

'I still have needlework,' Averil said. 'There is all the

table linen for my trousseau. The light on deck is so good it makes doing white-work monograms very easy.'

'I intend to carry on reading,' Dita said. 'Novels,' she added, daring him to comment.

'Sensation novels?' Alistair enquired, ignoring her challenging look.

'Of course. I packed the most lurid novels I could find and I am devouring them shamelessly. I have an ambition to write one and I am reviewing plots to see what has not been covered. Perhaps I shall become an eccentric spinster novelist.'

'How about a story set on a pirate ship?' Alistair suggested, his expression so bland she could not tell if he was teasing her or not.

'Oh, yes, what a wonderful idea, and quite fresh, I think.' Dita cast round their little group for inspiration. 'My heroine—who will look just like Miss Heydon—has been carried on board by the villain—a tall, dark, dastardly character with a scar on his cheek—' Alistair raised one eyebrow, which she ignored '—who has chained the hero in the foul bilges.'

'How is she going to escape his evil intent?' Averil asked, missing this byplay.

'The hero escapes, but, single-handed, even he cannot overpower the villain,' Dita said, improvising wildly. 'So he must haunt the ship, stepping in only to save her at critical moments.

'There will be storms, sea monsters, desert islands, the villain's lascivious attempts upon the fair heroine's virtue…'

'Perhaps she flees him and climbs into the rigging?' Alistair suggested. 'And he climbs after her and forces her down to the deck before pressing his foul attentions upon her in the cuddy.'

'It sounds highly improbable,' Dita said frigidly. 'Although the foul attentions sound…characteristic.'

'No, it's brilliant,' Callum contradicted. 'It will make a perfect cliffhanger. She hits him with the soup ladle and escapes to barricade herself in her cabin.'

'I was thinking of a carving knife,' Dita said with a tight smile at Alistair, who smiled back in a way that had the hair standing up on the back of her neck. *A hunting smile…*

'It sounds wonderful,' Averil said, breathless with laughter as she dabbed at her eyes with the napkin she was working on. 'You must write it, Lady Perdita.'

'In instalments,' Daniel added. 'And read one every evening. We will all contribute plot ideas as the story develops and take on roles. The hero is, of course, so perfect that none of us can approach him, but I see myself as the flawed, but ultimately noble first lieutenant of the ship, Trueheart. He loves the heroine from afar, knowing he is unworthy, but will redeem himself by the sacrifice of his life for her in about episode sixty-three.'

'Very well,' Dita agreed. 'I will do it. It will be a three-volume epic, I can see.'

The novel proved to be an absorbing occupation. Averil patiently embroidered the corners of innumerable handkerchiefs and table napkins and Dita wrote while they sat under their awning in the heat.

By the time they crossed the Equator Averil had moved on to pillow cases, the passengers, sustained by

3 Months Free

when you subscribe for 12 Months

SAVE OVER £47

SEE OVERLEAF FOR DETAILS

www.millsandboon.co.uk/subscriptions

SAVE OVER £47

Subscribe to Historical today to get 4 stories a month delivered to your door for 12 months, saving a fantastic £47.88

Alternatively, subscribe for 6 months and save £19.16, that's still an impressive 20% off!

FULL PRICE	YOUR PRICE	SAVINGS	MONT
£191.52	£143.64	25%	12
£95.76	£76.60	20%	6

As a welcome gift we will also send you a FREE L'Occitane gift set worth £10

PLUS, by becoming a member you will also receive these additional benefits:

- 🌹 FREE P&P Your books delivered to your door every month at no extra charge
- 🌹 Be the first to receive new titles two months ahead of the shops
- 🌹 Exclusive monthly newsletter
- 🌹 Excellent Special offers
- 🌹 Membership to our Special Rewards programme

No Obligation- You can cancel your subscription at any time by writing to us at Mills & Boon Book Club, PO Box 676, Richmond. TW9 1WU.

To subscribe, visit
www.millsandboon.co.uk/subscriptions

turtle soup, began to think hopefully of home and Dita had filled pages of her notebook.

Every afternoon after dinner the passengers retreated to their cabins out of the sun to recruit their strength before supper. Dita found that a difficult routine to settle to, despite having followed it for a year in India. Here, on the ship, she was too restless to lie dozing in her canvas box. And for some reason the restlessness increased the longer she was on board.

She was not afraid of her family's reaction when she got home, she decided—that was not what was disturbing her. Papa would still be angry with her—that was only to be expected, for he had taken her elopement hard—but Mama and her brothers and sisters would welcome her with open arms. Nor was it apprehension about her reception in society; she was ready to do battle over that.

No, something else was making her feel edgy and restless and faintly apprehensive in a not unpleasant kind of way, and she very much feared it was Alistair. The memory of their lovemaking on Christmas Eve should have served as a constant warning, she told herself. Instead it simply reminded her how much she wanted his kisses and his caresses. And Alistair, maddening man, had not tried to lay a finger on her, so she could not even make herself feel better by spurning him.

Had he turned over a new leaf and decided on celibacy? He was not flirting with anyone else; she knew that because she watched him covertly. Or was he deliberately tantalising her by apparent indifference? If so, he was most certainly succeeding.

Her only outlet had become the novel. The plot became

more and more fantastical, the perils of Angelica, the fragile yet spirited heroine, became more extreme, the impossibly noble, handsome and courageous hero suffered countless trials to protect her and the saturnine villain became more sinister, more amorous, and, unfortunately, more exciting.

Three days after they crossed the Equator, with the Cape Verde Islands their next landfall, Dita found herself alone in the canvas shelter on deck. A sailor adjusted the sailcloth to create a shady cave and she settled back on the daybed the ship's carpenter had made and looked out between the wings of the shelter to the rail and then open, empty sea.

She lay for a while, lulled by the motion of the ship, the blue, unending water, the warmth on her body. Then, insidiously, the warmth became heat and the familiar ache and need and she shifted restlessly and reached for her notebook and pencil.

The roll of the ship sent the little book sliding away and she sat up and scrambled to the end of the daybed to reach for it. 'Bother the thing!'

A shadow fell over the book as Alistair appeared and stooped to pick it up. 'Ah, the *Adventures of Angelica*.' When she tried to twitch it from his fingers he sat down on the end of the daybed, held it just out of her reach and opened it.

'Give it back, if you please.' It was hard to sound dignified when she was curled up with her slippers kicked off, her petticoats rumpled about her calves and no hat on. Dita scrambled back towards the head of the daybed, pulled her skirts down and held out one hand.

'But I want to read it.' He flipped to the end and read while Dita pressed her lips together and folded her hands in her lap. She was not going to tussle for it. 'Now, let's see. So, Angelica has escaped on to the desert island and Baron Blackstone is pursuing her, so close that she can hear his panting breaths behind her as she flees across the sand towards the scanty shelter of the palm trees. How is she going to escape this time?'

'The gallant de Blancheville has sawn his way through the latest lot of shackles and is rushing to her rescue,' Dita said with as much dignity as the ludicrous plot would allow her.

'I cannot imagine why Blackstone hasn't thrown him overboard to the sharks,' Alistair commented. He leaned back, one hand on the far edge of the daybed, his body turned towards her, the picture of elegant indolence. 'I would have done so about ten chapters back. Think of the saving in shackles.'

'Villains never do the sensible thing,' Dita retorted. 'And if I kill off the hero, that's the end of the book. With you as captain of this ship the drama would be over on page three; de Blancheville would have walked the plank and poor Angelina would have thrown herself overboard in despair.'

He curled a lip. 'The man's prosy and disposable. Have her falling for Blackstone. Think of the fun they could have on a desert island.'

'I really wouldn't—Alistair! That is my ankle!'

'And a very pretty one it is, too. Has your chaperon never told you it is fast to shed your shoes in public?' He ran his hand over the arch of her foot, then curled his fingers round it and held tight when she jerked it back. 'Relax.'

'Relax—with your hand under my skirts?'

'Don't you like this?' His thumb was stroking the top of the arch of her foot while his fingers brushed tickling caresses underneath. It was disturbingly reminiscent of the way he had caressed her more intimately.

'I'll scream.'

'No, you won't.' He slid off the daybed, knelt beside it, bent and lifted her foot. 'Pretty toes, too.'

'You can't see my toes,' she said in a brisk, matter-of-fact tone, which became a muffled shriek when he began to suck them through her stocking. 'Stop it!'

In answer his hand slid up her leg to her knee, tweaked the garter and began to pull down her stocking.

'Alistair, stop that this minute…. Oh…' Her stocking was off, her toes were in his mouth and he was sucking and licking each one with intense concentration. It was wonderful. It was outrageous and she should stop him. But she couldn't, Dita thought as she flopped back inelegantly on to the pile of bolsters, not without creating the most dreadful scene by struggling.

Why having her toes sucked should be so inflammatory, she could not imagine. And Alistair must enjoy doing it, although she could not see his face, only his dark head bent over her foot as he sucked her big toe fully into his mouth. *'Aah…'*

He released her and went back to stroking her instep and ankle. 'Tell me the story.'

'How can I concentrate when you are—?'

'Do you want me to stop?' He glanced sideways, his eyes full of wicked mischief.

'Yes! No…no.'

'Go on then.' He closed his lips around her toes again, but did nothing more than nibble.

'Um…' She forced herself to concentrate. 'I think we need a sword fight. De Blancheville has been freed by—oh, that is wonderful, don't stop… Freed by Tom the cabin boy, who is really the lovely Maria in disguise. She has stowed away to follow Trueheart, whom she loves from afar, and thinks that if de Blancheville removes Angelina then Trueheart will stop wanting her and… ah, oh, *please*…be Maria's.'

'Please?' He lifted his head again, put down her foot and shifted up the daybed. 'Please what, Dita?'

'I don't know!' He was sitting on the edge now, his hip against hers. Her voice shook as he leaned in. 'That was my *toes*. Toes aren't—'

'Erotic? Oh, but they are. Every inch of your body, inside and out, is erotic, Dita. Think what fun we could have finding out about eyebrows, or earlobes or the back of your knees.' His hand slid up her leg as he leaned closer. 'And all the places my tongue wants to explore.'

'After Christmas Eve, I don't think it is wise,' she managed to say. Eight years ago his lovemaking had not been so sophisticated. He had been practising, of course.

'Don't think.' His breath was on her lips now; his hand cupped her intimately. She closed her eyes on a shuddering sigh as something, distant, banged.

Alistair moved so fast that he was on his feet, tucking her stocking under her skirts, pulling them down round her feet, before she realised that it was the door of the cuddy banging to.

Dita sat up, pulled her feet under her and fanned her flushed face with both hands. Alistair, apparently engrossed in her notebook, was sitting on one of the chairs at the mouth of the canvas shelter as the approaching voices resolved themselves into the Chattertons and Averil.

'Oh, here you are, Dita,' Averil said, peeping into the shelter. 'What have you been up to?'

'Plotting,' Alistair said easily. 'We have just decided that the novel needs a duel.'

The others clustered round with exclamations of agreement. Dita made an effort. 'This swashbuckling is all very well, but someone will have to write the duel for me because I have never seen a sword fight.'

'We will choreograph it on the poop deck tomorrow,' Callum declared. 'And you can take notes. I've got my foils. Dan?'

His brother groaned. 'You know I'm useless with a rapier.'

'I'll fight you,' Alistair said. 'No reason why we can't do it after breakfast, is there? The chaperons aren't going to object to a harmless bout of fencing.'

'I would love to try it,' Dita said wistfully. Any kind of violent exercise appealed just at the moment. 'Would you show me, Mr Chatterton?'

'Of course!' Callum had loosened up considerably over the course of the voyage. He was not the only one, she thought, fanning herself. 'No reason why a lady cannot try a few of the moves with perfect propriety.'

'No.' Alistair still lounged in his chair, but his voice was definite. 'I will show you, if you insist.'

'Lady Perdita asked me,' Callum stated. The atmosphere became subtly charged.

'I will fight you for the privilege,' Alistair said.

Callum narrowed his eyes, his whole body tense, but Averil clapped her hands and laughed. 'How exciting! Shall we lay wagers? I will venture ten rupees on Lord Lyndon.'

'And I wager the same on my brother,' Daniel said. In the sunlight Alistair's amber eyes glinted like those of a big cat and she shivered.

'Will no one else back me? Lady Perdita?'

'Ten rupees on Mr Chatterton,' she said.

'Then if I win I will claim a forfeit from you,' Alistair said.

'Indeed?' Dita tried to sound dignified and knew she simply sounded flustered. 'I am sure you will choose something that is perfectly proper, my lord. *If* you win, that is. Gentlemen, perhaps you would excuse us? There is something I wish to discuss with Miss Heydon.'

The men took themselves off, Alistair with a sidelong smile. He made as if to slide the notebook into his pocket and then bent and put it on the end of the daybed. 'What is this? Someone must have dropped it. Is it yours?'

Her blue garter ribbon dangled from the tips of his fingers, the fingers that only moments before had been caressing her intimately.

'Certainly not.'

'Oh well, I had better keep it, then.' He put it in his pocket and strolled off while Dita seethed.

'That was a garter,' Averil whispered.

'I know. Mine. I have taken my shoes off, and a stocking. Very fast, I know, but it is so hot.' She retrieved her stocking from under her skirts and pulled it on. Perhaps Averil would assume her raised colour was due to the embarrassment of being almost caught shedding clothing.

'What was that about?' Averil asked, sitting down on the end of the daybed. 'One could cut the atmosphere with a knife, all of a sudden.'

'I expect the men are getting bored.'

'It wasn't that, I don't think. Lord Lyndon sounded as though he was challenging Mr Chatterton to a duel; his eyes positively made me shiver. I do wish you would not tease him so, Dita.'

'I do not tease him. I am going out of my way not to do so, but he is being extremely provoking.'

'May I ask? Have you and Callum Chatterton an understanding?'

'No!' Dita laughed. 'Of course not.'

'Why of course?' Averil put her feet up and curled her arms around her legs. With her chin resting on her knees she looked like a curious cat. 'He is intelligent and obviously destined for preferment. His brother is an earl, he is charming and good looking and he doesn't flirt like his brother. You like him, don't you?'

'Of course. I would be foolish not to. But I couldn't possibly *marry* him.' It occurred to her as she said it that she had looked at Callum, back in Calcutta, with interest. And close contact had only heightened her regard for him. So why couldn't she contemplate him as a husband?

'You would be a very good match for him and could only help his career.'

'You forget my reputation,' Dita pointed out.

'If you were the daughter of Mr Blank, with a dowry of five hundred pounds and freckles, then possibly that would be fatal. If he thought the worse of you for it, then he would not be so friendly, and if he had less honourable intentions, surely you have become aware of that by now?'

'True. But I do not love him.'

Averil was silent for just long enough for Dita to realise how tactless that was. They both spoke at once. 'I am sorry, I did not mean—'

'I am sure I will be very happy with Lord Bradon,' Averil said with stiff dignity.

'Of course you will,' Dita said. 'You are marrying with a strong sense of duty to your family and he is a most suitable choice and you have the type of character that will create happiness. I do not have a duty to wed and I do not have your amiable nature.'

Averil bit her lip. 'Is it Lord Lyndon? You and he seem to have so much in common.'

'Our only common ground is shared memories, and our only compatibility appears to be in the bedchamber,' Dita said, goaded. And not just the bedchamber. Here, in the open air, at the dinner table when he only had to look at her from under sensually drooping lids for her to ache with desire. Anywhere, it seemed.

Averil blushed and investigated the lace at her hem intently. After a moment she said, 'That is not enough, is it?'

'No, it is not.' Dita began to gather up her pencils.

'Alistair is not jealous, he is just territorial and I seem to have become part of that territory.'

'Oh dear,' Averil sighed. 'And I do love a romantic ending.'

'Never mind.' Dita conjured up a smile from somewhere. 'When you are married you can find me just the man.' *If he exists*, she thought as Averil, cheered by that idea, smiled.

Chapter Eleven

Alistair took one of the foils from Daniel Chatterton and tested the button on the point. It seemed secure and he brought the blade down through the air with a swish, pleased the weapon was light and well balanced in his hand. They were an expensive pair: Callum must take his fencing seriously.

Word of the bout had spread and most of the passengers were on deck to watch. One young lady had even brought her sketchbook and Dita was perched on a stool, notebook and pencil in hand, her face in shadow under a broad-brimmed hat.

Doctor Melchett had taken command of the wagers, which were growing prodigiously. As no one, except Daniel Chatterton, had any idea of the proficiency of either of them, it was hard to know on what basis people were staking their money.

'You are the favourite,' George Latham, one of the more senior Company clerks, remarked as he passed Alistair on his way to a place at the rail. 'Everyone's heard about the tiger, no doubt.' He glanced at Callum, who had discarded his coat and was rolling up his shirt sleeves. 'Chatterton looks competent though.'

'I am sure he'll give me a good bout,' Alistair said. He did not care if the man was the East India Company's foils champion, he was not teaching Dita to fence and getting his hands all over her in the process.

'How is the winner to be decided?' someone called.

'It is in the nature of a masquerade,' Daniel said. 'Lord Lyndon plays the villain, my brother the hero. They fight over the heroine, played by Mrs Bastable, who sits here.' He indicated a chair at the foot of the main mast where the lady dimpled and waved to her friends. 'She is the villain's captive. To win, one man must either disarm the other, or land a hit that in the opinion of our learned medical advisor—' Dr Melchett bowed '—is fatal or incapacitating, or must obtain the other's surrender.'

Callum picked up his foil, walked forwards and took his position. Alistair faced him and raised the foil for the salute. As Chatterton's blade came up Alistair saw the focus in the other man's eyes and blanked everything beyond his opponent from his mind; however this had started, it was not a game now.

'En garde!' Daniel called and the blades touched. Alistair stepped back sharply and Callum cut to his right. *So it begins,* he thought, watching the other man for balance and strengths, knowing he was being assessed in the same way as they cut and parried, shifting around their circle of deck.

He let his guard waver deliberately, took a touch to

the arm that would have been a slash with an unguarded weapon and confirmed his suspicion that Chatterton was weaker on the left foot. But it was a damnably close match. Alistair pinked his opponent on the left shoulder, took another hit on the forearm and then, as Callum was extended from that lunge, shifted his weight and drove him back hard towards the hatch cover.

In a flurry of blows they were toe to toe, face to face, their hilts locked. On either side the spectators drew back, uncertain which way they might move.

'Just what are your intentions towards Lady Perdita?' Alistair asked between clenched teeth as they each thrust forwards against the weight of the other.

'My *what*?' Callum gave ground and recovered.

'You heard me.'

'Entirely honourable—if that's any of your damned business,' he retorted. 'What are yours?'

Alistair stepped back, lowered his weapon without warning and Callum stumbled, caught out by the sudden shift in weight. Alistair ducked under his guard, there was a sharp flurry of strokes and he had the button of his foil against Callum's jugular. *What the hell* are *my intentions?* 'Neighbourly,' he said, showing his teeth. *And that's a lie.*

For a long moment his opponent stared into his eyes as though trying to read his mind. Then Callum gave a half-smile, let his foil fall to the deck and spread his hands in surrender. 'You win,' he said, then dropped his voice, 'Just don't try and run me through if I smile at her, damn it. She's a delight—and I freely admit that it would take a stronger man than I to take her to wife.'

They went to get their coats, the antagonism between

them vanishing as rapidly as it had built. Doctor Melchett was besieged by those who had laid wagers and the two duellists were buffeted from all sides by well-wishers.

When Alistair finally made it to the comparative peace of the poop deck, he found Dita sitting scribbling in her notebook. 'Was that helpful?'

'Yes, it was. And extremely exciting.' She closed the book and looked at him, her green eyes dark and troubled despite the steadiness of her gaze. 'You have a forfeit for me, I believe.'

'Yes.' He had been thinking about that, ever since he had thrown the challenge at her. 'You will allow me to show you how to defend yourself.'

'I am not likely to be carrying a sword if I find myself in trouble, Alistair!'

'No, but you have your teeth, your feet and your elbows and you will usually have a hat pin, or a glass of wine or your reticule.' He regarded her seriously. 'You are too attractive, Dita. That and the scrape you got into mean that men will try to take advantage of you when you get to London.'

She shifted uncomfortably. 'Surely not. I am not pretty—'

'I know that. And you know perfectly well how attractive you are, which is an entirely different thing—you didn't get that way without working at it.' Dita opened her mouth and closed it again. 'I will teach you a few fencing moves, as Chatterton could have done perfectly well, but I will teach you to fight dirty, too.'

'Where, might I ask?' She sounded outraged, but looked intrigued.

'In my cabin—if you dare.'

'You are teaching me how to repel unwanted advances—aren't you worried that you might find your own lessons turned on you?'

'Of course, you can try. You won't best me though. Besides, my advances are not unwelcome—are they?' he said with a deliberate arrogance designed to provoke.

Dita shook her head at him, but a smile she could not control twitched at the corner of her mouth. He felt something shift inside his chest, something almost like a twinge of fear. *Damn it, what am I getting myself into?* He gave himself a mental shake: she was not a virgin, he was not going to risk getting her with child, she was willing. What was there to worry about?

Dita stood up. She felt curiously shaken. It was probably the fight. Even though she knew there were buttons on the foils and that it was essentially a game, there was something primal and stirring about two men fighting with deadly skill and elegance. Especially, she had to admit, over her. Even more so when one of them was Alistair. She did not want to investigate that thought too deeply.

'Would you care to try the foils now? You do not mind an audience?'

She hardly had time to nod before he was gone, to return with the swords and Mrs Bastable, both Chatterton twins and Averil at his heels. Alistair placed one foil in her hand and she exclaimed at how light it was.

'The point is to impale your opponent, not bludgeon him to death,' he said, and she snorted with nervous laughter as he put his hand over hers to adjust her grip. 'Good, check the button is secure, you do not want to run Mr Chatterton through just yet.' Callum grinned, picked up the other foil and stood opposite her. 'Now stand sideways, with your feet like this...'

Alistair nudged her into position, his hands warm yet impersonal on her shoulder, at her elbow. She had thought he would need to hold her more closely and found herself oddly piqued that he did not. *'En garde,'* Callum said, bringing his foil up, and she imitated him.

'Now lunge.' Alistair moved behind her, his body suddenly as close as she could have wished, one arm bracketing her, his hand over her fingers. Their weight shifted together, Callum moved, his foil coming across to deflect her blade, and Alistair pulled her back. 'Bring up your foil; he is going to counter-attack.'

'Oh!' It was alarming, seeing that blade coming towards her, even slowly. Hers met it at right angles. 'Push,' Alistair said in her ear and she did, as he twisted her wrist, moved their balance and Callum, caught unawares, found his foil flicked out of his grasp.

'Now, in for the kill!' Instinctively she straightened the blade, let her body go with the thrust of his and Callum was standing there, the button of her foil pressed against his heart.

'I've killed you!' She jumped up and down in glee before she realised what she had said. 'Oh! I am so sorry, Mr Chatterton, I didn't mean—'

'You, Lady Perdita,' he said with a grin, 'are quite lethal, with or without a weapon. I think I will let my brother stand as your opponent in future—he has no reputation as a swordsman to lose.'

'I think that is quite enough,' Dita said. 'I know what it feels like to hold a sword now, and I would like to learn more—but I do not think that proper lessons would be quite—'

'Proper?' Alistair released her and reversed the foil over his arm for Callum to take before he went to retrieve the fallen one. 'Thank you,' he added, holding out his hand to shake the other's. 'That was good sport.' He nodded to Dita and strode off.

'What was that about?' Dita demanded when she found herself alone for a moment with Callum while Daniel wiped the blades with an oiled cloth and laid them back in their case. He looked at her blankly. 'Mr Chatterton, one minute you and Alistair are bristling at each other like two tom cats on a wall and the next you are shaking hands and appear to be friends for life.'

'Oh, that.' He took her arm and strolled to the rail where they could look down on the main deck. 'He thought my intentions towards you might be less than honourable, I suspect. Now he believes me when I tell him they are simply those of friendship and I believe *him* when he tells me that he is acting purely as a concerned neighbour.'

'A neighbour?' Dita stared at him. 'Lord Lyndon has been no neighbour of mine for the past eight years.'

'He obviously feels he still has a responsibility to look after you, Lady Perdita,' Callum said with a perfectly straight face and laughter in his eyes. 'If you will excuse me.' He bowed and left her a victim to considerable confusion.

Why on earth did Alistair feel he had to warn Callum off, and why did he want to teach her to defend herself? Was he a rake or a reformed man? Or a rake who was trying to lull her into a false sense of security? Whatever the answer, it was intriguing. Not that she should give in to her regrettable attraction to him again.

She was still leaning on the rail and brooding when Alistair came back. 'That empty cabin is still unoccupied and no one is around down there. Do you want to attempt to disarm me now?'

Dita followed him warily, but the space was brightly lit by three lanterns and there were an array of props on the unmade bunk. It seemed he really did have a self-defence lesson in mind.

After ten minutes he had her in fits of laughter as he demonstrated the best way to wield a hat pin to deter a pest sitting next to her in a pew at church, the easiest way to tip a glass of wine down a gentleman who was standing too close whilst making it seem like an accident, the most painful part of the foot to stand upon with a French heel and how to free one's hands if they had been seized. It was all fun and extremely useful.

'Girls ought to be taught this sort of thing instead of endless embroidery,' she remarked as Alistair rubbed a twisted thumb.

'That will deal with the pests,' he said. 'What I will show you now is how to deal with an over-amorous gentleman who completely oversteps the bounds of decency.'

'Indeed?' Dita raised an eyebrow. 'You intend to stop kissing me and…other things, do you?'

Alistair studied her without amusement. 'Tell me that anything I have done has been unwelcome and I will not speak to you, or approach you, for the remainder of this voyage.'

That was handing her her own with a vengeance. Dita searched her conscience, then shook her head. 'You have done many things that are shocking, unwise and outrageous, and I have not been unwilling.' It was difficult to meet his eyes, but when she did the tension had vanished from his face.

He nodded. 'After this, should you change your mind, you will be able to give me a very pointed hint. There are a number of places where a jab or a blow is extremely painful and will win you time to get away. If you will allow me to take you in my arms, like so—'

Dita knew she was still flushed, and it was hard to remember that she was supposed to be fighting and not yielding.

'Make your fingers stiff and jab here, then raise your knee...' Her hand and knee hardly made contact before he twisted away, eel-like. 'You have it to perfection. Now, let's try again.' Alistair took her in a firm embrace, turning so his broad shoulders were to the bunk. 'Try for the solar plexus.'

'You are holding me too tightly,' she protested. 'That isn't fair!' It was no longer a game, but she could not have said quite why not. She felt hot and bothered and far too close to him. Her nipples, she could feel, were peaking hard against her bodice, her breathing was all over the place and the wretched man was stroking his fingers down her spine.

'Rakes don't play fair, Dita,' he murmured, bending to nibble her ear. 'Stop palpitating and think about what I showed you. I have all the time in the world while you decide what to do.' His tongue traced hot and moist down to the lobe and she jumped as though he had pinched her.

'You...' *Think, Dita, your hands are free. He said something about ears... Oh my lord, he is sucking my earlobe...* She raised her hands, grabbed both Alistair's ears and twisted. The result was instant.

'Aagh!' They stood, a foot apart, glaring at each other, then Alistair began to laugh. 'Excellent.' He rubbed his ears with a grimace. 'You see, there is no point pussy-footing about. If you are serious, then act and put everything you have into it. What you should have done, the moment I released you, was to use your knee. If you had done it hard enough, I would be rolling about on the floor by now and you would be out of the door.'

'Thank you, ' Dita said. 'If I ever encounter a wolf, I will know what to do now.' She still felt unsettled and aroused and simmering beneath that there was anger with herself for feeling that way—and with him for manipulating her so. She turned and opened the door. 'A wolf, or any other kind of deceiver. Good day, Alistair.'

'Wait.' He took her arm and pulled her back into the cabin, pushing the door to with the flat of his other hand. 'What exactly do you mean by that? Who has been deceiving you?'

'Why, you, of course. You make love to me and then you lecture me on defending myself against rakes. Are you a lover or a seducer? A friend or is this just a game? You made love to me here before and you know full well you could have ravished me if you had wished it—I had no defences. You caressed me on deck until I was a trembling wreck and you held me in your arms just now and made me melt for a foolish second. You know how to make me react to you, you seem to understand me all too well, but I do not know who you are any more.'

'I am an awful warning, that is what I am,' he said with no humour whatsoever. 'I want, Dita my dear, to make love to you and because I know you are not a virgin I want to take advantage of that. So far, I have had enough self-control not to risk leaving you with child. So, yes, I am a rake and a seducer. And yes, I know I should not make love to you and I know I will try to kill any man who does, because part of me remembers that I grew up defending you. So that makes me a hypocrite as well.'

'You remember me as a child?'

'Yes, of course I do! We have discussed this—how could I forget the trouble you got me into, time and again?'

'I was sixteen when you left. Do you remember me then?'

'Not really.' He frowned. 'I'd been to Oxford and then I was away—London, travelling, staying with friends—for much of the time after that. When I came back you were still too young for parties and balls, so I didn't see you at those. You had grown up, I can remember that: all eyes and hair and gawky long legs.'

'We kept bumping into each other, though,' she reminded him. 'Out riding and walking, in the grounds. You seemed happy. Excited even.'

His face became expressionless. 'Oh, yes, I was in wonderful spirits.'

He had been different, she had sensed that. Laughing, light-hearted, even, she could see in retrospect, just a little flirtatious. She had been falling in love with him, all unknowing that that happiness and flirtation had not been for her. Another woman?

'The last day. The day before you left,' she persisted. 'Do you remember…meeting me that day?'

He frowned, troubled. 'No. I was angry and I was devilish drunk by the evening, that I do know. I woke up with one hell of a hangover. It is all very fuzzy. You were there though, weren't you?'

'Yes,' she conceded. 'And, yes, you were angry and a little drunk.'

'I am sorry. You obviously went away and left me to it—very wise. I got a lot drunker.' Alistair turned and began to put the cabin to rights.

He did not remember. He did not recollect her finding him in the garden of Lyndonholt Castle with a bottle in his hand and another at his feet, distracted, both furious over something and desperate with grief. She had pulled him towards the house, worried that he would stumble into the moat, and somehow had towed him up the stairs to his bedchamber. As she had pushed him in through the door he had turned and the pain in his face had torn at her heart. Her friend was hurting. And so she had stood on tiptoe and kissed his cheek, for comfort. Only she had missed and found his mouth and feelings she had never known flooded through her and she had put her arms around his neck and he had pulled her to him and into the room and…

As she stood there now, all she wanted to do was walk into his arms and turn up her face to his again. He would kiss her, she was certain. She should leave, she knew that. He was no longer a desperate, drunken young man who did not care what he was doing. But there was a question she had to ask, even though she dreaded the answer and knew that if she asked it, things would never be the same again.

'If you want me so badly,' she said before she could lose her nerve, 'why not marry me?'

It rocked Alistair back on his heels. She saw him recoil and found she had bitten her lip. It hurt, but not as much as his reaction.

He recovered in the blink of an eyelid. 'Is that a proposal?' he drawled.

'No, it is a rhetorical question; there is no need to panic. When I marry—if I marry—it will be a love match. I do not have to settle for less.' She put up her chin and stared back into the cynical amber eyes that watched her. 'I want you, but I do not love you. Half of the time I do not even like you, as the child I was did.'

'And there you have it. You want love and emotion and devotion.' He shrugged. 'I do not. Love is a fantasy, overrated at best, poison at worst. Those giggling girls on board would tell me they loved me if I gave them the slightest encouragement, and they would convince themselves they meant it, any of them. What they *love* is my title and my money.

'Friendship and loyalty now, those are another matter. I like you, Dita. I want you and I am doing my damndest to balance those two things because I owe you loyalty.'

'You call licking my ear—'

'I never said I was a saint,' he said with a grimace. 'I take my pleasures where I can. And you, my darling Dita, are certainly a pleasure.'

'Oh, you…you maddening man. Just keep out of my way from now on. No help, no defending me from other men, no teasing, no games. *Nothing*. Do you understand me?'

'But of course.' Alistair sketched a bow. 'Behold, your most indifferent servant—until you ask me to behave otherwise. May I hold the door for you, or is that too demonstrative?'

Dita glared, beyond any retaliation. Inside something hurt. She wanted the old Alistair back, the boy, her friend. Instead she had this man whom she desired beyond safety or reason and who she could not understand any more than she understood herself just at the moment.

'Far too demonstrative,' she snapped, opened the door and swept out.

Chapter Twelve

Alistair was as good as his word. His manner was polite, impeccable, indifferent and drove her wild with desire. The cynical part of her wondered if he knew that. However, he still attended the evening meetings of what Daniel Chatterton had christened the 'editorial committee'. As they left Madeira behind them the novel reached chapter thirty, enlivened now by the swordfight, pirates, the attempted keelhauling of the hero with a dramatic escape and the unfortunate Angelina still barely eluding the clutches of the evil Blackstone.

'Who is not exerting himself very hard in that direction,' Dita heard Alistair mutter to Daniel as they left the deck after a spirited discussion of the day's incidents.

Neither are you, thank goodness, she thought, attempting to be glad of it. But the fact that Alistair was behaving perfectly did not mean that her own treacherous feelings were as obedient. She still wanted him, still longed to touch him. And she wanted their old friendship back as well. She wanted, she was well aware, the moon.

The light was fading fast and Dita reminded herself they were not yet halfway through March. It was chilly now they were in the Bay of Biscay, the ladies put heavy cloaks over their shawls before venturing out and Averil, brought up from childhood in India, shivered.

'How much longer, Captain?' she asked as they crowded into the cuddy, cheerful and warm with its lamps burning in their gimbals and the smell of the baked goods the cook had sent up with tea.

'Impatient, Miss Heydon?' He smiled. 'We have made good time, you know. Provided we do not run into any trouble with French warships, or privateers—and the captain of British navy brig we encountered two days ago thinks we should not—and the wind holds, then I expect to sight Land's End in two days and you should be on land in Plymouth the day after that.'

Most of the passengers, Dita included, would disembark at Plymouth and travel overland to their destinations, even those heading for London. After so long at sea the chance to be free of the ship more than made up for the trials of road travel.

'Are you London-bound, Lady Perdita?' Alistair asked her as she sipped her tea. He passed her the cakes, taking care not to touch her hand, she thought. Or perhaps she was being too sensitive. This distance was what she wanted, wasn't it?

'No. I shall go home to Combe,' she said, with a smile of pleasure at the thought. 'We will go up to London for the Season a little late, but Mama did not wish to make firm plans—the length of the voyage is so unpredictable.'

'I will escort you then. I am returning to Lyndonholt Castle.'

'There is no need,' Dita protested, then caught herself. Her alarm at the thought of being in a close carriage with Alistair for a long day's journey must sound as though she did not trust him. It was herself she did not trust. 'Thank you, but I would not want to inconvenience you. Mr Bastable must get up to town immediately we land, but Mrs Bastable is going to stay with Averil and me until we are collected. My father will come for me and Averil's betrothed will presumably send a carriage and a maid for her.'

'But do you want to wait?' Alistair passed her a biscuit, but she shook her head, too undecided to think about food. 'Mrs Bastable can select a reliable maid that your parents would approve of. I will hire a chaise for you and a horse for myself.'

'Thank you. I must admit that when I have landed I am sure I will not want anything more than to be home.' She put her hand on his forearm and felt him stiffen. She lifted it away. 'You are very kind, Alistair.'

No,' he said, his smile thin. 'I am a selfish devil; you would do well to remember that, Dita.'

'Are you cold, too?' Averil asked. Dita jumped and stopped watching Alistair's back as he left the cabin. 'You are shivering as much as I am. Shall we change into something warmer before supper?'

Wednesday 15th March—off the Isles of Scilly

'We will put into Hugh Town on St Mary's tomorrow, Mrs Bastable,' the captain said as the steward cleared the cheese board from the supper table. 'That storm last night has taken us west, and it will be as well to check the ship in quiet waters before we enter the Channel, but it will not delay us long.'

Alistair stretched his legs under the table, bumped feet with Daniel who was discussing fox hunting with George Latham, and grimaced. Oh, to be on land, stretching his legs. To run, to ride, to feel grass under his feet and a gentler sun on his skin. To have the freedom to be alone without the constant need to make conversation and allowances. Without the constant, aching, nearness of Dita Brooke. *Marriage.* Her question had both surprised him and made him wary. She wanted love, and that he could not give her. It was unfair to dally with her, to tease her into an unconsummated *affaire*, he kept reminding himself. So far that resolution had held.

'English soil at last,' the matron said with a sigh, dragging her shawl more tightly around her shoulders. 'An English spring. It is twelve years since I last saw one of those. Can we not go into harbour tonight, Captain Archibald?'

'No, ma'am, I'm afraid not. We must wait here at anchor until a pilot rows out to us at first light. The waters around the Isles are littered with reefs and rocks and sand bars and are not safe to be approached in the dark.'

'I had no idea spring in England would be so chilly,' Averil remarked. 'I thought the sun would shine and it would be warmer than this.'

'Not on a March night, Miss Heydon,' Callum said with a grin. '*Ne'er cast a clout til May be out*, is the saying. It will be a while before we have temperatures that you might consider even passably warm enough for you to break out your pretty muslins.'

She sent him a smile that froze as the ship gave a sudden lurch, sending the wine glasses sliding. Alistair saw Daniel's head snap round to met his brother's eyes and exchange a silent message. He put down his own wineglass and watched the captain.

Archibald was frowning. 'What the—?'

He was on his feet even as a sailor appeared in the doorway. 'Mr Henshaw's compliments, Captain, but the wind's got up and she's dragging the anchor and will you come at once?'

Several woman gave little shrieks, but not, Alistair noted as he got to his feet, Dita. She had gone a trifle pale, but she was calm.

'What should we do?' a man asked from further along the table, his voice rising in barely controlled alarm.

'Nothing,' Alistair said, thinking furiously. Through storms and wild seas the ship had never felt so strange under his feet as it did now. Something was very wrong, but panic would only make it worse. 'I expect it will be a trifle unsettled while they put out another anchor or shift position to find a better hold on the sea bed. Better not to retire to our bunks just yet, in case it becomes rough for a while.'

He exchanged a swift glance with the Chatterton twins. The three of them were the youngest, fittest men amongst the civilian passengers in the cuddy. If there was any danger, they would help the officers get the women to the boats.

'Should we go on deck?' Mr Crabtree, a middle-aged merchant, asked.

'Why, no,' Alistair said easily. 'Think how underfoot we would be. There are all the sailors rushing about doing whatever they do with yards and sheets and anchors. We should just settle down for a while until the captain comes back.'

He strolled across to where Callum was stooping to look out of the window. 'What can you see?' he murmured against the babble of conversation. Across the cabin Daniel was teasing the ladies about their plans for London shopping, but he had stayed on his feet and Alistair could sense his tense alertness.

'It is as black as the devil's waistcoat, except for that light over there.' Callum nodded at a spot on the port bow. 'And that's moving.'

'Wreckers?'

'No, it's us. We're going before the wind and closer to the light and the land. I don't like the feel of this.'

'Neither do I. We're all up here, aren't we?'

'Yes.' Callum cocked his head towards the door to the Great Cabin from where a babble of voices and the sound of a crying child could be heard. One of the lieutenants walked briskly through the cuddy and they heard his feet clattering down the companionway.

'He'll sort them out down there,' Alistair said. 'There are enough able-bodied men to help. Up here there's seventeen if you don't count the three of us.' He jerked his head towards Daniel. 'Just in case, we'll divide them up, five or six each. You have a word with your brother and we'll start to cut them out and get them into groups without them noticing, with any luck.'

Callum nodded and strolled over to speak to his twin under cover of a lively discussion about London hotels. Most of the other men knew what the danger was, Alistair was pretty certain, but they were staying outwardly calm. They were tough, experienced characters, all of them, even those who were older and fatter. Certainly he received slight nods of acknowledgment as the three younger men edged the ladies into little groups and the motion of the ship became stronger.

Dita made her way to his side and whispered, 'You think we are in danger, don't you?'

'Best to be careful,' he murmured back, 'and not to panic.'

'Of course,' she said. She had gone even paler, but she kept her chin up and a smile on her face as though they were discussing a trivial matter, and he felt a flash of pride in her courage. 'I'm sure there is nothing to be—'

The *Bengal Queen* shuddered to a stop as though she had run into a wall, sending Dita stumbling into his arms. For a moment there was silence, then one of the older women began to scream and was shushed by her husband.

'Up on deck now,' Alistair ordered, setting Dita on her feet. 'You all with me. That group there—*Mrs Bastable!*—with Daniel Chatterton. You five with Callum. Hold tight as you go. We'll get the ladies into the boats first.'

The cabin shifted, throwing them all into a heap, half on the deck, half sprawled across table and chairs. A lamp crashed down, burning oil spilled out, and Dita yanked the shawl from Mrs Bastable's shoulders and smothered the fire. Without a word the men began to get the fallen to their feet. Beside him Alistair was aware of

Averil helping an older woman, her voice calm as she took her arm.

Dita had blood trickling from her forehead. 'Dita? Are you—?'

'It is nothing.' She brushed off his hand and went to get Dr Melchett upright.

'Hurry.' Daniel was at the door, braced against the worsening tilt of the deck, his hand stretched out to pull the others towards him until he had his little group of six, then he gave way for Alistair to get his charges on deck. At his side Callum hauled and pushed until everyone was huddled around the main mast.

It was dark, lit only by the moving light from the lanterns, and the wind that had come up so fast was cold and gusting. Hair and shawls flapped wildly, men's faces came in and out of focus as the sailors fought with the ropes to lower the boats. Passengers from the Great Cabin began to pour out, milling around, adding to the confusion.

While Alistair fought to keep people together and sort the women and children and the frail from the more able-bodied, the twins helped load the first boat, with four of the sailors to row and some of the older men to help the women down the ladder and into the wave-tossed boat. It pushed off from the side and vanished into the darkness.

'Now you.' Alistair pulled Dita towards the side as the second and third boats were lowered. Their feet slid on the tilting deck; water was coming over the side as waves hit the ship broadside. Then the moon came out from the clouds and he saw the rocks as its light lit the breaking surf.

'No, get the older women on this one.' Dita twisted from his grasp and went to help Mrs Bastable and a grey-haired lady who was sobbing wildly. It took longer this time—the angle of the ship was greater, the wind seemed to be gaining strength. Or perhaps, Alistair thought as he fought his way to Daniel's side, they were losing theirs.

At last the boat was loaded and away, and another lowered to be crammed with the Great Cabin passengers. Alistair found Lieutenant Henshaw at his side. 'All the rest of the passengers into the next one,' he ordered.

Alistair pulled Dita and Averil up the tilting deck to the rail. 'I'll go first,' he said, holding Dita's eyes with his. 'I'll keep you safe.'

'I know.' Her smile was shaky, but real, and he felt a stab of fear for her that was almost painful.

Alistair climbed down the ladder into the pitching boat with the sailors. He was cold and soaked; how the women were coping he had no idea. *Dita.* He blanked emotion from his mind and concentrated. The *Bengal Queen* was shifting on the rock that had snared her; he could hear the grinding sound, like a great beast in agony in a trap.

Daniel landed in the boat beside him, his face white as he stared up at his brother, still on deck. Callum began to help people over the rail, shouting encouragement over the crashing of the waves. Dita came sliding down the ladder into Alistair's arms; he pushed her back on to a seat. 'Hang on!'

Then Averil Heydon was clinging to his neck, gasping. 'I'm all right,' she shouted above the noise as she stumbled away to join Dita. The two girls wrapped their arms around each other as they huddled on the plank seat.

'Cal! Come on!' Daniel shouted, his hands cupped around his mouth.

Alistair saw Callum raise a hand in acknowledgment and put one hand on the gunwale, ready to climb over. Then he froze, staring out with a look of blank shock. Alistair swung round. Coming towards them was a foaming wall of water, black and white in the stark moonlight.

'Dita—' The wave hit, picking the boat up like a toy. They were falling, tossed up and over. Bodies crashed into him as they tumbled helplessly into the sea. He reached out as he fell, grabbed, almost blind, on nothing but instinct, and a hand fastened around his wrist. He saw Dita's face, stark with horror, and then they were in the water and all rational thought ceased.

Chapter Thirteen

'Dita! Dita, open your eyes.' She was dreaming about
Alistair. She wished she could wake up because in her
dream she was freezing cold, and her whole body ached
and he was shouting at her. 'Dita, darling!' Now he was
shaking her. She tried to protest, to push him away. It
hurt and the blanket must have fallen off the bed which
was why she was so cold…

'Dita, damn it, wake up or I am going to slap you!'

'No,' she managed and opened her eyes on to near-
darkness. It was not a dream, she realised as fitful moonlight caught Alistair's face. His hair was plastered to his
head, his shirt was in tatters. 'What?'

Water, even colder than she was, splashed over her
feet. Her bare feet. It all came back: the ship and the fear
and the great wave that had hurled them out of the boat
into the sea.

'Thank God. Can you crawl up the beach?' Alistair
asked. He was kneeling, she realised. 'We need to get
away from the sea into some shelter. I don't think I can

carry you, I'm sorry.' His voice sounded harsh and pain-ful as he hauled her up into a sitting position against his shoulder.

'Don't be,' Dita murmured against the chilled skin. He must be exhausted, beyond exhausted, and he was still asking more of himself. 'You saved me. I can crawl. Oh—' She leaned over and was violently ill, retching sea water until she was gasping. 'All right…now.' Her throat hurt; she must sound as bad as he did, she thought, aware of Alistair holding her, shielding her with his own shivering body against the cold wind.

The beach was sand, thank heavens—she did not think she could have managed if it had been rock or shifting pebbles. As she struggled Alistair half-lifted, half-dragged her, her arm around his shoulders, their free hands clawing at the gentle slope until the texture changed. 'Grass.'

'Yes.' He staggered to his feet and pulled her the rest of the way until she lay on the short, salt-bitten turf. 'Hell, I can't see any lights.' He turned, peering into the gloom. 'But there's something over there, a hut perhaps. Can you stand now?'

She managed it, climbing up his body until he could hold her against his side, and there, fifty feet beyond where they stood, was the sharp edge of a roof line. With an aim in sight they moved faster, stumbling across the turf, stubbing bare feet on rocks.

'It's not locked, thank God.' Alistair pushed against the door and it creaked open. 'Hold on here.' He placed her hands on the door jamb and went inside. Dita heard curses, a thump, then a rasping sound. A thread of light became a candle, then another. 'There's a lamp,' she said and he lit that, too.

'A fisherman's hut, perhaps,' Alistair said. 'Here, come and lie down.' He came across the room to help her to the rough cot and she saw him clearly for the first time. He was still wearing his evening breeches, but his shirt hung on in shreds and tatters, his stockings clinging to his calves. Dita looked down and found she only had her petticoats, much ripped, her stays and, under them, her chemise. Beneath that her questing fingers found a row of tiny globes. The necklace was safe.

'And get those clothes off,' Alistair added. 'They'll only make us colder. There are blankets. And, by St Anthony, the fire's laid and there is wood.'

Beyond modesty, Dita began to claw at the sodden fabric with shaking fingers. Alistair turned his back, knelt and set a candle to the fire. 'You, too,' she managed between chattering teeth as she furled a stiff and smelly blanket around herself. 'If we pull this cot to the fire, we can both get in and share the heat.'

Between them they dragged the rough-framed bed to the hearth. Alistair heaped the firewood close so he could reach out and throw it on, and then he stripped, the rags of his shirt disintegrating under his cold-clumsy fingers.

Dita stared as he stood there in the firelight. 'You are covered in marks.'

He glanced down, unselfconscious in his nakedness. 'The long boat hit me as we went in, I think. That's probably the ribs.' He prodded and winced. 'The rest is rocks. There was a bad patch just after we were thrown out.'

'Come to bed.'

To her astonishment he managed a wicked grin. 'I thought you would never ask, Dita.'

'Idiot,' she said and found she was near to tears. 'Come and hold me.'

He threw the other blanket over her and then slid in under it so her back was to the fire. Dita pulled open the blanket she was wrapped in and wriggled close until she was tight against his long, cold, damp body.

'Mind you,' he said, as he reached out to drag the covering over them, 'this isn't how I imagined our first time in a bed would be.'

'We've been in a bed,' she mumbled against his chest. *Twice, if only he remembered.*

'Not naked and not in it.' Alistair wrapped his arms around her tightly. 'What's this?'

'Your pearls. I had them made into a necklace in Cape Town and I've been wearing them ever since.' She had put them under her clothes because she hadn't wanted to give him the satisfaction of seeing how she prized his gift. That seemed so petty now.

'Next to the skin?'

'It improves the lustre,' she said, daring him to comment.

But all he said was, 'Are you all right?'

It was an insane question, she thought, then smiled. The hair on his chest tickled her lips as they curved. 'Yes. Yes, I am.'

'So am I. Good being alive, isn't it? Sleep now, I've got you safe.'

He had kept her safe through that nightmare, her childhood terror made a thousand times worse, in darkness, in numbing cold. She pressed her lips to his skin in a kiss as she closed her eyes and tried to piece together her jumbled memories.

She had been thrown out of the boat, Averil's screams in her ears, and a hand had fastened around her wrist. She had known it was Alistair—those strong fingers, that implacable grip that did not loosen as they sank and then were thrown to the surface. How he had got her to shore she had no recollection. She must have passed out, but they could not have been in the water long or they would surely have died of the cold.

'The others,' she said, tensing in his arms. 'Averil, the Chattertons, Mrs Bastable…'

'We are safe, they may be too,' he said, tucking her head more firmly under his chin. 'And the other boats got clear of the rocks before that wave hit us. There are a lot of islands, it isn't as though we went down in mid-ocean.' His hand stroked down her back. 'Sleep, Dita. There is nothing you can do about it now.'

She slept and woke to find herself warm, with Alistair leaning over her on one elbow to toss another branch on the fire. There was a faint grey light in the room, coming through the thick salt-stained pane of glass in the window. The candles had gone out and the lamp burned pale in the dawn.

'Hello,' he said, looking down at her. 'How are you?'

'Alive,' she said and smiled up into his stubble-darkened face. 'You look a complete pirate.'

He grinned. 'You sound like one. Your voice is as hoarse as mine feels. I'll have a look round in a minute,

see if there is anything to drink. Then I'll go and find if
there is anyone living on this island. I don't know which
one it is.'

Instinctively her arms tightened around him. 'Don't
leave me.'

'It won't be for long—they are all small, I'll be back
soon.'

'I'll come, too.'

'You need to rest, Dita.' He looked down at her as she
lay back against the lumpy pillow. 'You've got a lion's
heart, but not its strength.'

'I can manage. Alistair—I don't want to be alone.'

'Dita—oh lord, don't cry, sweetheart, not now we're
safe.' He bent over her, his amber eyes soft with a concern she had never seen before, not in the adult man.

'I'm not.' She swallowed, looked up, lost herself in
his gaze.

'No? What's this?' He bent and kissed the corner of
her eye. 'Salt.'

'We're both salty,' she murmured and, as he moved,
she lifted her head and kissed his mouth. 'You see?'

Alistair went still, his eyes watchful. 'Dita?' There
was a wealth of meaning in that question and he did
not have to explain any of it to her. She was warm now,
and her blood ran hot and she was alive and she wanted
him—because she was *alive* and because he had given
her that gift. Against her body she felt him stir into
arousal.

'Yes,' she said. 'Oh, yes, Alistair.'

He rolled, pinned her under him and she ignored
the protests from battered, bruised muscles and wriggled until her hips cradled him and the wonderful hot

threatening promise of his erection pressed intimately against her.

Alistair took his weight on his elbows, which rocked his hips tighter into hers, and she gasped at the pleasure of it. 'You are so lovely,' he murmured. 'You look like a mermaid, washed up at my feet.'

She almost protested. She was sticky with salt, her hair a tangled, still-damp, mess. She knew how she looked every day, scrubbed from the bath with no artifice of hairdressing or jewellery or the subtle use of cosmetics. The lack of balance in her face, her long nose, her wide mouth—he would see all that with complete clarity. But he appeared sincere; he appeared to see her, at this moment, as *lovely* and she could not protest, not when the man she loved was about to make her his.

'What is it?' She must have gasped. 'Did I hurt you? Am I too heavy?'

'No. No.' Dita stared up at the face above her, the man she had known virtually all her life. Her friend, the man she had thought she simply lusted after. *I love him? Oh my God, I love him.* And he would make love to her now and this time it would be perfect, because it was Alistair. He would heal that long-ago nightmare.

He smiled, that wicked smile that had drawn her after him for all those years of her childhood, driving away the other, so-familiar, expression from his boyhood, that of concern for her. *He's saved me from every scrape I have got myself into—except Stephen. And when he led me into trouble, he got me out of that to, except that once. He could have ravished me on the ship, but he didn't…*

Alistair began to kiss her throat, one hand sliding

between their bodies, intent, she knew, on weaving sensual delight that would make her mindless, blissful, until she was his. *He is practiced, he won't hurt me,* she thought as the first shiver of apprehension mixed with the pleasure. It had been a long time.

He will realise I am not a virgin, but then, he thinks that I slept with Stephen. Thank goodness she had fought Stephen off, thank goodness the man she loved had been the only one. She stiffened at the memory of Stephen's groping hands.

'Dita? Don't worry, I won't risk a child.'

Alistair's lips closed around her right nipple and she gasped as he sucked, her mind wiped blank for one exquisite moment. Then she fought through the sensation. It was important, because she loved him, that he did not believe that she had given herself to Stephen

'I need to tell you something.'

'Now?'

'Yes, now, Alistair. You know that I am not a virgin.'

He lifted his head from her breast, intense, serious, his eyes dark and heavy with arousal. 'I know. The scandal—that character you eloped with.'

'Stephen Doyle. I never slept with him.'

Alistair sat up and she tried to see his expression in the gloom.

'Then why the hell didn't you say so and put a stop to all the gossip?'

'I suppose because I was too proud to explain that after an hour alone in the chaise I realised that I had been completely deceived in him. I spent two nights fending him off with the cutlery, but no one but my family would have believed me and I would have lost my dignity along with my reputation.'

'Dignity? But if you were still a virgin—' She saw the memory of her words come back to him. 'Who was it, then?'

'You.' She had not meant to blurt it out, but the word simply escaped.

'*What?* Don't be ridiculous, Dita. When, for heaven's sake? I would have remembered.'

'Not if you were drunk and angry and very upset about something else,' she said and watched his face change as he realised when she must mean.

'Are you saying that the night before I left home I took your virginity? And I don't remember it? Don't be ridiculous, Dita. You were a child—I wouldn't have done such a thing.' He sounded furious. Dita watched as he flung himself off the crude bed and went to light the lantern, her stomach a tight knot of hurt misery.

'I was sixteen,' she said flatly. 'I found you in the rose garden in the base of the ruined tower. I had never seen you like that—drunk and upset and so angry. You were almost incoherent and I couldn't make any sense of what you were saying. I didn't want any of the servants to see you like that, so I helped you inside and up the back stairs to your room.

'And then I pushed you inside and you turned around and—Alistair, you looked so unhappy, I kissed you. I just meant to comfort you, like I would if you had fallen off your horse or something. But I missed your cheek and found your mouth and then something happened. It didn't feel like comforting a friend any more. You were not the same. I was not the same. I didn't understand, but you seemed to and you pulled me inside and closed the door.'

'And ravished you? Is that what you are saying?' He stood there, naked, fists clenched, his body very visibly losing all interest in what they had been doing a minute before.

'No, of course not. I wanted it, too. I didn't really understand, but I wanted you.' She thought back to the excitement and the apprehension and the sheer delight of his caresses. There had been pain, but there had been the joy of being in his arms and realising that she was a woman and she loved him and he must love her, too. 'I don't think you knew who I was, not at first. Afterwards you just stared at me and said…something. So I left.'

'What did I say?'

Dita bit her lip. The words had haunted her for years; now she had to repeat them to the man who had used them on her like weapons. 'You said, "Of all the bloody stupid things to do. You. I must be mad. Get out." There were other things, I don't recall very well—I had my hands over my ears by then. You were so angry with me and the next day you had gone.'

'Oh dear God. I don't remember,' he said, his face pale in the lamp light. 'Dita, I swear I don't remember. I kept having dreams, but they were so confused I didn't believe them. I just thought they were fantasies. Hell, I might have got you with child.'

'Fortunately not,' she said with as much calm as she could muster. 'That never occurred to me until years later. I was very innocent, you see.'

'Innocent! You don't need to tell me that,' he said bitterly. 'You might have told me all this before I made love to you on board,' he said. 'Damn it, all that held me back was my fear of getting you with child. Now I know I should never have laid a finger on you at all.'

She stared at him. 'But you thought I had slept with Stephen. Why would this make any difference?'

'Because it makes you my responsibility. Don't you see that?'

'No, I do not. It was eight years ago, Alistair. And you were drunk.'

'That makes it worse. Why didn't you tell me straight away?' He paced the small hut, ignoring his nakedness.

'In Calcutta? What would you suggest I should have said? Good evening, Lord Lyndon. Don't you recall the last time we met? You were kicking me out of your bedchamber after taking my virginity?'

'No! I mean before we made love.'

'I did not want to talk about it. I wanted, not to forget it exactly, but to put it behind me. And then it got rather out of hand,' she admitted. 'I was not expecting to feel like that: so overwhelmed. I hadn't got much experience, even now, remember?'

'Don't rub it in,' he said with a bitter laugh, as he turned away to pick up his breeches. 'Thanks to me, you have now.' He hauled the damp, clinging fabric over his hips, picked up the remnants of his shirt and tossed it away again. 'Get dressed, you are shivering.'

She was, Dita realised, and not just from cold. Why was he so angry with her? Was this her fault, too?

'Pass me my clothes, then,' she said, suddenly shy of her nudity. He gave them to her and she wriggled into the camisole and then the petticoats. They had fared better than Alistair's breeches; their thin cotton had dried in the warmth from the fire, although the salt made them feel unpleasant against her skin. The corset was still damp and she tossed it aside with a grimace of distaste.

'We must get married as soon as possible. It is fortunate your parents are down in Devon and not in London; we can organise something quietly.'

'Marry you?' She sat there in her damp undergarments and shivered at the tone of his voice. 'Why?'

He did not love her, for if he did, surely he would have said so. And when he had made love to her not one word of love or tenderness had passed his lips, only desire.

'I told you. I as good as raped you and that makes you my responsibility.' This was not what she needed to hear in his voice.

'So I must be yours because of one drunken incident eight years ago?'

'Exactly.' Alistair turned and began to rummage around the shelves and dark corners of the hut while she dressed. 'There's nothing to drink, but I've found a knife.' He took a blanket and cut a slit in the middle, then dropped it over her head. 'That's better than trying to walk with it wrapped round you,' he said, doing the same for himself. He opened the door. 'Come on.'

In the full daylight she could see his face clearly. Unshaven, bruised, grim. And, no doubt, he could see her very clearly, too, as she stood up. Did he realise that she was not shivering, but shaking with anger?

'I will not marry you,' she stated flatly. 'I cannot believe you would insult me by offering it.'

'Insult?' He stopped in the doorway, every muscle tense.

'Yes. I would not marry you, Alistair Lyndon, if you went down on your knees and begged me.'

'You will have no choice. I will tell your father what happened.'

'And I will say that you got a blow on the head in the shipwreck and are having delusions. They know the truth about Stephen, but they also know that no one else believes I did not sleep with him. I will tell them you are being gallant as an old friend, but that I do not want to marry you. They are going to believe me—what woman in her right mind would turn down Lord Lyndon, after all?'

'So when you made love with me on the ship, when you returned my kisses—what was that?'

'Desire and a curiosity to see if there was any difference in the way you make love sober and with some experience.' That was not the truth, of course. She must have been in love with him for weeks. But it was not *her* feelings that were at issue here. 'You don't think I was in love with you, do you? No, of course not—you'd have avoided me like the plague.'

He could have had no idea how she felt about him, she supposed, seeing his mouth tighten into a hard line and his head come up. But then, neither had she, until a short while ago.

'And do I make love better sober?' Alistair made himself drawl, made himself sound cynical and blasé when all he wanted was to shout and rage and shake her until her teeth rattled. How could she have kept that from him? Everything he believed about himself seemed to crumble. He had been capable of behaving like that and had not even remembered it.

By any objective standards Dita looked ghastly—pale, bruised, serious, her hair hanging in tangled, sticky clumps—but her dignity and her anger shone through. He would have been happier, he realised, if she had been weeping. That did not make him feel any better about himself either.

'Oh, considerably. It was very nice the first time, but this was better,' she said. 'I haven't any grounds for comparison, you understand, but the sobriety would have helped. And, of course, no doubt your technique has improved with age and experience.'

'You little cat.'

'Meow,' she said bitterly as she got to her feet with none of her usual grace. For a moment he glimpsed the ungainly child as she adjusted the grey blanket.

He hardened his heart. Dita, who valued love and emotion in marriage, had rejected him. Foolish, headstrong, romantic idiot of a woman. Did she think he *wanted* to be leg-shackled to a passionate, troublesome, headstrong female? *A narrow escape*, he told himself, feeling sick. But it wasn't. She had thrown his honour back in his face.

'Ready?' He made his voice as brisk as he could with his throat rasped raw by salt water and emotion. 'We will discuss this later.' She shot him a mutinous look. 'Now the sun is up I can at least tell which direction we're facing. Last night I couldn't make head nor tail of the stars—I have been away from northern Europe too long, I suppose.'

'Or possibly you were a trifle weary for some reason,'

Dita suggested with some of the old spirit back in her voice as she came out of the hut to join him.

'Could be that,' he conceded. Now was no time to pursue this shattering argument; he needed to get her safe. 'Now, that's a good-sized island over there and that's east, so, if I recall the map correctly, it must be St Mary's, which is the biggest. Which makes this one Tresco, and if I'm right it has a fishing village at the northern end.' He glanced down at her, but her face was averted. 'It won't take me long; you should rest here.'

'I am coming,' Dita said with an edge to her voice that warned him that she was close to the end of her tether.

'All right,' he said and began to walk. It was hard now he was actually moving. Everything seemed to hurt, he was desperately thirsty and shaken to the core over what Dita had told him. But she kept up with the slow pace he set, doggedly putting one foot in front of the other, and he wondered whether any of the other women on the ship would have shown the same stoical courage. Averil Heydon, perhaps, but none of the other young women had the sheer guts. Probably they wouldn't need them; thanks to Averil and Dita, they had gone off in the first boats.

'I should have insisted you went off in an earlier boat,' he said, following his thoughts.

'How? By picking me up and throwing me into it?' she asked in a valiant imitation of her best provocative voice. 'You must learn you cannot order me about, Alistair.'

'So you say,' he snapped. It was bite back or take her in his arms and kiss her until her voice lost that little quaver that cut straight through his anger and shame and frustration. And he knew where that would lead. 'Damn it, Dita, you must marry me.'

Her silence was almost more loaded with anger than a retort would have been. Then after a few more steps she said, 'I doubt I will ever marry. If a man asks me to marry him, despite the scandal, and I love him, then I will marry him. Otherwise, I will just have to stay a spinster. I am not going to marry you in order to ease your guilty conscience, Alistair.'

They plodded on for a few more painful steps along the turf above the high-water mark. The sea was grey and choppy after the storm and he kept his body between it and her as much as he could. 'So you propose a test if someone proposes—does he love you enough to marry you despite Doyle?'

'I suppose so. I had not given it much thought; I just know that is what I would do.'

Would he have passed her test? he had wondered. If, before this shattering revelation, he found he loved Dita Brooke and wanted to marry her, would the thought of one lover in her past make a difference? He thought of his one love, his past love. She'd had another lover, and that had broken his heart. But then, look who the man was—

Love was a fantasy and a trap. Dita must agree to marry him whether she liked it or not.

'I hear voices!' Dita looked up, alert. 'Over there, past those rocks.'

They stumbled forwards, his arm around her shoulders, and, as they reached the low tumbled headland three men in blue came over it. Sailors. 'They've set the navy to search,' he said as the men broke into a run. 'It is all right now, Dita, you're safe.'

'I was always safe with you,' she said, her voice thready, then, as he held her, she went limp and fainted dead away.

Chapter Fourteen

'...Several ships at anchor in St Mary's Pool, so the Governor ordered off crews to all the islands to check along the shorelines.' The confident West Country voice soothed Dita with the longed-for cadences of home.

'How many survivors?' Alistair's voice rumbled against her ear. He must be holding her, she realised, coming out of the hazy dream-state she had been in. *Hiding*, she reproved herself. *Coward*. But she did not move. He was warm now, and it was not blanket she was snuggled against, but good woollen cloth. *I love you, I hate you, I need you... Why couldn't you have told me you loved me and made it all right?*

'Can't say for sure, my lord. All the longboats that went off before yours got in to harbour—some to St Mary's, some to Old Grimsby on Tresco. But an elderly man on one of those had a heart seizure and a lady perished of the cold, so I hear. There are injuries as well—I don't know how serious. The crew all got off safe after your boat was swamped.'

'There was a passenger left with the crew—any news of him?'

'No, my lord, I'm sorry, I don't know. But they'll be picking people up all along the beaches, I'll be bound. You'll hear the news when we get you back to the Governor's house. Not long now, this is a good strong crew.'

The strange rocking motion made sense now, and the breeze on her face: she was in a boat. Dita opened her eyes and moved and Alistair's hand pressed her cheek tighter against his chest. 'Don't be afraid. We're nearly there.'

'I'm all right.' She shifted again and he relaxed his arms so that she could sit up straight on his knees. She wanted to move away from him, but there was nowhere to go. They were in a navy jolly boat with smartly dressed sailors at the oars, making good progress towards a rugged little jetty dead ahead. Opposite her a lieutenant with red hair and a crop of freckles looked at her with concern on his plain face. 'I am sorry to have been so feeble,' she apologised. 'I think it was relief.'

'It will be that, my lady,' he said. 'Lieutenant Marlow, ma'am. You probably don't recall, but we took you to Mrs Welling's cottage and she found you some clothes— not that they'll be what you are used to. You'll be wanting a nice hot cup of tea, I expect.'

'A nice cup of tea.' She quelled the urge to laugh; if she started she might not stop. Of course, a nice cup of tea would make everything all right. 'Yes, that will be very welcome.' It was an effort to speak sensibly—her frantic, circling thoughts kept pulling her away from the present. She wondered if she was going to faint again.

Why did I tell him about that night? But I have to be honest with him. I love him.

'Have this now.' Alistair pressed a flask into her hands and she made herself turn to look at him. Someone had lent him clothes, too, and he had shaved and washed and combed his hair. If it wasn't for a black eye and the scrapes and bruises, he might be any gentleman out for a pleasure trip. 'It is cold tea and you need the liquid,' he said prosaically, steadying her.

'Thank you,' she said, as politely as a duchess at a tea party, and took the flask. It was cold, without milk or sugar, and it slid down her throat like the finest champagne.

When the boat bumped against the fenders at the quayside Dita made herself stand up and picked her way over the rowing benches to the side, determined to put on a brave face and not make an exhibition of herself in front of all these strangers. But curiously her fear of being in a small boat had gone and she stepped on to the stone steps without a qualm or an anxious look at the water slopping against the jetty. Perhaps after that great wave anything else was trivial, or else it was the emotional impact of that confrontation in the hut.

There was a crowd at the harbour side: onlookers; small groups of sailors with their officers, apparently being briefed for the next part of the search; some harassed clerks with lists and men holding half-a-dozen donkeys.

'It's very steep up to the Garrison,' Lieutenant Marlow said. 'Best ride a donkey, my lady.'

'Very well.' She let Alistair take her arm as they

walked to the animals. She knew she should be strong and not lean on him, not encourage him in his delusion that he was responsible for her, but his strong body so close was too comforting just now to resist. He boosted her up to sit sideways on the broad saddle. 'Alistair! Look—there's another boat coming in with people in it. Who is it?'

'Stay here.' He walked to the edge of the jetty and stared down, then came back. 'Mrs Edwards, a merchant's wife whose name I don't recall, and one of the Chattertons. He looks in bad shape.' He hesitated. 'They all do. Best you go on up to the house; the Governor's people will look after you.'

'See whether it is Daniel or Callum,' Dita urged. 'Find out how he is.' It must look bad if Alistair was trying to get her away.

This time he took longer, waiting as the three were lifted out of the boat and carried up the steps. None of them could walk. She saw Alistair bend over the limp form of the man as they shifted him into a cart, then he went to speak to the clerks and walked back, his face sombre.

'It is Callum. He's unconscious now and very cold. He must have dived in when we were overturned. They found him clinging to the upturned boat with the two women—he was holding them on. No sign of Daniel or Averil yet. The Bastables are all right, although she broke her arm or her ankle—the man isn't sure—getting into the boat. And they found Dr Melchett clinging to an oar, alive and kicking. He's a tough old buzzard.'

'Oh, thank goodness for those, at least.' She bit her lip as the donkey was led away, Alistair walking by her side. 'How soon will the news reach the mainland? I must write and let my family know I am safe before they read of the wreck.'

'The Governor will have it all in hand, don't fret,' Alistair said as they wound up the narrowed cobbled street.

He must be exhausted, Dita thought. *He shouldn't have to keep soothing me.* 'Of course, I should have thought of that.' The final turn took them to the bottom of a slope so steep that even the sure-footed little donkey struggled before they came out through the gate in the castle walls and on to the wide expanse of grass and workshops that surrounded the strange little Elizabethan castle on the top of the promontory.

The man leading the donkey turned left to follow the line of the battlements, past gun platforms, to a great wide-fronted house set back against the slope and commanding a view over Hugh Town straggling between its two bays.

Footmen ran out to meet them, helped Dita down and ushered them into the warmth and the shelter of the Governor's residence. It seemed bizarre to be walking on soft carpets, past works of art and gleaming furniture and to be surrounded by attentive servants after the cramped cabins of the *Bengal Queen* and the crude hut that had sheltered them last night.

The Governor's secretary was on hand to greet them, to note their names and who they wanted notified of their safe deliverance. 'We are sending a brig to Penzance every day,' he explained. 'Anyone who is fit to travel can go in it and we send news to the mainland as we get it.' He snapped his fingers at a footman. 'Take Lady Perdita to Mrs Bastable's room—I hope you do not object to sharing, ma'am, but I understand she is your chaperon? And Lord Iwerne to the Green Bedchamber—again, my lord, I trust you do not object to another gentleman in the same chamber? The house is large, but with so many to accommodate—'

'What did you call me?' Alistair demanded and the man paled.

'You did not know? My lord, I must apologise for my tactlessness. The marquis passed away over a month ago.'

'Alistair.' Dita put her hand on his arm. His face was expressionless, but under her palm he was rigid. 'Why do you not go to your room now? You will need to be quiet, a little, perhaps.'

'Yes.' He smiled at her, a creditable effort, given the shock he had just received. 'Will you be all right now?'

'Of course. Mrs Bastable and I will look after each other.'

He nodded and she watched him walk away, his shoulders braced as though to shoulder the new burdens of responsibility that were about to descend on them. Even less, now, should he think of marrying her, she thought. He needed a wife he loved to support him in his new role.

Mrs Bastable, her bandaged arm in a sling, was tearful and shaken and Dita found relief that day and the next in helping her and attempting to boost her spirits. She had the happy idea of suggesting they nurse Callum Chatterton, who was confined to bed. He was almost silent, asleep—or pretending to sleep—for most of the time. But tucking him in, harassing the maids and bringing him possets kept the older woman's mind a little distracted from her worries about Averil.

By the next evening the Governor called together everyone who was able and read the list of those who were dead and those who were missing.

'Every beach has been walked and every rock that remains above high water inspected,' the Governor said, his voice sombre. 'We must give up hope now for those who have not been found.'

Dita sat quite still, the tears streaming down her face. They had not found Averil, but they had recovered Daniel's body just two hours before.

'I'll go and tell Callum,' Alistair said. He put out his hand as though to squeeze her shoulder, then dropped it without touching her and went to break the news. He had not touched her since she had mounted the donkey, she realised.

'There will be a service tomorrow in memory of those who have been lost,' the Governor continued.

'I will attend that,' Dita whispered to Mrs Bastable, who was mopping her eyes, her hand tight in that of her husband. 'And then, dear ma'am, we will take the ship to the mainland the day after, unless Mr Chatterton needs us.'

Callum, pale, limping, frozen, it seemed to Dita, in shock at the loss of his twin, still managed to attend the service at the church overlooking Old Town Bay. 'I'll take him home tomorrow,' he told Dita as she walked back with him, her arm through his, trying to lend him as much warmth and comfort as she could. 'Lyndon— Iwerne, I should say—has been like a brother, you know. No fuss, no prosing on, just good practical stuff, like finding a decent coffin and—I'm sorry, I shouldn't speak of such things to you.'

'Not at all,' Dita murmured, looking out over the sea and wondering where Averil was now. She had written to her friend's family in India and to her betrothed, but even now, it still seemed impossible that she would not hear her voice again. 'We cannot pretend it has not happened, and we need to speak of those we have lost. Daniel was betrothed, was he not?'

'Yes.' Callum sounded even grimmer. 'And Sophia has waited a very long time for him. Now I must tell her that she has waited in vain.'

Dita had thought she would be afraid to go on a sailing vessel again, but there was too much else to think about to allow room for nerves: Mrs Bastable, frail and anxious on her husband's arm; Callum grimly determined to behave as though he was completely fit, to get his twin's coffin home and to comfort Daniel's betrothed; Alistair, who would not speak to her about his father and who was going home to a life utterly changed.

And Averil. 'I cannot believe she has gone,' Dita said when Alistair joined her in the stern to watch the islands vanish over the horizon. 'We were such good friends— surely I would know for sure if she was dead? It feels as though she is still *there*. Alive and there.' She gestured towards the islands.

'She'll always be there for you, in your memory,' he

said. 'Come inside now, those borrowed clothes aren't warm enough for you.'

He was practical and kind and firm with all of them and as distant as a dream.

When they arrived in Penzance, Alistair took rooms at a good inn and then hired maids for both Dita and Mrs Bastable. He procured a chaise and outriders and sent the older couple on their way to their daughter's home in Dorset and found a carriage to carry Daniel's coffin and a chaise for Callum and dispatched that sad procession on its way to Hertfordshire.

Finally, at dawn the next day, Alistair helped Dita and Martha the maid into a chaise before swinging up on to horseback to ride alongside.

'Isn't his lordship going to sit inside?' Martha enquired. She stared wide-eyed at Alistair through the window. 'He's a marquis, isn't he, my lady? Surely he isn't going to ride all that way?'

'He has been shut up on board ship for three months,' Dita said. She, too, was watching Alistair; it was very easy to do. 'He wants the exercise.'

And doubtless he did not want, any more than she did, to be shut up together in the jolting chaise with all those things that must not be spoken off hanging in the air between them. He should be resting, of course, but telling Alistair to rest was like telling a river to stop flowing.

She let her fingers stray to the pearls and found some comfort in running the smooth globes between her fingers. She wore them outside her clothes now; he knew she had them, after all. *The only thing of his I possess,* she thought. *If things had been different I might have a child of his. An eight-year-old child to love.*

'Those are lovely pearls, my lady,' Martha remarked. She was proving talkative, Dita thought, not sure whether to be glad of the distraction or irritated. 'I thought you'd lost everything in the shipwreck, ma'am.'

'I was wearing them,' Dita said and went back to staring out of the window. Alistair had ridden ahead and there was nothing to distract her now, just the small fields, the windswept trees, the looming mass of the moorland. Home. She thought about her family. Mama, Papa and her youngest sister Evaline, who would be coming out this Season, rather late because they had to wait for Dita to come home. Then there was Patricia, two years younger and already married to Sir William Garnett. Perhaps Dita was going to be an aunt and did not know it yet.

And the boys, of course. Serious, tall George, the heir and a year older than her, and Dominic, sixteen now, and a perfect hellion when she had left. Had they changed? Were they well and happy?

She thought about them all fondly for a while, then let her memory explore Combe, the old sprawling house that had been extended by generations over the years. It snuggled into the protection of the wooded valley that surrounded it and shielded it from the winds from the coast to the north or from the moors to the south.

There were thick woods, meadows, small, tumbling streams and buzzards mewing overhead. She loved it, bone deep. Perhaps she could stay there until she could face life without Alistair.

But, no, that would be selfish. She could not keep her family from London and Evaline's Season, and she could not bear to be apart from all of them either. She must draw what strength she could from Combe and then she would go and face London and the gossip and the snide remarks and the men who would think she was fair game.

At least if anyone tried to take liberties she was prepared now. Dita thought about Alistair's lesson, the strength of his hands on her body, the feel of him, pressed so close to her, and sighed.

'He's ever so handsome, isn't he, my lady?' Martha, with her back to the horses, must be able to see Alistair riding behind the post chaise.

'Martha, if you have ambitions to become a lady's maid in a big house—*my* maid, for example—you must learn not to make personal remarks about gentlemen, or to gossip. Do you understand?'

'Yes, ma'am.' The girl bit her lip. 'Might you take me, my lady? If I'm quiet enough?'

'I'll give you a fortnight's trial and see how you manage my hair and clothes,' Dita said, yielding a trifle. Martha's references from the agency were good and at any other time the maid's pert observations would have amused her, but she was in no mood for chitchat about Alistair now.

It had been a long day's journey, broken only by the need to change horses and to snatch a bite to eat at two o'clock. Alistair must have been saddle-sore, but he rode on, attentive to her needs at each stop, but as impersonal as a hired courier. His eyes promised that this silence would not last.

'We are almost there,' Dita said as the light began to fade. 'Here are the gates.'

Her brothers appeared on the threshold as the party drew up, her parents and Evaline just behind them. Dita tumbled out of the chaise without waiting for the step to be let down and the family ran down to meet her, catching her up in a chaotic embrace. They had never been a family to stand on ceremony, or to hold back on displays of physical affection, and it was several minutes before she emerged, tear stained and laughing, from her father's arms. He had forgiven her a little, it seemed.

'Mama, Papa, here is Alistair Lyndon—Lord Iwerne, I should say. You must know that he saved my life not once, but twice—in the shipwreck and in India, from a mad dog.'

The Earl of Wycombe strode over to where Alistair stood at his horse's head, apart from the family reunion. 'My dear Lyndon!' He enveloped him in a bear hug that, after a moment, Alistair returned. 'We can never repay you for bringing us our Dita home safely.' Her father held the younger man by the shoulders and regarded him sombrely. 'You have been through a most terrible ordeal, and now to come home to the news of your father instead of the reunion you must have longed for so much—it is a bad business. You may rely upon me for any assistance I can give you.'

'Thank you, sir. I appreciate your generous offer.' He looked directly at Perdita and then, with reluctance, it seemed to her, came across and took her hands in his. 'Home safe, Dita. Your courage will see you the rest of the way. We will talk later.' He bent and kissed her cheek, bowed to her mother and walked back to his horse.

'But, Lord Iwerne,' Lady Wycombe called, starting across the gravel towards him, 'will you not stay tonight with us? I know it is only a matter of a few miles, but you must be so weary.'

It was one mile by the direct route: jumping the stream, scrambling up and down wooded slopes, cutting through the kitchen gardens. Dita had done it often enough as a child and she guessed that that was the way Alistair would take, not troubling to ride the six miles round by road, through the lodge gates and up the winding carriage drive to the castle.

'Ma'am, thank you, but I should go home.' It seemed to Dita that he hesitated on the last word, but perhaps it was her imagination. 'And, besides, you will want to be alone with your daughter now.'

He swung up into the saddle, touched his whip to his hat and cantered off down the drive. *Off into his new life*, Dita thought. *His English life. A new title, a new role and a new wife when I can persuade him that I am not his responsibility.*

'Oh, I am so glad to be home,' she said, turning and hugging George. 'Tell me absolutely everything!'

Chapter Fifteen

Alistair kept the tired horse to a slow canter across the Brookes' parkland, then slowed as they entered the woods. The ride had narrowed to a narrow track now, proof of the lack of recent contact between the two estates. He wound his way through, then cut off to send the horse plunging down to the boundary brook, up the other bank. On this side, his land, the track became a path that eventually led him to the high wall of the kitchen gardens.

Strange how it all came back, he thought, as he leaned down to hook up the catch on the gate with the handle of his whip. It creaked open as it always had and he ducked his head as they passed through. It was almost dark now and no one was working amidst the beds and cold frames, but there was a light in the head gardener's cottage.

The horse plodded along the grass paths to the opposite gate, patient as Alistair remembered the knack of flicking the catch open, then it was a short ride to the looming bulk of the stable block.

The grooms were just finishing for the night; most of the doors were closed, the yard almost deserted, although there was light spilling from the tack room door and the sound of someone whistling inside. A lad was filling buckets at the pump and looked up at the sound of hooves.

'Sir? Can I help you?'

Alistair rode closer, then dismounted where the light from the tack room caught his face. The boy gasped. 'My lord?' So, his resemblance to his father had strengthened as he had grown older. He had thought it himself, but it was interesting to see the confirmation in the lad's face.

'Yes, I am Alistair Lyndon,' he said. Best to be clear, just in case the lad thought he was seeing a ghost.

'And right welcome you are, my lord,' said a voice from the tack room door as a burly man came out. 'You won't remember me, my lord, but I'm—'

'Tregowan,' Alistair said, holding out his hand. 'Of course I remember you, you were a groom here when I left. Your father taught me to ride.'

'Aye, my lord.' The groom clasped his hand and gave it a firm shake. 'He died last November and I'm head groom now.'

'I'm sorry to hear he is gone, but he'd be proud to know there's still a Tregowan running the stables here.'

'Fourth generation, my lord. But you'll be wanting to get up to the house, not stand here listening to me. Jimmy, lad, you run ahead and let Mr Barstow know his lordship's home.' The boy took to his heels and Tregowan walked with Alistair towards the archway.

'I did hear that your letter arrived yesterday, my lord, all about the shipwreck. I'm powerful sorry to hear about that—you'll have lost friends, I've no doubt.' Alistair gave a grunt of acknowledgment. 'Her ladyship took a proper turn. As bad as she was when your father died, from what they say.' His rich Cornish burr held no shade of expression.

'Indeed. Well, I had better go and reassure her that I am safe and alive.' Alistair kept his own tone as bland. 'Goodnight, Tregowan; I look forward to seeing the stables tomorrow.'

As he rounded the corner the front of the castle came into view. In 1670 the Lyndon of the day had extended and fortified the old keep that had suffered so badly at the hands of Cromwell's forces. His grandson had added an imposing frontage in the taste of the early eighteenth-century and successive generations had added on, modernised and improved until any lover of Gothic tales would have been hard put to find a draughty corridor, a damp dungeon or a ruined turret in the place.

Alistair thought about Dita's sensation novel, lost now, and wondered whether she would try to rewrite it. He stopped to get the feelings that thinking about her evoked under control. How could he have done that—and how could she not have told him? What did it take to preserve a perfect social façade with a man who had so brutally taken your innocence?

The thought had come to him on today's interminable ride that perhaps she had gone to his arms on the ship in order to prove something to herself, to lay a ghost.

Or perhaps, when his thoughts had been darkest, she intended him to fall in love with her so she could punish him by her refusal.

She was certainly punishing him now; his conscience and his honour demanded he marry her, but without her consent he was left with few options. He could tell her father, he could abduct her, he could seduce her and get her with child…

His face must have been grim as the massive front doors opened and he strode up the steps and into the Great Hall. The butler, who was a stranger to him, froze and then stammered, 'My lord. Welcome back to Lyndonholt Castle, my lord. I am Barstow.' He looked beyond Alistair, into the gloom. 'Your luggage, my lord? Your man?'

'I have neither. If there is one of the footmen suitable, I'll have him as valet for the moment; he can find me evening wear in my father's wardrobe, I have no doubt. My compliments to her ladyship and I will join her at dinner. I would like a fire lit in my room and hot water for a bath immediately.'

'My lord.' The butler stepped forwards as Alistair made for the stairs. 'Her ladyship gave no orders about his late lordship's bedchamber. It is exactly as he left it, the bed is not made up—'

'Then see that it is,' Alistair said, allowing his displeasure to show. He had no fear of ghosts and he had every intention of stamping his ownership on this house from the start.

'Her ladyship is still occupying the adjoining suite, my lord. And she has taken over his late lordship's—

your—sitting room and the dressing room,' the butler said, looking wretched.

'I see.' Alistair put one booted foot on the bottom step. 'I have no wish to inconvenience her ladyship at this hour. I will take whichever of the guest chambers is easiest, Barstow.'

'My lord, of course. The Garden Suite would be most comfortable, I believe.' He began to gesture to footmen. 'Gregory, you will act as his lordship's valet for the time being. Fetch his lordship whatever he needs from the Marquis's Suite. I will have the decanters sent up, my lord. Her ladyship dines at eight.'

Alistair began to climb past the lavish trophies of arms and armour on the wall. *So, she had won the first round, had she?* Even as he thought it there was a flurry of rustling silk and the patter of slippers on the stair. He looked up as he reached the first turn and saw the black-clad figure of his stepmother.

'Alistair!' She held out her hands and waited while he climbed the stairs to her side. It allowed him ample time to appreciate the picture she presented, as no doubt she intended.

'Stepmama,' he said, bowing over her hand. 'My condolences.'

'So cold, so formal,' she said, but there was something very like fear in the wide blue eyes. 'There was a time when you called me Imogen.'

'Indeed, but that was before you married my father,' he pointed out politely.

'I know I broke your heart,' she murmured. 'But are you still angry after all this time?'

'Do you really wish to discuss it here?' he asked.

'Allow me to walk you back to your retiring room. Or, should I say, mine?'

'Alistair, are you going to grudge me one tiny room?' The fear had gone, perhaps when she realised he was not going to treat her to some Cheltenham tragedy. Where had the affected wide-eyed manner come from? Eight years ago Imogen had been sweetly naïve—or so he had thought.

'Not at all,' he said with a smile as he opened the door for her. 'You will have the whole of the Dower House all to yourself.'

'What?' She turned like a cat as he closed the door behind them. 'You cannot throw me out of here!'

'I most certainly can require you to move to the Dower House,' Alistair said. 'I will have it overhauled for you immediately.'

God, but she is lovely, he thought, studying her dispassionately. For over a year the thought of her had torn his heart. Petite, vivid, with big blue eyes and glossy black hair, she had a certain something that transformed her piquant little face from merely pretty to a loveliness that took men's breath away. She had certainly deprived him of both breath and sense as an idealistic twenty-year-old.

'But how can you exile me? After all I have been to you!' The flounce was new as well, although it gave the most excellent opportunity for any onlooker to admire the curves of her figure.

'A stepmother?' he enquired, deliberately obtuse. 'Do sit down, Imogen, because, frankly, I would appreciate the chance to.'

'You loved me,' she declared in throbbing tones

as she sank on to the *chaise*. 'I know I broke your heart, but—'

'I was infatuated with you eight years ago when you were nineteen,' Alistair said flatly. 'Young men are liable to be taken in by lovely faces and you are, my dear, very lovely.' She cast her eyes down as though he had made a passionate, but slightly improper, declaration. 'It was a shock to discover that you had been—shall we say, *flirting*?—with me when all the while you were in my father's bed. I had not thought myself so unobservant, I must confess.'

'Alistair! Must you be so crude?' Imogen lifted one hand as though to ward off a blow. 'I had no idea of the depth of your feelings and my lord was so…passionate and demanding.'

'Let us be frank, Imogen.' He found he had no patience with her games. 'You thought my father might not come up to scratch, so you strung me along as your insurance policy. Either that or you thought a marquis in the hand, even if he was old enough to be your father, was a more certain bet than the heir.'

Her guilty colour was proof enough. The daughter of the local squire three parishes away, Imogen Penwyth had been an acknowledged local belle and her parents were avid in their ambition for her. At the time he had been too angry and wounded to think this through, but he had had time since to realise just what had been going on.

'Mama was simply anxious to do the best for me,' she whispered. He wished he could believe she had not been as ambitious and unscrupulous as her parent.

Between them his father and this woman had made

him deeply cynical about love, but he knew how gullible he had been. *An idealistic young idiot, in fact*, he thought with wry affection for his youthful self.

That young man had been serious, rather studious and puzzled about where his life was going to lead him, given that he had a vigorous, tough father who had shown no desire to hand over any part of running the estates to his only child. He knew then that he wanted to travel, to explore. His interest in botany was already leading him to read widely on the subject, but it never occurred to him that he could—or should—leave England.

His duty was to be at his father's side, he had assumed, aware that the other man despised him for not being the hard-drinking, wenching gambler he was himself. The marquis had been unable to condemn his son for being a milksop, however, not when Alistair was acknowledged to be the best shot in the county, rode hard and even, much to his father's loudly expressed relief, conducted a number of discreet *affaires*.

But he had paid off his current mistress when he had come face to face with Imogen Penwyth at a dance. She was too lovely, too pure for him to even look at another woman when he loved her.

'You don't understand,' Imogen said, petulant now.

'I understood perfectly well what was going on when I walked into the library and found my father with his breeches round his ankles and you spread all over the map table with your skirts up to your ears,' Alistair replied. He was too tired for this, but if he didn't make it quite clear to Imogen that he was no longer a slave to her charms life was going to get even more complicated. 'And don't try to tell me he forced you, or your parents forced you or you had no choice in the matter,' he added. 'Frankly, I don't care.'

'Oh!'

'Let us be clear,' he said, getting to his feet and wishing he could just fall into bed and sleep for a month. 'I will spend a week or so here to deal with the most pressing business and I will put the refurbishment of the Dower House in hand. I will then go up to town for the Season. When I get back I expect you to have moved out.'

She turned huge, imploring eyes on him and he noticed the sapphires, just the colour of those eyes, dangling from her ears and adorning her neck. 'And I expect to be able to account for every item of entailed jewellery when I get back,' he added. 'My wife will be requiring them.' Her mouth dropped open, probably the first genuine expression he had seen on her face that evening. 'I will see you at dinner, Stepmama.'

As he closed the door behind him something hit the other side—a dainty slipper, no doubt.

Gregory was bustling round the Garden Suite, looking nervous when Alistair reached it. 'Your bath is ready, my lord.' He gestured towards the dressing room door. 'Are these clothes acceptable, my lord? And shall I assist you to undress, my lord?'

'They look fine.' Alistair gave them a cursory glance. His father, he was sure, had kept his lean figure to the end and they had been much of a height. 'I am quite capable of undressing and dressing myself, thank you. And one *my lord* every twenty minutes will be adequate.' The footman bit his lip and Alistair smiled, getting a grin in response. 'I'll shave myself, too.'

He glanced at the clock. Half past seven. No time for dozing in the bath then. 'Get a jug of cold water, Gregory, in ten minutes.'

He sank into warm water, soaped himself lavishly and felt himself drift off. *Dita*. How would Imogen have coped with everything that Dita had been through over the past few months? He thought of her in that hut on the island, soaked, shivering, courageous and the most desirable woman he had ever seen.

And the most pig-headed and defiant and proud, too. She was his whether she wanted to be or not. Or whether he wanted it either. God, life would be hell with Dita, resentful and furious and intelligent enough to get up to any madcap scheme that took her fancy. Her face seemed to shimmer on the inside of his closed lids—

'Aagh!' The cold water was like a slap in the face. Alistair reared up out of the tub, spluttered and shook himself like a large dog as Gregory backed away, clutching the jug like a shield. 'Good man,' Alistair said as he climbed out and grabbed for a towel.

'My lord?' Gregory was staring at him.

Alistair glanced down. The bruises and abrasions were spectacular and the scars from the tiger's raking claws always went red in hot water. 'Shipwrecks tend to have that effect.'

'Arnica?'

'Does it do any good?' He began to towel himself dry.

'My old gran always swears by it, and there's some in the stillroom,' Gregory volunteered.

'We'll try it tomorrow,' Alistair said, amused at the thought of Gregory's 'old gran'. He was a pleasant young man with a sense of humour and might be worth keeping on as a valet. It was time to put the East behind him, at least for a few years, and concentrate on learning to be an English gentleman again.

Gregory made himself scarce while Alistair dressed, although the silence that was presumably him holding his breath while the neckcloth was being tied was almost as distracting as chatter would have been.

He reappeared with a box in his hands. 'Mr Barstow said I was to be sure to put these into your hands, my lord. He says to say they have been in the silver safe under his lock and key since his late lordship died.'

'Did he, indeed?' It sounded as though the butler had taken his mistress's measure and that his loyalties lay with the new marquis, not with her. Alistair opened the box and found tie pins, fobs and one old, heavy signet. He had never seen it off his father's hand before. It slid on to his with a cold rightness, the almost black stone heavy on a hand unused to rings. But it made a point: he was Iwerne now.

Just in case Imogen missed it, he lifted out the heavy gold watch with its chain and fobs and put it in his waistcoat pocket, arranged the chain across to the buttonhole, then took a modern piece, a fine amber-topped pin, and set it in his neckcloth.

'Goes with your eyes, my lord,' Gregory said chattily as he locked the box and was thus spared Alistair's frown. 'There's an amber brocade waistcoat in the clothes press, that would suit you, too.' He offered Alistair the key. 'His late lordship used to put it on his watch chain.'

There was a certain sardonic amusement in contemplating what his father would say if he saw him in his clothes and jewellery. 'Dead men's shoes,' he said under his breath as he tried on the evening slippers and found they fitted.

There was a choked snort from Gregory, who looked appalled at his own reaction. Alistair raised an eyebrow at him and went down to deal with Imogen with a grim smile on his face.

Chapter Sixteen

'I am so glad you've cheered up, Alistair,' Imogen said as he strolled into the drawing room.

'Are you?' It was hardly a witty rejoinder, but it was better than *Go and get some clothes on!*, which was his immediate reaction to the sight of Imogen's gown. She might be in deep mourning, but his stepmother was interpreting that solely by the unrelieved black that she wore. The gown was cut so low that Alistair suspected close examination would reveal the edge of the aureole of her nipples, not that he had any intention of getting near enough to verify that. 'My new valet keeps me in a constant ripple of amusement,' he added, straight-faced, and saw her pretty brow wrinkle for a second. Imogen had never had much of a sense of humour.

'Dinner is served, my lord,' Barstow announced and Alistair offered Imogen his arm, walked her briskly to the foot of the table, saw her seated and retreated to the head, a considerable distance away.

'We must have some leaves removed, this is too long,' Imogen said to the butler.

'I prefer it this length.' Barstow bowed and retreated to the sideboard while the footmen began to serve soup. 'The dining room in the Dower House is more compact, as I recall,' Alistair added. 'You will be able to have a smaller table there, Stepmama.'

'I am not at all convinced that will be convenient.'

'The dining room or the table?'

'The Dower House,' she snapped, her colour high, all traces of wheedling quite vanished.

'Then you must tell me in what ways it is lacking and we will remedy them. You will not wish to be coming up to London, of course, not at this stage of your mourning, but do not hesitate to let me know when you would like me to obtain a town house for you next year.'

'Not come to London? However shall I dress?'

'Decently, I trust,' Alistair said with an edge to his voice. 'Send for a modiste, send to town for fabrics. I will not be ungenerous with your allowance.'

'My—' Imogen stared at him.

'But of course,' he added, 'if you are able to carry the cost of travel to London and accommodation while you are there—for I fear Iwerne House will be undergoing extensive works—I can only assume you require no allowance from me.'

'You… I…I must obey you or be a pauper, is that it?'

The complete lack of expression on the faces of Barstow and the footmen gave Alistair the clue that scenes of this sort were not unknown in the household.

'You have only to do what your natural good taste

and the dictates of society tell you,' he added soothingly, 'and all will be well.'

'In that house!'

'Indeed.'

Imogen sulked for the rest of the meal, treating Alistair to an exhibition of frigid disdain that would have amused him if he were not so tired. As soon as the dessert, which she merely picked at, was removed, she got to her feet.

'Goodnight, ma'am,' Alistair said, rising. 'I will see you at breakfast, perhaps?'

'I doubt it, I rarely rise before noon.' She swept out, quivering with affronted dignity.

Alistair stayed on his feet, poured himself a glass of port and carried it to the other door. 'Barstow, send Gregory to me in my chamber, if you please. I will take breakfast at eight.'

The footman bustled about, turning down the bed, shaking out a long silk robe, trimming the candle wicks as Alistair shed coat and neckcloth. 'Is there anything else, my lord? Goodnight then, my lord, your nightgown is on the bed.'

Alistair gave him a minute, then got up and turned the key in the lock, walked through to the dressing room and locked the outer door there, too. He sat for a while at the desk, savouring his port and making lists, one eye on the clock. As it struck midnight there was a light scratching on one panel, repeated when he made no move to open it. After a moment the handle turned. Silence, then he heard the handle in the dressing room rattle.

It was as well he had taken precautions. Perhaps, he thought, his smile thin, he should find himself a chaperon. Once he had thought he would die for that woman. What nonsense love was.

'We must call at the Castle,' Lady Wycombe said, two days after Dita's return, when the family had finally stopped talking. 'We should not be neglectful in welcoming Lord Iwerne formally to the neighbourhood again—and, of course, we must thank him once more for all he has done for us.' She smiled fondly at Dita.

'Must we, Mama?' Evaline wrinkled her nose. 'Lord Iwerne, by all means, but her *ladyship*...'

'Is she so very unpleasant?' Dita asked, curious. 'I met her, of course, now and again. She is beautiful.'

'And empty-headed and spiteful,' her sister retorted.

'Evaline! Oh dear. Yes, well, she is not a female I would wish my daughters to associate with, if I am to be honest,' Lady Wycombe admitted. 'As you are both grown up now and none of the men are here, I will not disguise the fact that I fear her morals are not all they should be either, even when the late marquis was alive.'

'Really? Surely he was not a man to stand for that sort of thing?'

'Sauce for the goose, my dear,' her mother said with startling frankness. 'Once it became clear she was barren, they appear to have agreed to find their pleasures where they chose. It was obvious the lack of children was not his fault, for, although Alistair's mother died before she could have more babies, there are enough bastards of his in the area to crew a brig.'

'Mama!' Dita said on a gasp of shocked laughter.

'While Alistair is in residence we must show every courtesy.' Lady Wycombe smiled. 'And, Evaline, lend Dita your new emerald-green afternoon gown and the villager hat with the velvet ribbons, I'll not have Imogen Lyndon sneering at how my daughters dress. Oh, yes, and the pearls.'

Elegantly gowned, and with Evaline in a delightful rose-pink ensemble beside her, Dita regarded her mother fondly as the carriage rattled over the drawbridge to the outer gatehouse of the castle. Her frankness and lack of prudery had made Mama easy to confide in during the aftermath of her ruinous elopement when her father was still coldly angry with her. She had assured her mother that she had not slept with Stephen, and that had tempered her father's ire somewhat, but even so, he had taken longer than her mother to come to terms with her foolishness.

Now she looked forward to seeing Mama deal with the widow. And she ached to see Alistair again, even though it was certain to be difficult. They had not been apart for three months, she realised—now two days seemed an eternity. Whatever else lay between them, she could not forget that she loved him. That emotion was not the product of the shock of the shipwreck, she knew that for certain now. She loved him, in spite of everything.

Lady Wycombe asked for his lordship, not her ladyship, when Barstow opened the door to them, an interesting breach of etiquette. His lordship was At Home and would be with them directly, the butler informed them as he ushered them through to the drawing room.

When Alistair came in Dita found she could not take her eyes off him as he shook hands with her mother. The space of those two days seemed to have sharpened her focus. He looked fine-drawn and there was a pallor under his eyes that spoke of late nights and worry; in the darkly formal clothes, he looked older, too. They must be his father's, she realised, and wondered if he minded very much having that intimate connection to a man from whom he had been estranged.

'Lady Perdita.' He took her hand and she looked into his eyes. Was he happy? Was he looking after himself? Was her expression betraying how much she needed him? There was something in his face that warned her that he had not forgotten, or changed his mind. He was going to do something to force a marriage, whatever she had to say about it.

'Lord Iwerne. Have you settled in yet? I expect, like me, you are having to borrow everything from slippers to combs.'

He nodded and smiled. 'Yes—it feels very strange, does it not? Lady Evaline.' His eyebrows rose a trifle as he turned to her sister and Dita felt a sudden, quite shocking, pang of jealousy. Evaline looked lovely, and sweet, and the perfect image of the kind of young lady Alistair had been talking of marrying. The sort of young lady he *ought* to be marrying. 'May I say that you have grown up quite considerably since I last saw you? And very charmingly, too.'

Evaline blushed and lowered her lashes, but she did not simper or stammer. 'You are very kind, Lord Iwerne, but as it is eight years, I think a little change is to be expected.'

Alistair laughed and they settled around the tea table as the footmen brought in the urn and china. 'Before we say anything else, I must thank you for everything that you have done for my daughter,' her mother said with her usual directness. 'I know now that if was not for your courage and endurance Dita would have drowned—or met a horrible death if that dog had bitten her. My husband will be calling, of course, but I felt I had to say what I feel as a mother: I will never forget and if there is ever anything the family can do for you, you have only to ask.'

Alistair was silent, looking down at his clasped hands on the table. Dita saw the unfamiliar ring on his signet finger and how he rubbed it, absently, as though it helped him think.

After a moment he said, 'If I have been able to be of service to Lady Perdita, it is an honour. You should know, ma'am, that your daughter is a lady of courage and integrity. Great courage,' he added. 'She put herself at risk to save a child.' The silence grew uncomfortable. Evaline gave a little sob, Lady Wycombe cleared her throat. 'And talent,' Alistair added. 'Did you realise that Lady Perdita is a novelist?'

'Really?' Her sister turned, wide-eyed. 'You have written a book?'

'It is at the bottom of the sea, I fear,' Dita said. 'Although that is probably the best place for it.'

'Never say that!' Alistair began to tell the story of

Adventures of Angelica and soon had Evaline and Lady Wycombe in a ripple of laughter while Dita buried her face in her hands and implored him to spare her.

'It sounds *wonderful*,' Evaline declared as the door opened and a lady walked it. She was quite, quite lovely, Dita thought, staring at her for a startled moment before she recognised her, *and* her mood. The marchioness was furiously angry.

'My dear Lady Wycombe!' She advanced with hands outstretched, a charming smile on her lips, ice in the big blue eyes. 'I am so sorry! My fool of a butler announced you to Alistair and not, as he should, to me. Really...' she turned her gaze on Alistair '...the man is incompetent—you must dismiss him.'

'You are labouring under a misapprehension, Lady Iwerne,' Lady Wycombe said. 'I asked for Lord Iwerne. We have come to welcome him home and to thank him for everything he has done for Perdita.'

'I see. I quite long to hear all about these adventures. Will you walk with me in the garden, Lady Perdita? I am certain your mother and sister will not want to listen to the tale all over again.'

It was the last thing Dita wanted to do. She opened her mouth to invent a twisted ankle and was suddenly seized by curiosity. This self-centred female most certainly did not want to hear about her, so what *did* she want? 'I would love to see the gardens, Lady Iwerne,' she said, getting up. Her skirts brushed Alistair's knees as she passed and he looked up and frowned at her. So he did not want her walking alone with his youthful stepmother. That was interesting.

* * *

'I am glad you have come home,' Imogen began, the moment they were on the terrace. 'I so need a female friend of my own age to confide in.' She was a couple of years Dita's senior, but she was not going to correct her—this was too intriguing.

'How flattering,' she murmured, 'but I will be going up to town very soon with my parents and sister.'

'You will?' The prettily arched eyebrows rose. 'But— forgive me—I thought you were no longer in society… after the elopement.'

'That little affair?' Dita laughed. 'I am used to deal-ing with gossip; I will not regard it. And besides, I am not husband-hunting.'

'Oh? Perhaps that is wise, under the circumstances. But I am quite cast down, for I shall be so lonely, shut away in the Dower House.'

She made it sound like a prison. Dita was vividly reminded of *Adventures of Angelica*—how well Lady Iwerne would fit into such a melodrama. 'Shut away? Surely not. You are two months into your mourning; the first year will soon go. And besides, there is this lovely park, the gardens…'

'Ah, but you do not understand.' Imogen cast a hunted look around, as if expecting to see assassins appearing from behind every topiary bush. 'I must shut myself away for my own protection.'

Dita pinched herself. No, she was awake so she could not be dreaming that she had strayed into a Minerva Press novel. 'From what? Or whom?'

'Alistair,' Imogen declared, as she sank on to a

bench and pulled Dita down beside her. 'May I confide in you?'

'I think you had better,' Dita said. 'You can hardly leave it there.'

'When I was a girl, he loved me, you see,' Imogen said. 'He adored me, worshipped the ground I walked upon. It was a pure love. A young man's love.'

'Er...quite,' Dita said, feeling vaguely nauseous. 'It would be if this was before Alistair left home.' At least, he was only twenty, so *young* was accurate, although whether his affections were entirely pure, she had her doubts—very few young men of that age had a pure thought in their heads in her experience. 'And you loved him? Encouraged him?'

'I was flattered, of course, although I had many admirers.' She simpered and Dita folded her hands together firmly—the urge to slap was tremendous. 'Perhaps I was too kind and he misunderstood.'

Dita said nothing, thinking back. She had no memory of Alistair mooning about, love-struck, but then she had only been sixteen and she never saw him at dances or parties. But he had seemed different, somehow. That fizzing excitement, the way he was almost flirtatious. Had that been it? He had been in love and she had sensed it. Perhaps that had awakened her own new feelings for him.

'Then another man declared himself and I was...' she sighed '...swept away. He was older, more sophisticated, titled.'

The realisation of what Imogen was saying hit Dita like a blow. 'You are saying that Lord Iwerne courted you at the *same time* as his son? It wasn't after Alistair left home that he paid his addresses?'

'No.' Imogen produced a scrap of lace and dabbed her eyes. 'It was dreadful. My lord found me alone and his passions overcame him. He held me to him, showered kisses on my face, declared his undying devotion—and Alistair walked in.' She went extremely pink.

'He was doing rather more than rain kisses on your face, was he not?' Dita said with sudden conviction. 'He was making love to you. Where?'

'In the library,' Imogen whispered.

So that was it. He found his father and the woman he loved in an act of betrayal and he walked out, furiously angry, and got drunk. And then I found him. And when she had given herself to him the disgust he must have felt with Imogen, with women in general and with himself, had swept over him. He had thrown her out of his room and the next day he had left.

Of course he had. How could he live in the same house as his father when he had seduced the woman Alistair loved? How could he accept Imogen as his step-mother after that betrayal? He had been in an impossible situation. Any other man he could have punched, or called out, but this was his father.

'So he left and made a new life for himself abroad,' Dita said, thinking out loud. 'And now he is back.' How hideously embarrassing for both of them. 'But I am sure with tact on both sides you can put it behind you.'

'But he still loves me,' Imogen said. Dita stared at her. Impossible. 'He desires me,' the young widow whispered. 'I am afraid to be in the house with him, that is why I must take refuge in the Dower House. I told him, it is wrong, sinful. I am his father's widow. But—'

'That,' Dita said with conviction, 'is nonsense. Of course he no longer loves you. Or desires you.' Her certainty wavered a little there—Imogen was very lovely. No, surely Alistair had better taste now he was an experienced man.

'Oh!' Imogen glared at her. 'I see what it is—you want him yourself and cannot face the fact that he is besotted with me. Well, you beware, Lady Perdita, he is dangerous.' She sprang to her feet and swept off along the terrace, silken skirts swishing.

Dita sat and stared after her. 'Dangerous? No, but you are,' she murmured. After a few minutes she got up and made her way back to the drawing room. 'Lady Iwerne was a little tired and went to lie down,' she said. Alistair looked at her, questions in his eyes, but she produced a bright smile, incapable of thinking what to do about this revelation.

Alistair was charming to all three of them, saw them to the door, waved them off, but Dita had the impression that his gaze rested on her with speculation.

'What on earth did that woman want with you?' her mother demanded, the moment the carriage door was closed.

'Oh, to poke at me and be catty,' Dita said. 'She is bored, I have no doubt—I do not grudge her the amusement.' She fiddled with the pearls for a while, then asked, 'Will she be moving into the Dower House?'

'I imagine so. Alistair said something about having it renovated,' Lady Wycombe said.

That sounded likely. A planned renovation for the Dowager to move into before Alistair came home with a bride was only to be expected. Surely, if Imogen felt threatened in any way, she would have fled there immediately. No, for some reason she was feeling the need to attack Alistair and he ought to know what she was saying.

Inwardly Dita quailed at the thought of discussing that day when he had made love to her, but if Imogen spread this vicious nonsense some of the mud might stick. How could she? she railed inwardly, more furious the more she thought about it. How she must have changed—or had Alistair been blinded by love, all those years ago? She would have to think how to tell him, but she must do it tomorrow. It would be a sleepless night.

Chapter Seventeen

❧

Please meet me at the hollow oak by the pond, the note read in Dita's impatient black hand. *Ten o'clock this morning. It is very important. D.*

Alistair studied it while he drank coffee. That could only be the old tree that he and her brothers had used as a shelter when they fished in the horse pond as children. Dita would tag along, too, but it was one of the few occupations that would drive her away with boredom after half an hour.

What did she want that was so urgent and that could not be discussed in the house? Had she thought better of her situation—or realised how determined he was—and had decided to accept him?

He suspected not. Dita was stubborn. No doubt a frustrating encounter lay ahead, but it would get him out of the house with its increasingly poisonous atmosphere. Alistair found himself longing for the moment when he could, with a clear conscience, leave the estate and go up to London.

He strolled down to the stables and spent an hour with Tregowan, looking over his father's horses, but he found he was too restless to concentrate.

Was Dita unhappy? He missed her, he found, more every day. There was no one to wake him up with tart observations over breakfast, no one to make him laugh or to freeze him with a sharp look from green eyes. No one to stir his blood as only Dita stirred it. *Green-eyed hornet*, he had thought her that evening in Calcutta. She would certainly sting when he finally had her trapped.

Alistair shifted restlessly, changed his position leaning against the mounting block, and considered how long it would be before he could go to London and set up a mistress. It would be a short-term arrangement until he took Dita as his wife; he despised men who took marriage vows and then immediately broke them.

'I'll take the grey hunter out now, Tregowan.' It was early, not half past nine, but he'd gallop the fidgets out before he met her.

Dita was already sitting under the oak when he got there, her back against the trunk, her knees drawn up with her arms around them as she'd been used to sit, watching the boys fish until her patience gave out. It made him smile despite everything, just to look at her. She turned her head at the sound of hooves, but did not move position. The long skirts of her riding habit pooled around her feet and his horse snickered a greeting to her mare, tied to a nearby willow.

'He's handsome,' she said in greeting as Alistair dismounted and threw the reins over a branch.

'Very,' he agreed and came to sit next to her on the

turf. 'My father had an eye for horseflesh.' *And female flesh, too.* 'Are you all right?' She was silent and he turned his head against the rough bark for a better look at her face. 'You are not, are you? Couldn't you sleep?'

'No,' she agreed, 'I couldn't.'

'Nightmares? Or have you made up your mind to do the right thing and marry me?' He put his arm around her shoulders. She sighed and leaned in to him for a second and he felt himself relax.

'No. A dilemma.' After a moment she sat up straight, pushing herself away from his arm. 'Alistair, I am worried about Lady Iwerne.' When he did not reply, she added, 'She told me a very unpleasant story about you. If she is spiteful enough to spread it, she could do a lot of damage.'

'What is she saying?' he asked, surprised his voice was not shaking with the temper that flashed through him.

'That you were in love with her, eight years ago, and that you left home when you realised she was going to marry your father, which in itself is quite understandable,' Dita said flatly. 'But she told me that she is frightened of you now and feels she has to flee to the Dower House to be safe from you forcing your attentions on her.'

Alistair swore. 'Quite,' Dita said. 'The question is, what are you going to do about it?'

'You don't believe her?' He had to ask.

Dita made a scornful little noise. 'I believe you were in love with her, yes. She is quite extraordinarily lovely and I expect then she was prettily behaved and flirted with a sweet sort of innocence. You were in such a state when you realised the truth that your emotions must have been deeply involved.

'But now? I can imagine that she is distractingly beautiful to have around the house, but she is foolish and empty-headed and you have higher standards than that. I would guess that she irritates you greatly. Leaving aside the small matter of it being incest to lie with your father's widow.'

The relief that Dita so categorically believed in him distracted Alistair from how she had phrased it and it took a while for her words to sink in. 'Thank you for your faith in me.' He found her calm intelligence both bracing and refreshing after Imogen's tantrums. 'But how do you know how I reacted to the realisation that she and my father—'

'I saw you that day, don't forget.' She kept her voice carefully neutral, but Alistair winced. 'Imogen said that your father found her alone, his passions overcame him and he swept her into his arms and showered kisses on her face while declaring his undying devotion. It was rather more than that, I imagine.'

'I walked into the library and found him taking her on the map table,' Alistair said. 'I turned right round and walked out and didn't go back until I was sure I wouldn't do something stupid, such as hit him.'

'And so you went and got drunk.'

'Yes. And, unfortunately you know more about what happened next than I do.' He got to his feet and walked away from her. 'I must have sunk at least two more bottles after you left me.'

'I am so sorry. Look at me,' Dita said. 'It is all right,' she went on as he turned, and he saw she was studying him gravely. 'I told you after the shipwreck—it wasn't your fault. And it wasn't your fault that I realised that I was in love with you and that you broke my heart.'

'What?' He sat down with a thump on a tree stump.

'Along with every other impressionable girl for twenty miles around,' Dita explained with flattening calm. 'You were very handsome then, you know. You still are, of course, but so many of the boys and young men we knew had spots, or kept falling over their feet or were complete boors. I didn't see it because I was still thinking of you as my friend, you understand. Or like George. Only, when you kissed me like that I realised that you most certainly were not my brother and I didn't want you to be. That is why I came to you. Don't think you forced me.'

Alistair knew he was gaping and had no idea what to say. 'I was *sixteen*, Alistair. Girls that age are all emotions and drama and there is nothing they enjoy more than the agonies of exaggerated love. We grow out of it, you know. You broke my heart, of course, when you went away. I thought it was all my fault, because I didn't know about Imogen. But then I heard Mama and Papa talking about some row you had had with your father over land and I saw it was nothing to do with me. Girls that age fall in and out of love four times a month.'

'You were in love with me? Then why the hell won't you marry me?' he demanded. 'That's what you want in marriage, isn't it? Love?'

'I told you—I fell out of it soon enough. And I was rather hoping for a husband who loved me,' she said tartly. 'Mind you,' she added, 'it did make a lasting impression, making love with you. You know how if ducklings hatch and there is no duck around they become fixed on whatever they see first and think the cat or a bucket is their mother?' He nodded, bemused. 'Well, I think I must have become imprinted with the image of tall, dark, handsome men with interesting cheekbones— because Stephen looks a bit like you, I realise now. And I don't find blond men very attractive.'

He shook his head as though to dislodge an irritating fly. 'Look, you know you have to marry me. You love me.' The thought filled him with terror.

'You were not listening,' she reproved. 'That was eight years ago. Calf-love. But that doesn't matter now. How are we going to neutralise Imogen before she spreads this tale round half the county?'

Alistair dragged his mind—and his body, which was taking an entirely inappropriate interest in the thought of how Dita might demonstrate love—back to the problem. 'I need a chaperon,' he said. 'In fact, half a dozen of them. I'll invite a houseful of men, sober professional men, to stay immediately. I'll get in my London man of business, an architect, someone to advise on landscaping the grounds, the steward here, my solicitor—they'll drop everything if I call. I'll have the vicar to stay, while I'm at it, tell him I want to discuss the parish and good works, or something. I've got the devil of a lot of business to see to—I'll do it here and now.'

'Of course!' She clapped her hands together. 'They won't be a houseparty of bucks or rakes but deadly dull businessmen of the utmost respectability. There is no way she can accuse you of harassing her with them in the house. And, I've just thought of another idea—why not bring her to call on us and ask Mama's advice on finding a suitable companion to live with her? Mama can tell everyone quite truthfully how thoughtful you are and how concerned that Imogen is looked after and how you are exerting yourself to make the Dower House comfortable for her.'

'Yes, that should put a stop to her nonsense. We make a good tactical team, you and I.' There it was again, the sense of connection that he so often felt with Dita stealing over him, as though their minds were touching. 'I don't understand her—she seems to be reacting with spite because I haven't fallen at her feet. But she must know perfectly well that any sort of relationship other than the obvious one is impossible—and scandalous.'

'She has a guilty conscience.' Dita rested her chin on her knees and tipped her head to one side, thinking. 'She knows she betrayed you and that both she and your father acted badly—it is much easier to attack the person you have wounded rather than beg forgiveness. I feel sorry for her. At least, I feel sorry for the girl she was, and it is sad that she did not have the character and intelligence to mature into a happy person now.'

'Sorry?' He stared at her. 'What is there to arouse your pity, pray?'

'It kept me awake last night, thinking about it,' she confessed. 'I was so angry with her, and so frightened at the damage I feared she could do you. But gradually I began to think about her all those years ago. She was very young and, I have no doubt, completely under the influence of her parents, as any well-bred girl would be. What they said was law. She fell for you and I am sure they encouraged it, for you were an exceptionally good match. And then someone—probably her mother—realised that your father's roving eye had fallen on her. Not the heir, but the marquis himself. They didn't care that he was old enough to be her father, or that she had a *tendre* for you. He was the better match and that is all there was to it.

'They would have told her to encourage him, she would have found herself alone with him when she might have expected to be chaperoned.' Dita shivered and looked up at him as he stared back at her, appalled. 'He had a reputation, did he not? This was not some kindly, fatherly figure. This was a mature rake and she was an innocent little lamb.'

'My God. She was unwilling?'

'She did as she was told, as was expected of her,' Dita said and he heard the anger quivering in her voice. 'I wonder if the fact that you look like him made it better or worse. But I doubt she ever thought she had a choice; young girls in our world do not, you see. They are raised to make a good match at all costs. That is what the Marriage Mart is, a market, and they are the lambs brought for sale.'

'All of them? What about you?' he asked and her fierce expression softened.

'I have exceptional parents.' She chuckled, 'And I am a disobedient and difficult daughter. Evaline is not like me,' she added, a frown creasing her forehead. 'She is the dutiful one, like Averil. I hope she will be all right; this is her first Season.'

'I won't be in London for another week at least, but I will keep an eye on her,' Alistair promised. 'And then you and I will talk and you will realise by then that marrying me is the right thing to do.'

Her face must have changed for the arrogant male certainty of his expression softened. 'Dita? Are you all right?'

'No. I am not,' she said. 'I am thinking about those young women like Imogen was. Like Evaline. All those hopes and expectations, all that duty and ignorance. A few months when they are the focus of attention, their virtue and their bloodlines and their dowries on display—and then a lifetime to live with the results of the bargains that are struck.'

'It is the way it has been done for people of our class for hundreds of years.'

'And it suits the men very well, does it not?' she flashed back. 'Listen to yourself: the complacent marquis. You will keep an eye on my sister and make sure she finds a suitable man, never mind her true feelings. You will satisfy your own pride and sense of honour by trying to force me to marry you. Not because you love me, or even because I am *suitable*, but because you took my virginity.'

Too angry now to sit at his feet, she scrambled up. 'Nothing else matters, does it? Such a little thing to make such a fuss about—a thrust, some pain. But that makes the woman your possession and you will duel and kill for that. Was that what it was with Imogen? Your father had her virginity and you did not even stop to think about her feelings? Damn you and your honour.'

'Honour and desire,' Alistair said, and closed the distance between them in two strides. He took her wrist and bent his head even as she reached to lash out at him. 'Let me show you.'

He had taught her well. She had him twisting to avoid

her knee, grunting as her stiffened fingers found his stomach, cursing under his breath as her teeth found the back of his hand.

'So you will force me now?' she panted as he crushed her back against the tree.

'But you want me. Tell me you don't want me.' Almost eye to eye the amber gaze held hers, demanded the truth, made her knees tremble.

'Damn you.' But she stopped struggling. *I love you, you arrogant creature. Why can't you love me? I want you.*

'Tell me to stop,' he said. His body heated hers; the thrust of his erection felt as though it had the power to pierce their clothing. Her mind emptied of everything but need.

'Let go of my arms,' she managed to say and he did, his eyes darkening at what he must think was her refusal. Dita curled her arms around his neck and brought her mouth, open, to his. There was a moment of stillness, then his tongue thrust in to take possession.

She expected urgency, roughness, anger. Instead, he stilled again, then began to lavish languid strokes into her mouth. She had time to taste him and savour every texture, the slide of her tongue across his teeth, the muscular agility of his tongue, the soft, wet interior of his mouth, the firmness of his lips. This was kissing as luxurious as the most decadent dessert and she surrendered to it with soft whimpers of delight.

His hands cupped her breasts, his fingers seeking her nipples, frustrated by the tight weave of her tailored habit. She slid her hands between them, fumbling with the buttons until the top opened and he could push aside the short habit-shirt and free her breasts from the constraint of the light corset she wore for riding.

In contrast to his mouth his fingers were not gentle as they found the peaking nipples, trapped them, rolled them until they became aching pebbles and the sensation lanced down through her belly to where she throbbed for him.

Dita found the fall of his breeches, opened it, clumsy with her haste, and sobbed with relief against Alistair's mouth as she closed her fingers round the hard silken shaft. He lifted his head as his hands left her breasts and took hold of her skirts, but the length and weight of the voluminous habit defeated him.

'Down,' he rasped, pulling her to the grass. 'Like this.' She found herself on hands and knees, her skirts up to her waist, her jacket hanging open as he bent over her. 'Dita.' He buried his face in the nape of her neck, biting softly as his hands cupped the weight of her breasts. 'You are mine.' She felt him nudge her legs apart and gasped. She wanted to look at him, to see his eyes, kiss his mouth, but the weight of him, the excitement of what he was doing was strange and arousing almost beyond measure.

He left her breasts, one hand braced on the ground as the other parted her. 'Such sweet honey.' She should be embarrassed that she was so wet for him, but she was beyond that now, pushing shamelessly against his probing hand. One finger slid into her, then another and she moaned as he caressed her deeply, withdrew, tormented the throbbing focus of her need, plunged in again. The exquisite feeling built and built to the point of pain and she gasped, wordless words that he seemed to understand.

Alistair shifted and she felt him against her, hard and implacable. '*Yes*, now!' And he surged into the heat and the tightness. There was discomfort, momentary; it had been a long time and he was a big man, but her body opened for him, sheathed him as he entered, and she shuddered with delight as he began to move, driving them both with his passion until the spiralling tension took her, shook her, threw all conscious thought from her as she felt him groan above her and pull away.

Dita came back to herself to find she was leaning back against Alistair's chest as he knelt, supporting her. 'I should have got you with child,' he said and his voice was not quite steady.

'You—' She did not know the words, could hardly speak.

'I withdrew,' he said, his arms tight when she would have twisted to look at him. 'It makes no difference. You must marry me now.'

So, that had not been a spontaneous expression of passion, perhaps concealing feelings she longed for, but which he was unaware of. It had been a calculated move to force her. The hurt was almost as great as that first rejection had been.

'Nothing has changed,' she said, finding her voice was as harsh as his. 'I am not a virgin and I am not with child.'

'Damn it.' He stood, pulling her with him. 'Then I should finish the business and do it properly this time.'

'Then you would be forcing me.' She moved away

and fumbled with her buttons. When she turned back he was stuffing his shirt into his fastened breeches, his face thunderous.

'How do you know I am not capable of that?'

'Because I know you,' she said. He made no move to stop her as she untied her mare and stood on a tree stump to mount. She did not turn back as she rode away into the woods.

She went back to Wycombe Combe by way of the ruined tower where she had found him that evening eight years ago. It was deserted, so she slid down and sat there amongst the flowerless rose bushes, out of sight of everyone and everything except the jackdaws, and got her weeping done, once and for all. There was a pool of rainwater, clear and fresh, on top of one of the tumbled walls, and she bathed her eyes afterwards and walked briskly home to plot with Mama against the spiteful, damaged woman who would try to ruin Alistair. The woman who had loved him once.

Chapter Eighteen

~~~~~~~

4th April—Grosvenor Street, London

'Lord Iwerne is in London.' Lady Wycombe spread the single sheet of notepaper open beside her breakfast place, not noticing Dita drop her bread and butter back on the plate.

A week apart had not made the separation any easier to bear, as she had hoped it would. Perhaps nothing ever would. 'Alone, I trust?' she said, making her voice light.

'Yes, this is a letter of thanks, I believe. He says that Lady Iwerne is settled in at the Dower House and is planning its redecoration with the assistance of Miss Cruickshank, whom he considers was an inspired choice of mine.'

What we need, Mama had said, *is a lady as apparently frivolous as Imogen, but with the sense to realise who is paying her very substantial wages and enough insight to hazard a guess as to why*. It appeared they had succeeded. 'It was a masterstroke of Alistair's to have expressed doubts about Miss Cruickshank,' Dita said. 'Lady Iwerne is quite content, thinking she has bested him in this.' Despite that earth-shattering incident in the woods he had still called with Imogen and Dita had done her best to help. It seemed they had succeeded.

'And is he at the Iwernes' town house in Bolton Street?'

'Yes, he writes it is in drastic need of redecoration and is tempted to send the entire contents to the Auction Mart. He also says that if we are attending Almack's this evening he will see us there and he hopes we will ease his initiation into the Sacred Halls, as he puts it.'

Evaline laughed. 'I do feel sorry for the poor gentlemen. They have to wear the stuffiest of evening dress, the food and drink is almost non-existent and they spend their entire time escaping from predatory mamas.'

'I hope that is not directed at me, my dear,' Lady Wycombe remarked with a chuckle. 'I cannot feel so sorry for them; they have every eligible young lady presented for their inspection—think of all the effort it saves them!'

Twelve hours later Dita overheard Evaline put this point of view to Alistair as they stood beneath the curving front edge of the orchestra balcony. Her sister had seemed rather subdued and thoughtful for the past few days, but teasing Alistair appeared to have revived her spirits.

'Rather it confuses the eye,' he retorted. 'All this beauty and vivacity dazzles the poor male brain.' He did not appear very dazzled to Dita, watching this exchange.

If anything, his expression as he surveyed the dancing in the centre of the ballroom and the chattering groups around it was detached and judgemental. She put out a hand and steadied herself against a pillar. It was hard to believe that this man was the one with whom she had shared those passionate interludes. How could their experiences together not brand them as lovers for every eye to see?

'So may a sultan inspect his seraglio,' she murmured, recovering herself. She waved her fan languidly.

'I have no need of one of those,' he said, not turning his head. 'My choice is fixed.'

'It takes two to make a contract,' Dita retorted. 'Where has Evaline gone?'

'Over there with that fellow with the crimson waist-coat.' Alistair pointed.

'Oh, yes. I wonder who he is,' she mused, more out of an instinct to keep an eye on Evaline than from any real curiosity.

'No idea, but then, I hardly know a soul here. Dita, I will call on you tomorrow.'

And I will be out, she vowed. 'Come and let me introduce me to some of our acquaintances.' She slipped her hand through his arm.

'Are you having any problems with gossip?' he asked bluntly as they strolled along the edge of the dance floor. She could feel his muscles under her palm and sensed he was every bit as tense as she was, despite appearances.

'Some. There are snide remarks from the usual cats, some of the chaperons look at me a little sideways, but I can ignore that. The men—' She shrugged, making light of it in case he reacted badly. There had been things said, hinted, glances and touches and several outright offers that were most definitely not honourable. Somehow she had coped, although it hurt. Sooner or later they would realise she was not available, she hoped.

'Lady Cartwright,' she said as they came up to a lively group, 'may I make known to you the Marquis of Iwerne, just returned from the East?' As she expected, Fiona Cartwright, a lively young matron, pounced on this promising-looking gentleman and promptly drew Alistair into her circle of friends. With that start he would soon know virtually everyone in the place and surely, once he did, he would see that there were many young women who took his fancy and this foolishness would cease.

A glance at the dancers showed that Evaline was partnered by the young man in the handsome waist-coat. With a mental note to find out who he was, just in case he should prove undesirable, Dita strolled on, in no mood to dance herself. She felt weary and out of sorts, her mood not helped when she saw Alistair walk on to the floor with the charming Lady Jane Franklin on his arm. It was just what she hoped for and the sight was like a knife in the stomach.

'Madam? May I assist you?'

Startled, she turned to find a gentleman at her side. He was slightly over average height, with light brown hair, hazel eyes and tanned skin. 'Sir?'

'I beg your pardon, but you sighed so heavily I thought perhaps…'

'Oh, no, I am quite all right. Just bored, if the truth be told.'

'Would you care to dance? I am sure I can find some-one to introduce me.'

'I fear I am not in a dancing mood this evening, sir. But thank you for offering.' Impulsively she held out her hand. 'Shall we forget propriety for a moment and introduce ourselves? I am Perdita Brooke; my father is Lord Wycombe.'

'Lady Perdita.' He bowed over her hand. 'Francis Wynstanley. You may know my brother, Lord Percy Wynstanley. I am quite a newcomer to Almack's myself; I have been in the West Indies for several years.'

'And I am just back from India, so I am equally out of touch,' Dita said.

A flash of crimson caught her eye and she saw it was the waistcoat of Evaline's partner—and he was dancing with her again.

'What makes you frown, if I may ask?'

'My sister, dancing a second time with a man I do not know. See, the blonde girl in the pale green and the man with the crimson waistcoat.'

'Oh, I can help you there. That is James Morgan, my brother's confidential secretary. Percy is much involved in politics, you know, and Morgan is his right-hand man. Good character and all that, nothing to be wor-ried about.'

'No, indeed. If you can vouch for him I am quite reassured.' But she was not. Confidential secretaries, however well bred, were not what her parents were look-ing for.

A week later her friendship with Lord Percy's brother was pronounced enough for her mother to be asking questions. 'He seems a most pleasant gentleman,' she observed. 'And intelligent. I spoke to him for a while at Lady Longrigg's soirée last night. Has he any prospects?'

'I really have no idea,' Dita said, with truth.

'I trust he is not some idler hanging out for a rich wife.'

'Mama, we are friends, that is all.'

But she was provoked enough to probe a little as they sat in the supper room at the Millingtons' ball. Alistair, she noted with a pang, was partnering one of Lord Faversham's daughters and Evaline had her head together with James Morgan, which was worrying.

'Do you make your home in London, Mr Wynstanley?' Alistair was flirting, she could tell, just from the back of his head—and the way the Faversham chit was blushing.

'I am doing the Season and living with my brother for the duration, but I have an estate in Suffolk I inherited from my maternal grandfather and I shall be basing myself there and seeing what is to be done to bring it about.'

'How interesting. It needs much work?'

He was a nice, intelligent, apparently eligible man. It would be pleasant, but unwise, to continue their friendship. Was this whole Season to be like this, fearing to make any male friendships while she watched Alistair find his wife?

'Good evening, Lady Perdita.'

Dita jumped and then managed a smile of welcome as Francis got to his feet. 'Oh…' *Pull yourself together!* 'Lord Iwerne, Miss Faversham, may I introduce

Mr Wynstanley? Mr Wynstanley: the Marquis of Iwerne, Miss Faversham.'

'Will you not join us?' Francis pulled out a chair for Miss Faversham and they all sat down again. Francis gestured to the waiter and wine and glasses were brought.

Dita met Alistair's eyes with what she hoped was tolerable composure, only to find he was at his coolest, one eyebrow slightly raised. She stared back defiantly and engaged Miss Faversham, who appeared very shy, in conversation. Beside her she was aware of Francis undergoing a skilful interrogation—damn Alistair, he would be warning the man off in a moment!

After what seemed like an hour, but was probably only fifteen minutes, Alistair rose. 'Might I beg the honour of a dance, Lady Perdita?'

'Why, yes.' Her instinct was to refuse, but that would show she cared. She consulted her card. 'The second set after supper?'

'Ma'am. Wynstanley.' He bowed and escorted Miss Faversham out of the supper room.

By the time Alistair came to claim her for the set she had lost her nerve. 'I have changed my mind,' she said, staying firmly in the seat where Francis had left her when he went to claim his own partner.

'Don't sulk, Dita, it isn't like you.'

'I am not sulking and you, Alistair Lyndon, are not my keeper; I'll thank you not to embarrass me by interrogating perfectly respectable gentlemen just because they are in my company.'

'I am going to marry you,' he said, taking the chair

next to her without being asked. 'And besides, you should not toy with men's affections this way. Wynstanley seems a decent enough fellow and he is within an inch of falling for you, if I am any judge.

'Well, we know you are not, don't we?' she countered, refusing to react to the declaration that he would marry her. 'You place no importance upon love.'

Alistair stretched his legs out in front of him, showing every sign of settling down for a long and intimate conversation. 'It is a chimera, a delusion. You will come to your senses soon enough and marry me, Dita.'

'What if I fall in love with someone else and want to marry them?' she demanded. 'Or are you so arrogant that you believe that would be a delusion that I must be saved from?'

It was not a possibility, of course. She had come to accept that she was not going to fall out of love with him and into love with some other man. Given that, marrying someone like Francis and settling down to a pleasant, if second-best, life might be possible if only she could square her conscience over hiding her feelings for Alistair from him. But to marry Alistair when she loved him and he did not love her would be misery. She would be constantly hoping that he would fall in love with her and every day she would be disappointed.

'If he is a decent man and if I was convinced you loved him, then perhaps.' He did not look happy about it. 'And if you gave me your word of honour that you did love him and were not simply trying to escape from me.'

'You trust my honour?'

'I thought I could trust it with my own,' he countered and there was no mistaking the bitterness now.

'So you place your honour above my happiness?' she asked. 'No, do not answer that, I do not think I want to hear it. 'Why not give some thought to your own happiness instead and then perhaps we can both sleep easy in our beds?'

Alistair sat down again as Dita swept off. Happiness. He had never thought of it as something to go out and seek. He had lived life as he wanted it and on his terms ever since he had left home and he supposed that for most of the time he had been happy. Certainly he had felt challenged, fulfilled, energised by the life he had lived.

Happiness, Dita appeared to be implying, required him to take a wife. He knew he needed one, but these little peahens were intolerable; he had observed them for two weeks and they bored him rigid. He studied the room, feeling like a punter assessing racehorse form. *Silly laugh, intolerable mother, rude to servants, never washes her neck...* None of them had Dita's class or intelligence. And she, with every reason in the world to marry him—except her fantasy of love—refused him.

He sat and watched the dancing until he caught sight of Lady Evaline Brooke waltzing, which he was fairly certain she shouldn't be, with that young man who only appeared to possess one waistcoat. He should extricate her from that flirtation before her mama saw her. Alistair waited until the music stopped and then walked across to cut into their conversation that was continuing as they left the floor.

'Lady Evaline.'

She jumped and looked guilty. 'Lord Iwerne.'

'Won't you introduce me?'

'Of course. Lord Iwerne, this is Mr Morgan, Lord Winstanley's confidential secretary. James, the Marquis of Iwerne.'

'My lord.' The young man made a neat bow. He was slightly stocky, dark—Welsh, perhaps, as his name might suggest—and met Alistair's cool regard with a expression that was polite but not cowed. *He's got some backbone, then.*

'Mr Morgan. Lady Evaline, I was hoping for a dance.'

'Oh. Well, my card is quite full, my lord.' She fiddled with it, nervous.

'How dashing of you, Lady Evaline.' He caught the dangling card and opened it. 'Are you sure you cannot spare me a single county dance?' Every remaining dance had JM pencilled against it. The uncomfortable silence dragged on. 'How did you expect to get away with that?' he asked.

'We were going to sit them out, my lord,' Morgan said. 'Over there.' He nodded towards a partly curtained alcove. 'Not outside, I assure you.'

'I suggest you have rather more of a care for the lady's reputation, Mr Morgan. Lady Evaline, you, I believe, will dance this set with me.' He swept her on to the floor, leaving Morgan white-faced on the sidelines. It was a country dance, not the best place for a delicate exchange, but he managed to ask, 'What would your mother say?'

'She'd be furious,' Evaline murmured. She was as

white as her swain, but her chin came up and she fixed a bright social smile on her lips. 'You are quite right to chide me, my lord.'

'I am not chiding,' he said. 'I'm rescuing you.'

The steps swung them apart and they said no more until the set was finished and he walked her off to find her mother. 'Hide that card,' he suggested. 'Lady Brooke, here is your youngest daughter, who has danced me to a standstill.'

'Thank you,' Evaline said as he stood looking down at her. 'You are quite right, I know.'

'I wouldn't want to see you come to harm,' he rejoined as her mother's attention was claimed by a friend. 'You matter to me.' She would be his sister-in-law if he had his way; it behoved him to protect her. Besides, he owed her mother much for her help with Imogen. Evaline blushed and lowered her eyes, but he was not displeased. She had seen the folly of that silly flirtation. Enough of acting the big brother for one evening, he thought, and went in search of the card tables.

Chapter Nineteen

'Good morning.'

Dita started and dropped her reticule. Her footman dived for it and Alistair removed his hat with a suave politeness that made her want to hit him for making her react so revealingly.

'Good morning, Lord Iwerne. This is an early hour to meet you in Bond Street—I would have thought at ten o'clock you would still be contemplating breakfast. Thank you, Philips.' She took her reticule from the footman and tried for a bright smile as she gestured for him to retreat to a discreet distance.

'I had some shopping.' He was carrying nothing, nor did he have a man in attendance, but perhaps he was having whatever it was delivered. 'Will you be at the Cuthberts' masquerade this evening?'

'We all will. Or at least, Mama and Evaline and I. It would probably take wild horses to drag Papa to such a thing.' They began to stroll along the pavement.

'And what will you be going as?' Alistair raised his

tall hat to Lady St John, who was observing them with interest from her barouche.

'A milkmaid,' Dita admitted with a sigh. 'Very pretty and conventional, but Mama thought it suitable.'

'You are still in trouble with the old tabbies?'

'Not really, but people are aware of me, I suppose. You saw Lady St John just now. Who am I with, what am I doing?' She shrugged. 'I don't care, but I should be cautious for Evaline's sake.'

'Then I cannot lure you off for a morning's delicious sin in Grillon's Hotel?' he suggested.

'No! Don't say such things, even in jest.' She eyed him sideways. 'That was in jest, wasn't it?'

'No. It was a perfectly serious invitation. And now you are blushing most delightfully. Come and look at the wigs in Trufitt and Hill's window while I make you go even pinker.'

'Certainly not. I have no desire to look at horrid wigs, or to have you put me any more out of countenance than I already am. I wish you would go away, Alistair, and stop tempting me.'

'Am I?' He sounded very pleased at the thought.

'Yes, and you know it and there is no need to be smug about it.'

'Very well, but not before I make you another, quite unexceptional, offer. I have sent for Indian silks and jewels from my house in south Devon. It is where I have my plant collection and where I shipped goods back to while I was away. Would you like a costume for the masquerade? I am going to wear Indian dress myself.'

'Oh, yes!' The thought of fine silks and fluttering veils made her heart race. To see Alistair dressed in

Indian fashion, to partner her... 'Oh, no. It would look as though we were a couple.'

'Not at all. Everyone knows we have been in India—what more natural that we should both chose to dress like that. We will arrive separately, after all.'

It was rash, possibly even reckless. She knew how she would feel when she put on those sensual, sensuous clothes, how she would feel when she saw him, a peacock in all his magnificence. Dita took a deep breath to say *no*.

'Yes, please, Alistair.'

'Mama.' Both Dita and her mother looked round at the tone of Evaline's voice. 'I am very well dowered, am I not? I mean, I do not have to hang out for a rich husband?'

The Wycombes' town coach, driving along Piccadilly, seemed a strange location for such a question. 'Yes, you are, my dear.' Lady Wycombe put down the book she had just bought and turned her full attention on her daughter. Dita twisted on the seat, puzzled. 'And it is important that you marry a man of equal status and at least the same resources as yourself.'

'But why, Mama? What if I met a young man of prospects?'

Oh dear, Mr Morgan, Dita thought. She had done some investigating and James Morgan was about as well paid as the average curate, was the second son of a country squire, had an excellent degree from Oxford and ambitions to enter government service. Papa would never countenance such an unequal match.

'It would depend on his connections and pedigree,

my dear. Have you met such a man? I am trying to think to whom you might be referring.'

'It was a rhetorical question,' Evaline said with a bright smile that to Dita was patently false.

'Dear Alistair Lyndon is quite another matter,' Lady Wycombe continued. 'Now he might well take an interest, I believe. He would be eminently suitable, a most superior catch. Your father would be delighted.'

'Yes, Mama,' Evaline said and Dita closed her open mouth with a snap.

Oh my lord, she thought. No, he wouldn't, surely? That morning in Bond Street he had given no sign of having changed his fixed intention of bending her to his will—the very opposite, in fact.

'I hope he will be at Lady Cuthbert's masquerade tonight,' Lady Wycombe said. 'Your shepherdess costume is charming, Evaline, but I wonder what Lord Iwerne will be wearing.'

'He is going as an India maharajah,' Dita said without thinking. 'I saw him in Bond Street this morning and he told me he has sent for a trunk full of silks and jewellery and so forth that he shipped home to England last year. He promised to send me a selection of Indian female garments and jewels so I could wear Indian dress tonight.' She prattled on, convinced her confused and jealous thoughts must be visible on her face. 'He's got a small house in south Devon he bought because it had a garden suitable for the plants he has been collecting. Whenever he sent things back they went there and not to the castle.'

'How interesting.' Her mother looked thoughtful. 'If Evaline wears the Indian garments it will be subtle, but it will put the idea of a pairing into his head. You can go as the milkmaid as we originally planned.'

She did not appear to notice Evaline's look of dismay. Dita only hoped her own expression was not as unguarded. 'Yes, Mama,' she said obediently. It was providential, it would save her from more temptation. She wanted to refuse and sulk and disobey. Instead she closed her eyes and made herself accept her mother's instructions.

Alistair swept into the ballroom at the Cuthberts' hired mansion with a considerable flourish, resplendent in brocades and silk, a turban with a large moonstone and an aigrette of feathers at the front, a curving sword thrust through his sash and hung about with enough jewellery to stock a small, if exotic, jewellers. All around him masked faces turned and a ripple of appreciation ran through the ladies. He looked the part, he knew, because everything was authentic, just as the silks and gems he had sent to Dita were those of a Mogul princess.

And there she was. He recognised the costume although her hair, flowing freely down her back, had been dyed black and her eyes were hidden by her mask, her lower face by her veil.

When he had met her that morning it had not been by accident, although he was certain she had no idea he had been following her with the aim of giving her the clothes for this evening. The masquerade was an opportunity to recall the sultry heat, the sensual pleasures, of India. Dressed in exotic silks, surrounded by the licence of a masked ball, reminded of the East and its delights, she would be more receptive to the seduction that tonight he was set on.

What had happened in Devon had not shifted her intransigence; his patience since had not caused her to yield, but she was not immune to him—her blushes this morning had shown him that. And this time he would not be careful; if he got her with child, then she would surrender.

Dita was beginning to fill his thoughts, obsess him. The truth of what had happened that night seemed worse the more he brooded on it. What if she had become pregnant? He had left the country—she would have been alone, ruined. He had prided himself on meeting his responsibilities and now he knew he had defaulted on something as fundamental as a lady's honour. No wonder his dreams had been haunted by her face, by erotic images that had left him ashamed of his imagination. But it was not imagination.

Alistair narrowed his eyes on the slim figure and felt his breathing quicken. He wanted her, and he would have her. It was like following a fish through a pond full of weed. Every time he almost reached her she slipped away and he was stopped over and over by ladies exclaiming at his costume and men asking questions about the curving scimitar. Finally he saw a flash of golden silk as she went through a doorway and followed. What the devil was she up to? Or did she know he was behind her? Was she leading him here?

Soft-footed in his doeskin boots, Alistair padded along a passageway that opened up suddenly into a conservatory. Dita was nowhere to be seen. He scanned the crowded palms and ferns as though expecting a tiger to emerge from them, but all he heard was a sob, and then another.

He eased closer, parted some greenery and found himself looking into a little arbour with a fountain and Dita locked in the arms of a shepherd. *What the hell—?*

'I'm sorry,' she said, still sobbing, 'it is impossible. You were right: I must marry someone with money and a title. Mama and Papa expect me to encourage Lord Iwerne and they believe he will offer for me.'

Evaline? And then the man embracing her straightened up and Alistair recognised James Morgan. 'They cannot force you,' Morgan said. 'He is years older than you—'

'Ten, I suppose,' Evaline said drearily, making it sound like fifty. 'But he is kind, I think. He isn't like his father, after all. I wouldn't mind so much if it was not for you. I love you so much, James.'

'And I love you.' He bent his head and Alistair let the greenery drop, trying not to listen. 'But I must do what is right for you,' Morgan said after a moment, his voice stronger. 'I cannot allow you to be estranged from your family. It will be years, if ever, before I can support you in the style you are used to. I was wrong ever to let it get this far.'

Alistair sat down on a stone bench and realised that the churning sensation inside was nausea. *He isn't like his father*, Evaline had said of him. No, please God, he wasn't. What had he done to make the Brookes believe he would offer for Evaline? Perhaps his shadowing of Dita had appeared as something else in her parents' eyes.

Whatever the reason, he had come within an inch of sundering a young couple and breaking two hearts. It was only temporary, that illusion of love, but Evaline was a sweet girl and Morgan was apparently an honourable and likeable young man and they would make a good marriage if they got the chance.

He thought of Dita when she was talking about Imogen and his own youthful heartbreak and found that now he could understand what might force a young and dutiful girl into the marriage bed of a man she did not want. He stood up and took off his mask as he walked round the edge of the potted plants and into the grotto.

Evaline gave a small scream of alarm, but Morgan stood his ground, only shifting to put out an arm and draw her behind him. He put his chin up as he faced Alistair. 'My lord, I hope you will believe me when I assure you that I am entirely to blame for what must appear to be a compromising situation, but—'

Alistair waved a hand dismissively. 'Six of one and half a dozen of the other, I imagine, if she's anything like her sister. Evaline, put your mask on and get back to your mama or Dita. Do not say anything about this and try not to look as though you have been misbehaving in the conservatory.'

Evaline gave a little gasp and ran. Morgan confronted him. 'My lord! If you wish for satisfaction—'

'Mr Morgan, I am not a suitor for Evaline's hand, just a friend of the family. If you want a wife at the end of this, please control your desire to shoot me dead, sit down here and listen.'

'Evaline, what is the matter with you?' Dita murmured under cover of Lady Wycombe giving instructions to the housekeeper. 'I know this is boring, but we did promise to help Mama write the invitations for the dinner party; if you sigh like that once more, I am going to scream.'

'I'm sorry, girls, can you manage without me?' Lady Wycombe left the room, still discussing missing table linen.

Dita looked closely at her sister. 'You don't look as though you slept a wink. Whatever is the matter?'

'I am in love with James Morgan,' Evaline blurted out. 'And Lord Iwerne caught us in the conservatory last night and I keep expecting there to be the most awful row.'

'Oh, Evaline, I didn't realise you truly loved him. Are you sure?' Her sister's face was pale and miserable and Dita hated herself for the ruthless way she had been thinking about James Morgan. How could she have wanted to blight her sister's happiness when she knew all too well what it was like to love hopelessly?

'Yes. I know it is impossible. We both know it. And James is so honourable and…and then Lord Iwerne was *horrible.*'

'I'm not surprised, if he caught you in the conservatory unchaperoned! What happened?'

'He looked all cold and distant. And he sent me back to Mama and I don't know what happened with James, because I didn't see him again and perhaps he's called him out and he'll kill him and—'

'Stop it!' Dita gave her a little shake. 'You'll make yourself ill. I will write to Alistair and ask him to call on me and find out what he means to do. He won't challenge James, I am sure. You weren't… I mean, he wasn't doing anything very—'

'He was kissing me,' Evaline said. 'That was all.'

'Oh goodness, that was the knocker. I'll say we aren't

at home.' They both stared at the door, waiting for the butler to open it, but nothing happened. After a few minutes Dita rang the bell. 'Pearson, who was that at the door?'

'Lord Iwerne, my lady, for his lordship.'

'Thank you, Pearson. That will be all.'

The next half-hour crawled by. A footman came to say that Lady Wycombe had been detained in the kitchen, discussing the dinner party menu with Cook, and would they please finish the invitations without her. Evaline, apparently beyond tears, sat tying her handkerchief in knots, Dita made a mess of three invitation cards and gave up. What on earth was Alistair doing? Telling their father about Evaline's shocking behaviour? Surely not offering for Evaline's hand? The nightmare idea that perhaps he had decided to tell her father what had happened eight years ago gripped her and she tried to stay calm. There would have been an explosion from the study by now, surely?

The door knocker sounded again and this time, after a few moments, Pearson came in without them having to ring. 'That was a Mr Morgan for his lordship, my lady.'

Evaline fell back on the chaise with a gasp. Dita asked, 'Is Lord Iwerne still with my father?'

'Yes, my lady. Both the gentlemen are now in the study with his lordship.'

'I am going to have hysterics,' Evaline announced after another twenty minutes of sitting staring at each other. 'I am definitely going to—'

The door opened and Lady Wycombe came in. 'Eva-line, please come to the study.'

'Dita—'

'No, you do not need your sister,' her mother said as she took her arm. She left the door open and after a moment Alistair strolled through, shut it behind him and collapsed on the *chaise* where Evaline had been sitting.

'My God, I need a brandy.'

Dita splashed the liquor in a glass and handed it to him. 'Are you going to tell me what is going on?'

'Come and sit down beside me and tell me how wonderful I am,' he said with a grin. 'I have just convinced your father that Mr James Morgan is an eligible suitor for your sister's hand. Now, do I not deserve a reward?'

'No! How?' Dita shook her head, 'But he *isn't* eligible. No money, no prospects, no connections...'

'Oh, yes, he has. As of him giving a month's notice to Lord Percy Wynstanley, he is my confidential agent and secretary on a most respectable salary and with a very nice little house on the south Devon estate, which I am giving them as a wedding present, and the use of the third floor of my London house, which I am finding is approximately four times bigger than any reasonable man would want.

'And the young idiot did not realise, until I did some research and pointed it out, that his second cousin is the Earl of Bladings and his mother is a connection of the Duke of Fletton. Apparently his parents like to rusticate and never bothered to mention the family tree.'

'And Papa said *yes*?' Dita flopped down on the cushions beside him and grabbed both his hands.

'That's better. He did. And your mother. I must admit, I gave them to understand my friendship with Mr Morgan is somewhat more long-standing than it is, but I think Evaline is a good judge of character and all my enquiries, and a very long conversation with him, convince me he is an honourable and hard-working young man who will look after her. And he's just the man I need to have beside me—the amount of work with the estates is significant and then if I am going to take my seat in the House of Lords—'

'Alistair, I do love you!' Dita threw her arms around his neck and kissed him on the mouth before she realised what she was doing and what she had said.

He kissed her back, hard, then lifted his head and stared at her. 'If I realised I got that sort of response every time I employ someone, I would do it daily,' he said slowly with the air of a man working something through.

'Well, I could kiss you for a month, I love you so much for making Evaline happy,' she said, hoping the qualification would blur her true meaning.

'Ah. And there I was thinking you had decided to accept my marriage offer.' There was an edge to his voice that told her he was not as light-hearted as he would have her believe.

'Of course not. Nothing has changed.' She sat up straight, away from him. 'It is so good of you—why did you do it when you have no belief in love? I would have expected you to say they were both deluded.'

For a moment the thick dark lashes veiled the amber glow of his eyes and then he laughed, a dry chuckle that sounded as though he was laughing at himself, not at what she had said.

'I remembered what you had said about Imogen and how she would have done what her parents expected of her. Those two in the conservatory renouncing each other out of a sense of duty—it made me feel about eighty.'

It had affected him more than that, she could tell. There was something behind the light words and the laughter. Sadness, self-reproach and perhaps something that would help heal that old wound.

'Never mind, it all came out well in the end.' What Alistair was thinking about, she had no idea, but the thought of Evaline's happiness warmed her right through.

'Your little sister is marrying before you,' Alistair said, moving along the chaise and closing the distance between them until she could feel the warmth of his thigh pressing against hers. 'Why not make your parents doubly happy and give in? You know you will eventually.'

'Why is what I want not enough for you?' she demanded. 'Why do you not believe that I think this would be very wrong? Are you so arrogant that you believe that women should have no opinions of their own?'

'No!' He flung himself to his feet and paced away from her. 'You must know that I value your intelligence and your courage and your wit. But this is not a matter of choice, this is a matter of right and wrong. I did something unforgivable and it can only be righted by marrying you.'

'I forgive you,' she said starkly.

'If you marry anyone else, he will not.'

'You wanted to make love to me on the ship, even though you believed I had lost my virginity with Stephen. You didn't appear to mind that!'

'I wasn't thinking of marrying you then,' he shot back.

His words told her nothing that she did not already know. Why then did it feel as though he had slapped her? Because it came from his own mouth, she realised, the confirmation that he did not love her, despite the pitiful fantasies that came in the early hours, the dream that really, he did care with his heart and not just with his head and his honour.

She felt the prickling heat behind her eyes and knew, horrified, that she was about to cry.

Then the door opened and her parents came in with Evaline and James Morgan. Alistair stood up. 'You will want to be alone. We'll meet tomorrow, Morgan, as we agreed.'

'My lord.' The young man looked faintly stunned, Dita thought as she sat digging her nails into her palms in an effort to control the tears.

'Lyndon, I insist,' Alistair said, shaking hands all round as he made his way to the door. When he got to Evaline he stopped and kissed her. 'You be happy now, even in ten years' time when he is old.'

Evaline blushed and laughed and came to sit next to Dita. Dita squeezed her hand and whispered, 'What was that about?'

'He overheard me saying he was old,' Evaline hissed back. 'Wasn't that awful? I could have died, but he did this for us!' They hugged tightly, then Evaline disentangled herself. 'Dita, this is James.'

'Congratulations,' Dita said, kissing him on the cheek. Her own cheeks felt as though they were cracking with the effort to smile. 'I know you will make my sister very happy.'

'I swear I will, Lady Perdita. I confess, I am stunned by my good fortune. You know Lord Iwerne well, I believe? I heard how he saved you in the shipwreck. Is he always this generous?'

'Call me Dita. I believe that he will always want to reward the deserving if it is in his power. You obviously impressed him, he is fond of Evaline and you seem to be the sort of man he needs to assist him. But he will not be an easy employer, I imagine—he sets his standards high and expects a lot.'

'He'll get it from me,' Morgan vowed, his eyes full of passionate devotion as he looked at Evaline. 'And I will never let Evaline down.'

For two nights running she saw Alistair at the social events they both attended: a soirée followed by a ball one night, a full dress dinner the next. Dita noticed that he paid a great deal of attention to attractive widows in their late twenties and early thirties, of whom there were half a dozen in society this Season. She tried to tell herself that this was a good thing: well-bred, worldly-wise women who knew how to go on in society and who presumably knew enough to keep him faithful for more than a few months. The fact that she wanted to scratch their eyes out, especially the very lovely Mrs Somerton, was neither here nor there.

Watching him made her feel restless and reckless. Perhaps, she wondered, eyeing the rakish-looking stranger who had been seated almost opposite her at Lady Pershaw's dinner party, she should flirt a little herself. She always had flirted, and enjoyed it, but since she had been back in England, she realised she had lost the taste for it. It might take her mind off a certain amber-eyed gentleman who was watching Eliza Somerton with lazy appreciation.

The stranger was a little taller than Francis Wynstanley, although of much the same colouring, and he had well-defined cheekbones, a square chin and deep blue eyes which, just now, were staring back at her. Their eyes locked and Dita let hers widen a little, just enough to show interest, before she looked away and began to discuss church politics with the nice, and very dull, rural dean who sat on her left. Was that enough to pique his interest? Well, time would tell.

Chapter Twenty

The gentlemen rejoined the ladies less than an hour after the covers were drawn, for Lady Pershaw liked a lively party and had given her husband strict instructions not to dally over the port.

Alistair, Dita noticed, went straight to Mrs Somerton, who was looking particularly lovely in golden brown silk with cream lace accentuating white shoulders and an adventurous degree of décolletage. She was making him laugh.

Out of patience with her own inability to forget, and wishing she did not care about either him, or his *amours*, Dita looked for the blue-eyed stranger and found he was watching her.

She looked sideways and caught the full force of a very blatant stare. 'Who is that?' she asked Maria Pershaw, a young lady who could be relied upon to know all the gentlemen. 'By the music stand.'

'Sir Rafe Langham,' Maria said. 'Delicious, is he not? He is said to be highly dangerous and Mama has strictly forbidden me to flirt with him, which is so provoking of her.' She laughed and moved on and Perdita deliberately turned her back and drifted over to the long windows that were ajar on to the terrace to let in some fresh air.

'Lost, my lady?' a deep voice enquired.

'You know Latin or perhaps you are a Shakespearian scholar?' Dita responded, turning slightly to find Sir Rafe beside her.

'Both. Perdita, the lost princess of *The Winter's Tale*, cast adrift upon the coast. Apt, I thought, in view of the shipwreck.'

'Wrong coast, however.' She kept her shoulder a little turned and her voice cool. It would not do to seem over-eager.

'Indeed. It is warm in here, is it not?'

Ah, a very fast worker! 'I do not believe we have been introduced, sir.'

'Sir Rafe Langham. I have been out of town for some time otherwise...' He let his voice trail off. 'I knew who you were, of course—your beauty had been described to me.'

Nonsense, you heard I have a shady past and you thought you would try your luck, Dita thought. But it was so tempting to play with fire, just a little. 'You make me blush, Sir Rafe. Or perhaps it is the heat in here.'

He needed no further encouragement. He opened the window wide and Dita stepped through and into the cool night air. 'How refreshing,' she said. The edge of the terrace was not far. It was well lit by the spill of light from the uncurtained windows, and should be quite safe, even with a gazetted rake such as this one.

'And what a delightful fragrance in the air. I wonder

if it is this shrub.' Before Dita could get her balance she was swept off to the side, out of the light and into the shadows of a little gazebo.

'Ah, no. It is your perfume and not a flower at all.' He gathered her to him with alarming competence.

'Sir Rafe! Stop it—'

He kissed her and his right hand fastened on her breast while the left, spread over her behind, trapped her intimately close to his body. Dita tried to raise her knee, but he had her too close. Alistair's lesson came back to her vividly: ears are very sensitive. She reached up, seized an earlobe and twisted, hard.

He released her mouth with an oath, grabbed her wrist and yanked her deeper into the shadows. 'You little hell-cat! So you like to play it rough, do you?'

I am going to castrate you with blunt scissors, Dita thought as she fought him. *If I can just get my fingers round this loose stone…* But she knew, with a sinking heart, that the only way she was going to get out of this was at the cost of another, possibly ruinous, scandal.

Where the devil was Dita going? Alistair removed his gaze from Mrs Somerton's face, which was lovely enough to compensate a trifle for her frivolous conversation, and saw Dita slip through the window on to the terrace with a man. The mouse-brown hair looked like Winstanley's. The devil! He thought she had stopped encouraging that milksop.

It would only be flirtation, the man was to be trusted, surely, and Dita could look after herself. He himself had been flirting, blatantly, hoping that he could provoke a reaction from her. It seemed he had succeeded rather too well.

Alistair shifted, uneasy for some reason. The thought of her in another man's arms, another man's bed, made his stomach churn. He swore softly under his breath.

'My lord?' Mrs Somerton must have been chattering on for minutes while he brooded.

'I beg your—' Francis Wynstanley strolled out from behind a large plant on a stand. Whoever Dita was outside with, it was not her lukewarm admirer. 'Excuse me.'

He crossed the room as unobtrusively as he could, stepped out on to the terrace and closed the window behind him.

There. Alistair strode across the flags towards the gazebo and the flutter of pale fabric he could just see in the darkness.

'Take your hands off me, you reptile, before I hit you again.' Dita's furious voice had him grinning despite his anxiety. The *again* sounded promising. He should have trusted her to fight back.

'I warn you, drop that stone or I'll make such a scandal out of this—'

Alistair didn't recognise the voice, but his night vision had recovered enough to make out the two joined figures clearly. He sent a crashing right over Dita's left shoulder. The man slumped back, Dita staggered into Alistair's arms and dropped something painfully on his toes.

'Alistair! Oh—thank you!'

Alistair hauled the fallen man to his feet. 'You, sir, will meet me for this. Name your seconds.'

'No, he will *not* meet you,' Dita said, all the gratitude

gone from her voice. 'I can do without the scandal, thank you very much. And I have hit him with that rock, wherever it has gone, and I twisted his ears as you showed me, Alistair.'

'It is not enough.' Alistair said through his anger. He wanted to kill this lout. 'What is his name?'

'Rafe Langham,' Dita said. Langham had one hand clamped to his bleeding nose and was in no fit state to say anything.

'Langham,' Alistair gave the man a shake. 'Apologise to the lady, now.'

'Sorry. Carried away.' It sounded as though he had teeth loose as well as a broken nose.

'You will certainly be carried away, if you so much as whisper a word to this lady's detriment,' Alistair said, twisting his hand into Langham's neckcloth. 'Do you know who I am?'

'Iwerne,' Langham choked out.

'Indeed. If you are not out of London by this time tomorrow I will find a reason to challenge you and then, I swear, I will kill you. Is that quite clear?' There was a nod. 'In fact, I find you so unpleasant that I think that if I ever see you again I will have to challenge you anyway. Clear?' Another nod. 'Then go now, and if there is the slightest rumour about this evening I will find you.'

Langham stumbled off into the darkness, leaving them alone in the gazebo. 'Thank you,' Dita said, putting out both hands to him. 'I really thought only to take the air and enjoy a mild flirtation—and it got quite out of hand.'

Alistair clasped her hands in his. 'You are cold, you are not used to these temperatures.' She shook her head, not meeting his eyes. 'Dita, if you want to flirt, flirt with me.'

'I should join the queue, you mean?' she asked. He should have felt triumph; she had seen him flirting with other women and she was jealous, but something of her unhappiness reached him. This was not petty, she really was distressed.

'Dita?' he put his arm around her shoulders, not amorously, but gently, His palm rested on the soft skin of her shoulder; as he pressed he felt the slender bones, the beat of her pulse. 'What is it?'

'I cannot play these games any more, Alistair. I will not marry you, do you not understand? If you care for me at all, even the slightest bit, you will stop asking me.' She sounded bitterly in earnest, a woman at the end of her tether.

'Why?' he asked. 'I know you talk of love, but you enjoy *making* love with me, you cannot deceive me about that. We share so much history, we are old friends. We could have a good marriage. What is it, Dita?' He tipped her face up and the light from the reception room flooded across it, unsparing on the tears glittering unshed in her eyes. He had seen her cry with grief over Averil, but never like this. 'Dita, is there someone you love?'

'Yes. Now let me go.'

'Does he love you?' Who the devil could it be? Who had she met that he had not noticed?

'No. Now, are you satisfied?'

'Not if you are unhappy. Never, then.' He felt sick and shaken. 'Dita, what can I do?' He would bring her the man on his knees if it would wipe that bleakness from her eyes.

'Leave me. Stop asking me to marry you.'

For a long moment he could find no words. He was not used to defeat and he had not expected it here, or to find it so crushing. But a gentleman did not rant or complain; he had asked her what she wanted and she had told him with a sincerity that was utterly convincing.

'Your scarf, Dita.' He picked up the gauze strip and put it around her shoulders, his fingers brushing the soft skin. That was probably the last time he could legitimately allow them to linger like that, he realised, and gave himself one more indulgence, as he touched the back of his hand to her cheek.

The party was still animated and the room crowded as he let himself back into it. No one appeared to be looking for Dita so he stood there feeling lost and wondering at himself while he massaged the bruised knuckles of his right hand.

She was out there thinking about the man she loved. The bastard who obviously did not care for her, or he would be with her, protecting her from rakes. Protecting her from Alistair Lyndon.

His vision clouded and it took him a moment to realise it was with tears. Appalled, Alistair strode from the room, into the hall, snapped his fingers for his hat, cane and cloak. 'Tell my coachman to drive home, I'll walk,' he said.

When he reached the street he strode out, uncaring where he was going. Damn it, she was his. He loved her—what was she doing, wanting another man? *He loved her.* Alistair stopped dead in the middle of the pavement.

So that was what this was, this restlessness, this feeling of peace when he was with her, the mingling of thoughts and the shared laughter. The passion. The need to protect her. Love, the emotion he did not believe that mature, clear-headed men felt.

'Want to be friendly, ducky?' He glanced down to find a sharp-faced girl looking up at him, her right arm crooked in the time-honoured invitation to take it and walk with her to some dark alley.

'No,' he said as he fished in his pocket and found her a coin. 'No, I am not inclined to be friendly at all.'

The street-walker bit it and walked off, casting a coquettish look over her shoulder, her skinny figure swaying in her tawdry finery.

On the ship Dita had asked him why he didn't marry her and then, without waiting for his answer, had told him why she wouldn't take him, even if he offered. *I want you, but I do not love you. I do not even like you, half of the time*, she had said.

And he had pressed her to marry him, over and over so that the passages between them when the old, uncomplicated friendship had seemed to return were marred by his insistence, her resistance. And for him that lingering friendship, the passion, the sense of duty, had changed into something more, so slowly, so naturally he hadn't even been aware of it. Perhaps that love had always been there, waiting to emerge.

Could he convince her? Woo her? But if she had given her heart to another man she would not settle for anything—anyone—less.

'Hell, I have made a mull of this,' he said to the empty street. How was he going to live without Dita?

* * *

He had gone, without protest, and left the field to some unknown man, Dita thought bleakly. Of course, he didn't even know there *was* a field. He didn't know she loved him, didn't know she longed for him to love her, too. Like the honourable man he was, he had rescued her from Langham, made sure she was safe and then walked away, finally accepting her refusal because she was in love. The perfect gentleman.

But that touch, that lingering, gentle caress… Had that been a farewell or a blessing? Both, perhaps. She stared, unseeing, into the darkness. It had always been Alistair, all her life. Now, she had lost him for ever.

She shuddered, but it was not the cold that made her shiver, it was the thought that there was nowhere in London to get away from Alistair, and the knowledge that she could not bear to see him find someone else to marry and to live his life with.

In the end she was too cold to think properly. She went inside to where her mother was deep in conversation with two friends. 'I thought St George's, Hanover Square, and the wedding breakfast at Grosvenor Street. They'll be going down to the house in south Devon, I expect, and then— Ah, Dita dear, I was wondering where you had got to.'

'Mama, I'm sorry, but I am not feeling very well. I think I might have caught cold. May I take the carriage and send it back?'

'You do look very pale, dear. I will come with you.'

Her mother swept her out with punctilious farewells to their hosts. 'I do hope you have not got anything more than a slight chill,' she said, tucking rugs around Dita in the carriage. 'At this stage in the Season it would be such a pity to miss anything.'

'I would like to go home, Mama. At once. To Combe.'

'Home now? But why?'

'I don't want to talk about it, Mama.' Her mother opened her mouth, but Dita pressed on. If she was asked any more questions or talked at, she felt she could not bear it. 'Now Evaline is betrothed there is no reason for me to stay in town, is there? There is no one I am going to marry, Mama. I am sorry, but I am certain of it. I need time to decide what I want to do and I cannot think in London.'

Nor can I bear to dance and flirt and smile and watch Alistair make his choice. Much better to hear about it at a distance. When he brings his new bride home I can come back to town or go to Brighton or something. Anything. Her hand crept to her cheek where his had touched. *Goodbye.*

Dita straightened her shoulders and made herself sit up. She was not going to run away and mope for the rest of her life. She had money, she had contacts, there was a new life out there if she only had the strength to find it. Widows managed it when they had lost the men they loved and so could she. She just needed some peace to plan, that was all.

Chapter Twenty-One

◦⬯◦

Alistair left it until eleven before he called. He had to tell her how he felt. It was hopeless, of course, if she was in love and not just telling him that to stop him insisting on their marriage. That it might be a ruse was the only thing that supported his spirits—until he remembered the tears on her cheeks. They had been so very real.

It was still far too early for a morning call, which properly, if illogically, should take place in the afternoon, but there was a limit to how much suspense he could take. Pearson answered the door. 'Good morning, my lord. I regret that none of the family is at home this morning.'

'None of them? I will return this afternoon.'

'I believe it unlikely that they will be receiving today at all, my lord.'

What the devil was going on? The only thing he could think of was that Dita had announced that she wanted to marry whoever it was, her father had objected and a major family upset was in progress. The fact that she must be holding out would indicate that she was serious, he thought, striding down St James's and into his club. It was going to be a long twenty-four hours.

The second day produced almost exactly the same result. 'His lordship is at the House and is expected back very late. Her ladyship and Lady Evaline are, I believe, shopping, my lord, and will be going on to afternoon appointments. Lady Perdita is not receiving.'

Frustrated, Alistair reviewed his options, other than breaking and entering. He did have, if not a spy in the camp, a source of intelligence, he realised.

The note he had written to James Morgan brought the young man himself around to White's in the early evening. 'How may I be of service?' he asked as they settled into chairs in a quiet corner of the library.

'I need to know what is going on in the Brookes' house,' Alistair said. No point in beating around the bush. 'Is Lady Perdita betrothed to someone, or is there a problem over some man?'

'I don't think so.' James frowned. 'But then, I haven't seen Lady Evaline today as she had various obligations. I can ask her tomorrow though—I am hiring a curricle and taking her driving in the park. Of course, if it is very delicate, she might not be able to say anything.' He hesitated. 'You could ask Lady Perdita, perhaps?'

'I would if she was receiving,' Alistair said, almost amused by the way James struggled to keep the speculation off his face. 'Never mind, I will call again tomorrow.' And this time, if he was still refused, he was going to go in through the tradesmen's entrance and find out, one way or another. But he had betrayed more than enough to his new secretary. 'Do you enjoy the play?' he asked. 'We could go to the Theatre Royal and then on to some supper.'

Pearson looked decidedly uncomfortable to find Alistair on the doorstep at ten the next morning. 'I am sorry, my lord, Lady Perdita is indisposed.'

'Seriously?' Alistair's blood ran cold. Had Langham hurt her and she had said nothing at the time?

'I could not say, my lord.'

The man was hiding something. Alistair smiled. 'Please tell her I called.' As soon as the door closed he went along the pavement to the area gate, down the steps into the narrow paved space and tried the handle of the staff door. It was unlocked.

'Here, you can't come through here! Oh. My lord...' One of the footmen stared in confusion as Alistair nodded pleasantly to him and took the back stairs, up past the ground floor, on up to the first where the ladies had their sitting room.

The door was ajar and he walked in to find Evaline trimming a bonnet at the table. 'Alistair!'

'I need to talk to Dita,' he said without preamble.

'You can't. She's not... I mean, she isn't well.' Evaline appeared decidedly flustered.

'Not here?' She bit her lip and then nodded. 'Where?'

'She left for Combe yesterday morning, first thing,' Evaline admitted.

'Why?' Evaline just shrugged, her pretty face showing as much bafflement as he felt. 'Is she betrothed to someone?'

'Oh, no.' She seemed glad to have something she could answer. 'Although it something about marriage, I am certain. I heard Papa and Mama… I should not repeat it.'

Alistair sat down without waiting to be invited, finding, for the first time in his life, that his legs were none too steady. As he realised it Person opened the door. 'Do you wish refreshments to be served, Lady Evaline? Good morning, my lord.' It was as close to a rebuke as he was going to deliver. Alistair smiled at him. Even disapproving butlers were to be tolerated now he knew that Dita was still not promised to another man.

'Not on my account, thank you.' He got to his feet and bent to kiss Evaline's cheek. 'I'll go and see she is all right.'

'Oh, good.' She beamed back at him. 'And tell her to come back to town soon—I need her help for all the shopping I have to do!'

The temptation to take his curricle was almost overwhelming, but Alistair controlled it. He had no idea how Dita would react when he arrived on her doorstep and he wanted his wits about him. Speculation about what was going on kept running round and round in his head, but he could make no sense of what was happening.

He ordered Gregory to pack for at least a week away, ordered a chaise and four and set out at midday with one terse instruction to the postillions. 'Make the best time you can and there's money in it for you.'

It took them fifteen hours to Bridgewater, and another five on the narrower, twisting roads, and then lanes, that led to the Castle.

By the time the chaise pulled up in front of the great doors it was eight in the morning, Alistair had taught his valet to play a variety of card games, they had snatched dinner in Bristol and had slept in moderate discomfort for the past five hours.

Two hours later, with breakfast inside him, bathed, shaved and dressed in buckskins and boots, Alistair rode up to the front door of Wycombe Combe. At least he had got inside the door this time before he was refused, he thought, confronting the Brookes' butler.

'Is Lady Perdita not receiving me, or is she not at home to anyone?' he demanded.

'Lady Perdita has given orders that she is not to be disturbed, my lord. She's shut herself up in the Library Suite in the tower, my lord. And she hasn't come down. We take her meals up to her and I have to knock; the door at the foot of the tower is locked, my lord.' Gilbert had known Alistair since he was a boy and seemed grateful for the prospect of some guidance.

The butler would have a master key, Alistair reflected, but he did not want to put him in a difficult position; besides, he was experiencing a strong urge to do something flamboyant to make his point to Dita. She wanted romance? Well, if she locked herself up in a tower like Rapunzel, romance was what she was going to get.

Her grandfather had added an incongruous tower at one end of the house in a fit of enthusiasm for the Gothic, inspired by his friend Hugh Walpole. It overlooked the miniature gorge that the river made and created the impression that one of the turrets of his own castle had taken flight and landed there. Dita's father had moved the library into the second floor and Alistair recalled from childhood games of hide and seek that there was a guest suite above that.

He wondered why had she abandoned her own rooms as he made his way along the frontage of the house, round the curve of the tower wall and along to a point where a mass of ivy clung to the stonework. Forty foot up a window was open. Alistair shed his coat and hat, gave the ivy an experimental shake and began to climb.

He had made harder climbs, and more dangerous ones, although the result of falling on to the slabs below would be terminally unpleasant, but the ivy was old and thick and made a serviceable ladder. He was within six feet of the window when a wren erupted out of the foliage, shrieking with alarm, a tiny brown bundle of aggression.

The ivy tore under his hands as he swung out reflexively, swearing, then he grabbed hold above the weak spot and threw his weight more securely across.

'What the devil are you doing?' Dita's voice, immediately overhead, almost had him losing his grip again.

'Climbing this ivy,' Alistair said, while his heart returned to its proper place.

'That is such a male answer!' He looked up and found her glaring down at him, her arms folded on the sill. 'The question, as you very well know, Alistair Lyndon, is *why* are you climbing the ivy?'

'To get to you. I want to talk to you—I am worried about you, Dita.'

'Well, I don't want to talk to you.' She straightened up and the window began to swing closed.

'I can't get down,' he called.

'Nonsense.' But she poked her head out again.

'Let down your hair, Rapunzel,' he wheedled.

'This is not so much a fairy tale, more a bad dream,' she retorted, vanishing again.

Oh well, if she was not to be teased into a good humour he would just have to climb up and hope she didn't slam the window in his face. Alistair climbed another four feet before it opened wide again. This time a cloud of brown silk billowed out, settled, and revealed itself as Dita's hair. His fingers clenched into the ivy as a wave of erotic heat swept through him. He had seen it down wet, sticky with sea salt, tangled into knots, and it had affected him deeply then. But now it was clean, glossy and smelled of rosemary.

Alistair fisted one hand into it and tugged gently. 'Don't you dare,' she said, and swept it back and over one shoulder out of his reach. 'I always wanted to do that as a little girl, but I never realised how painful the weight of a grown man on the end of it would be.'

'May I come in?' he asked.

'Yes.' Dita vanished, leaving the window wide, but as he breasted the sill she held out her hands to help him climb through. 'Of all the idiotic things to do! You might have been killed.'

'Easier than climbing rigging.' It was interesting that that made her blush. 'Dita, why are you here?'

It seemed, as she turned and walked back to the big table in the centre of the room, that she would not answer him. Alistair did not push her, but looked around. They were in the library, the walls lined with curving bookshelves to fit within the circle of the tower. On the table there were piles of books, maps weighted at their curling corners and pen and paper.

'I am not going to marry,' Dita said, her back still

turned. 'I realise I cannot compromise on what I need: marriage is too permanent, too important to settle for a lifetime of second best. And I don't want to hurt someone by not being able to offer them everything that I have to give. So I came here to think about what I want to do and I decided that I will travel. I will find a congenial older woman as a companion and I will discover this country first. Then, perhaps, the war will be over and I can go abroad.

'I enjoyed writing. I might well rewrite our novel, and I will write about my travels.'

'You may hurt someone else, by deciding not to marry,' Alistair said.

'Who?' She turned, puzzled.

'Me.' He said nothing more, but let her work it out for herself.

'You? You would be hurt by my not marrying? You are saying that you care for me?'

'You know that I care.' His voice was rough, and he knew he was not gentle as he closed the distance between them and jerked her into his arms. 'I am telling you that I love you.'

'But you don't *want* to fall in love,' she wailed. 'You don't believe in it. Don't do this to me, Alistair. Don't pretend and say this just because you think you must marry me.'

He looked furious and more nearly out of control than she had ever seen him. 'I will be all right, Alistair. I don't have to marry—'

'I. Love. You,' he repeated. 'Love: not like a friend, not like a neighbour—like a lover. I had no idea until I walked out of that garden knowing you were in love with someone else, and then I found I was shaking and sick and I realised that I had lost you because I'd had no idea that what I felt for you was love.'

Dita felt as though the tower floor was shifting under her feet, but Alistair was holding her. She would not fall while he was there. Alistair, who was telling her he loved her.

'Then Evaline said you were not betrothed to anyone, so I guessed he either does not love you or is totally ineligible. Take me, Dita,' he urged. 'We'll travel and I'll take you wherever you want. We'll write together— you can help me reconstruct my notes and I'll help with the novel. We'll make love. You like me, I know that. Desire me, too. I think you trust me. One day I'll make that enough for you. I'll make you forget him.'

'You don't know, do you?' she said, looking into his eyes and reading the truth and an utterly uncharacteristic uncertainty in them. 'When I saw you on the ivy I thought you must have guessed.' He shook his head, not understanding. 'It is you. I love *you*, Alistair. I've loved you all the time, even when I told myself I hated you, when I told myself it was just desire, when I knew it was hopeless.' Dita smiled at him, trying, failing, to conjure an answering smile.

'But you said you grew out of it.'

'I lied. Do you think I could bear you knowing and not feeling the same? I would have sunk with mortification.'

And then he did laugh, his whole body convulsing with it. 'I believe you—I can imagine how that would feel.'

'But you were prepared to risk it,' she said, sobering

as rapidly as he relaxed. 'You were prepared to risk your pride by coming here and telling me you loved me.'

'Because I realise my task in life, Perdita my darling, is to cherish you and protect you and love you and if that means carving out my heart and my pride and my honour and laying them at your feet, that's what I will do.'

'Oh.' Her voice broke as the tears welled in her eyes. 'That is so lovely.'

'Don't cry, sweetheart, not before I tell you your duties. You are fated to give me purpose, make me smile and restore my faith in the world as a good place.'

'I won't stop you being an adventurer,' she promise as she swallowed the tears. 'I'll never close the window and leave you to climb alone again or tell you to stay at home and be safe. But you'll take me with you, always, won't you?'

'I promise,' Alistair said. 'Do you want to get married at the same time as Evaline?'

'I don't know. I didn't know I was getting married until five minutes ago! Why?'

'Well, she is not marrying for about three months and I have every intention of taking you to bed as soon as I can find one—and I really don't want to be careful.'

'Careful? Oh, you mean children.' She had tried not to think about babies, the ones she would never have because she was not going to wed. And now she would have Alistair's children. 'No, I don't want to be careful either. We'll tell everyone we want to let Evaline have her day to herself and we'll be married as soon as we can, if you want.'

'I want.' Alistair swept her up off her feet. 'Now, where's this bed?'

'Upstairs.' Half-breathless, half-inclined to giggle, Dita let herself be carried. Alistair shouldered open the door and laid her on the bed. 'This is very romantic, my lord.'

'Something from our novel writing obviously rubbed off,' Alistair said as he sat on the end of the bed and pulled off his boots. He turned back to her, shrugging off his waistcoat. 'I'll take it slowly, Dita, don't worry. By the pond—I should have been gentler, more careful.'

'I have been waiting a very long time for you to love me,' she said, kneeling up to untie his neckcloth and undo the buttons of his shirt. 'Could we be fast first and *then* slow, do you think?'

'I won't tease you,' he promised, dragging his shirt over his head. Dita reached out to run her hands over his skin, raking her nails lightly through the dark hair on his chest. She saw the way he tensed as she brushed his nipples, heard the intake of breath as she hooked her fingers into the waistband of his trousers and the arrogant swell of his erection and closed her eyes for a moment to let the wave of pleasure and power sweep through her.

Alistair took her mouth, his hands swift and sure on the fastenings of her gown, and she opened her eyes on his closed lids, the sweep of his lashes sooty against his tan, and shivered in delight at the sensation of skin against skin as the simple cotton gown fell around her hips along with her petticoats.

'Better than in the hut on the beach,' she murmured as she pulled back to look into his face. 'Dry and warm and not sticky.'

'Sticky can be good,' he said as he pressed her back on the bed, pulled off her chemise and began to lave her nipples with long, wet, lavish strokes of his tongue.

Dita surrendered to his skill and to the sensation. She made no attempt to stifle the moans of pleasure as he began to suck and tease and nibble at the hard, aching knots, his hands cupping and caressing her breasts, lifting them to his hungry mouth. They were alone at the top of her fairytale tower and nothing, now, was going to stop the full consummation of their love.

It seemed the most natural thing in the world to be here, naked, with Alistair, all pretence and misunderstanding stripped away. She felt no shyness when he lifted himself on his braced arms to gaze down at her, nor alarm when he lay back beside her and began to caress her breasts again, then her belly, then the sensitive mound with its tangle of dark curls.

'Let me look at you,' he said. 'We have made love and every time, it seems, there has been no time, or our emotions were getting in the way of knowing each other.' He slid down the bed and parted her thighs. She opened to him, blushing a little as he touched her there, opening her with gentle fingers. 'So soft and plump and wet.'

Dita closed her eyes as one finger slid between the folds, exploring intimately. She tightened around him as he eased a second finger into the aching heat, but it was not enough—she wanted him, *needed* him, there. She tried to say so, twisting, lifting her hips, and he chuckled, a wicked, affectionate sound, and did that thing with his thumb that made her gasp with pleasure.

'Now, Dita?'

'Yes.' He moved up her body, covering her and she

wriggled to cradle him, relishing his weight and the sensation of leashed power in the muscles she could feel tense under her spread palms. 'Now,' she urged as she felt him nudge against her, large and hard and potent. 'Oh, now, Alistair.'

'I love you,' he said as he moved and she gasped at the sensation, still not used to lovemaking. But the pressure, the fullness, were exciting and she arched against him, wanting more, wanting all of him. He lowered his head to take her mouth and surged and they were one again and she laughed against his lips and felt his smile curve in response.

He was right; there had been so many things wrong when they had made love before—guilt and secrets and anger. Now she could think of nothing but Alistair's body, hot and strong and relentless, driving into her with a rhythm that was as elemental as the sea and as dangerously exciting. Her nostrils were filled with the scent of his body and the tang of their mutual arousal and her ears were filled with the sound of their breathing, the roar of her blood.

She felt him lift away, his arms braced. It pressed his pelvis tighter into hers, drove him impossibly deep within her and she opened her eyes to see he was watching her, his tiger eyes burning gold with passion. She was so tense it was painful, so tight that she felt she would die of it. *'Now,'* he said. 'Let go, Dita', and everything peaked and then untangled in an explosion of pleasure and she lost herself in it, in him—drowning, yet safe.

Dita woke and found herself hot and sticky and entangled in Alistair's arms, pressed as tightly against his body as she could be. 'Mmm,' she said, eyes closed, kissing damp, smooth skin and working out that it was his shoulder.

'Awake?' He lifted the hair away from her face and she wriggled round to smile up at him. 'I love you.'

'I love you, too. Which is,' she added thoughtfully, 'an extremely satisfactory coincidence.'

'I think satisfactory may be an understatement,' Alistair said. He rolled her gently on to her stomach and began to lick his way down her spine. 'What a very lovely back you have,' he mumbled, his voice indistinct as he kissed the sensitive dip right at the base. 'Let us try something very, very slow.' He slid one hand under her, found the place that gave such exquisite pleasure and began to tease it, his other hand holding her down.

'Oh, peaches,' he said, nipping the swell of one buttock with his teeth while she whimpered and writhed. 'Do you want me to stop?'

'Yes! No… Oh…no.'

'Are you hungry?' Dita said. She had no idea what the time was, but the shadows were lying long across the floor and the breeze from the open window was cooler now.

'Ravenous,' Alistair said. He was lying sprawled on his back, one arm flung across his eyes. 'You have exhausted me, you witch.'

'I don't think so.' Dita rolled over, propped herself up on one elbow and cupped her fingers around the weight of his testicles. 'Look—you have woken up.'

'Food, you bad woman,' Alistair said, and sat up to

swing off the bed before she could tease any more. 'Is there water?'

'Cold, but I expect that's no bad thing.' Dita got off the bed, too, conscious of stiff muscles and a not-unpleasant awareness of her insides. 'Here, in the dressing room.'

Half an hour later they returned to the library. 'We'll go down, shall we?' Alistair said 'It isn't fair to ask them to haul a big dinner for two up all these stairs.'

She was feeling far too happy to mind the studious way the footmen ignored the fact that Alistair had appeared, apparently out of nowhere, and the smooth way in which Gilbert announced that a dinner for two was even now in its final stages of preparation.

Alistair's valet came in as they were settling in the salon to wait for the meal to be served. 'A package has arrived for you, my lord. It seem to have been delivered after your departure from London and they had it sent down, post haste, in case it was urgent.'

Alistair turned the small parcel over in his hands. 'A London post office stamp and no seal impressed in the wax. I wasn't expecting anything.' He opened it, shedding several layers of brown paper and stared at what was revealed. 'Dita, look at this.'

It was the small oval box that she had given him. 'Open it,' she urged and he slid back the lid to reveal the Noah's Ark animals still packed tight inside. 'Is it the same one?'

In answer he turned the lid over and showed her the initials, AL. 'I marked it.' He took out the little carvings and shook the box. A few grains of sand fell out. 'It has been wet—see the stains on the wood?'

'But how?'

'I left it on the table in the cuddy. I had been showing it to Mr Bastable before dinner. It could have escaped the wreck and been washed out and on to a beach somewhere. But who would know to send it to me? And why anonymously?'

They eliminated everyone they could think of by the time dinner was announced. 'All the survivors took ship back to the mainland and no one on the islands would know it was mine.'

Dita twisted the miniature figure of Noah in her fingers. 'Averil?' They stared at each other, silent with the weight of speculation. 'I felt that she was still alive,' Dita murmured at last.

'A mystery.' Alistair took the scrap of wood from her and put it back safe in the box. 'We have had our miracle—perhaps, after all, against all the odds, Averil has experienced one, too. We can only wait and see.'

They were sitting at a small oval table, close enough to touch. Dita looked up and caught the butler's eye. 'Gregory, would you all kindly leave us for a few minutes?' They filed out, expressionless, and she got up, walked around and placed her hands on Alistair's shoulders from behind, bending down to rest her cheek against his.

'It *is* a miracle, isn't it?'

He put up his hands to capture hers. 'A miracle that we're alive, that we're together, that we love each other. Every day from now on is going to hold that magic for us.'

'And every night,' she whispered in his ear.

'Oh, yes, my love. Believe it. Every night.'

* * * * *

A sneaky peek at next month...

HISTORICAL

IGNITE YOUR IMAGINATION, STEP INTO THE PAST...

My wish list for next month's titles...

In stores from 2nd September 2011:

❏ Seduced by the Scoundrel – Louise Allen

❏ Unmasking the Duke's Mistress – Margaret McPhee

❏ To Catch a Husband... – Sarah Mallory

❏ The Highlander's Redemption – Marguerite Kaye

❏ His Enemy's Daughter – Terri Brisbin

❏ His Dakota Captive – Jenna Kernan

Available at WHSmith, Tesco, Asda, Eason, Amazon and Apple

Just can't wait?

0811/04

2 Free Books!

Get your free books now at
www.millsandboon.co.uk/freebookoffer

Or fill in the form below and post it back to us

THE MILLS & BOON® BOOK CLUB™—HERE'S HOW IT WORKS: Accepting your free books places you under no obligation to buy anything. You may keep the books and return the despatch note marked 'Cancel'. If we do not hear from you, about a month later we'll send you 4 brand-new stories from the Historical series priced at £3.99* each. There is no extra charge for post and packaging. You may cancel at any time, otherwise we will send you 4 stories a month which you may purchase or return to us—the choice is yours. *Terms and prices subject to change without notice. Offer valid in UK only. Applicants must be 18 or over. Offer expires 28th February 2012. **For full terms and conditions, please go to www.millsandboon.co.uk/termsandconditions**

Mrs/Miss/Ms/Mr (please circle)
_____

First Name
_____

Surname
_____

Address
_____

_____

                                              Postcode
_____

E-mail
_____

Send this completed page to: Mills & Boon Book Club, Free Book Offer, FREEPOST NAT 10298, Richmond, Surrey, TW9 1BR

Find out more at
www.millsandboon.co.uk/freebookoffer

Visit us Online

0611/M1ZEE